THE ART MERCHANT

A Detective Esther Penman Thriller

J.K. Flynn

D1287549

First Published in Great Britain in 2022 by Chingola
Publishing

Cover designed by J.K. Flynn.
Photo image by *Hands off my tags! Michael Gaida* from
Pixabay.

ISBN: 978-1-7391797-1-7

www.jkflynn-author.com

THE ART MERCHANT

PROLOGUE

SHE WAS DEAD.

Maybe it was the sound her head had made when it struck the marble-tiled floor, or the way her eyes had stayed half-open, lightless and unblinking, after she'd landed. Maybe it was the awkward angle of her body, or her slightly parted lips. Or simply the utter stillness of her as she lay there. Whatever it was, Jack Barry knew she was dead, and he didn't need to get any closer to be sure.

At first, he'd panicked. He had run from the kitchen and the dead woman lying in the middle of it, back to the SUV he'd jacked to do the job. He'd gunned it down the pebble drive, and made it as far as the stone pillars that towered over the front gates before recovering his wits. There, as clarity returned, he'd skidded to a halt.

Now he sat, heart pounding, sweat soaking every inch of him, gloved hands gripping the steering wheel so tight his fingers were beginning to hurt. He could still see the half-open patio door in the Jeep's wing mirror. He stared at it, desperately *willing* his victim to come staggering out. But there was no movement. No sign of life.

He forced himself to relax, to loosen his grip. To breathe. He wanted to rip the itchy balaclava from his face, but he had to leave it on. The job had been checked out beforehand, and he knew she was alone and that there were no cameras. But as his breathing and heart rate slowed, Jack began to realise that he was going to have to go back in, and try to make it look like an accident. Or like a burglary gone wrong. There was a big difference between murder and manslaughter, and as much as Jack hoped he would never get tied to this, a guy had to make contingency plans. He would need to keep the mask and gloves on until he was done, just to be safe. This was the careful and sensible thing to do.

He shifted the Jeep's gears and began backing up the drive.

The driveway was long and curved and covered in white pebbles. It was sheltered on both sides by laurel bushes and willow trees, giving further seclusion to a house which was already set well-back from the country road. Three miles from Belfield's city limits, the houses of this wealthy neighbourhood were spread well apart, and most were out of sight of the roadway. There was little or no traffic on the secluded route, which led up into the forests and the Norwick Mountains beyond. Still, it was better to keep the stolen SUV out of sight while he did what he needed to do.

He pulled up alongside the patio door again and killed the engine. As he stepped from the vehicle, he paused to listen. Just birdsong. Then he heard a car approaching, faint at first but growing quickly louder. Jack held his breath until the sound of the motor passed, fading away again into the distance, and then he set to work. Taking a deep breath to steel himself, he stepped through the patio doors and back into the kitchen.

She lay there, exactly as before. The only difference was a small pool of blood that had spread from beneath her dark curls, slipping into the grouting between the polished marble tiles.

He had been sent to put the frighteners on her, nothing more. To send a message to her husband. He'd been given very specific instructions. He had the cable ties in one pocket and a permanent marker in the other. It should have been simple. The instructions had made it sound simple. Grab her, tie her up and gag her, cut all her clothes off and write two words, one on each breast, using the permanent marker… WATCH OUT!

Nasty. There was no doubt about it. He didn't like it, but only taking jobs he liked was no longer a luxury Jack Barry had. Still, there were lines he wouldn't cross. Murder, torture, rape. He wouldn't do that. In fact, he had secretly intended to deviate from the plans and let the woman keep her underwear on. A certain decency was needed; he could always claim a misunderstanding if anything ever came of it. Not that he'd thought anything would. He had felt it was a safe enough change to the plan, one that wouldn't have any real consequences for him. How ridiculous his bellyaching over that little detail seemed, looking down at her now. Fully clothed—and stone dead.

Why hadn't she listened? He'd told her he wasn't

going to hurt her. He'd told her to be quiet. Instead, she had kept shrieking and thrashing, kicking and clawing. He had done his best to restrain her, but she'd torn loose and gone for the phone. When he tried to grab it from her, they'd spun about the kitchen in a ridiculous dance, until finally he had lost his patience and smacked her one.

Her head had struck the marble worktop on the way down. He could see the dash of blood where she'd hit it, and the mark below her eye where he'd punched her. Her nails were all broken from when she'd clawed at his wax jacket.

He couldn't do anything to save her now, but he could still do something to save himself.

He set to work, pulling open drawers and rifling the contents. He didn't want to go further into the house, but there was a living room linked to the kitchen by a set of open folding doors and he moved through it next, pulling open cabinets and clearing out the crystal and china ornaments. He tossed the place, good and proper. Then he noticed the huge flatscreen TV on the far wall. He tugged it down roughly, ripping the cables, and it came away with a snap of broken plastic. Hauling the giant TV out to the drive, he chucked it into a laurel bush halfway to the gate, as though burglars had ditched it at the last moment.

He paused then, and glanced around the garden, breathing hard from his exertions. He turned and considered the half-open patio door. Better to leave it like that. It would fit with the disturbed-burglary scenario. That ought to do it, he told himself, ignoring the little voice in his head that told him he just didn't want to go back into the house and have to share the kitchen with the dead woman again. The woman he'd killed.

He shook his head. Done was done. He needed to get out of there.

Hurrying back to the Jeep, he climbed in and closed the door, before pulling off his gloves and mask. He heaved a breath as though he had just been underwater, but didn't allow himself any more than a moment. Rolling gloves and mask up into a bundle, he set them into the passenger foot well. He would burn the vehicle and everything in it later. He fished out the keys and started the engine. Driving carefully to the stone-pillared gate, he waited. He slid both windows down and listened. No traffic.

Pulling out, he drove steadily. Not too fast, but not too slow either. On towards the mountains, and the original plan he'd made for discarding the evidence.

The boss was going to be furious. As Jack Barry drove further up the winding mountain road, he began to sweat again. He realised that he would rather face a kitchen full of dead bodies than have to make his report back to the boss now.

1

BEFORE SHE EVEN opened her eyes, Esther knew she wasn't in her own bed. The smells, the feel of the sheets against her skin, and the sounds outside the window were all unfamiliar to her. These details occurred to her as quickly as her dream faded, but she didn't open her eyes straight away. Instead, she tried to dredge up some recollection of the night before... Clipped and blurry memories of a bar, or possibly two different bars... Snatches of a nightclub... Dancing... But there was nothing after the club. No sneak previews of who she might be about to wake up next to. And she'd had some howlers recently, like the two-hundred-and-fifty-pound trucker she'd met at that biker dive last month. She shuddered and flicked through the disconnected fragments of last night's memory again. Had she been a computer, her fierce and persistent attempts to access her memory bank from the early hours would simply be returning an ERROR message. Of course, computers didn't emerge from sleep with hangovers like this one. That was another reason for delaying the inevitable: she knew that once she opened her eyes, the headache and nausea would hit harder. She knew this from extensive experience.

Shifting her position slightly, she registered the silky-smooth sheets against her nipples and thighs. She was naked. Of course she was. How often had she woken up in a stranger's bed with her clothes *on?*

She took a deep breath. Screw it! She couldn't drift in this purgatory any longer. *Hangover and fat naked truckers be damned...* She opened her eyes.

Yeah, she'd never been in this bedroom before... she was ninety-nine per cent sure. Ninety-five, at least.

On the plus side, the room wasn't spinning as much as she feared it would, and the ache in her head didn't hammer home with the exposure to light as much as it might have.

She stared for a moment at the high ceiling. The light fixture hanging at its centre was housed in some arcane, Middle Eastern-style metal cage. Interesting. She dropped her gaze. At the foot of the bed stood an elegantly painted oriental wooden screen next to a rosewood chest of drawers. The bedroom itself was neat and tidy, and hardly darkened at all by the paper-and-bamboo blinds that covered the tall dormer window.

Fuck, she thought, *this guy's married.* But when she turned her head on the pillow, she was forced to revise this assumption. Not guy. Girl. Esther carefully propped herself up on her elbows to get a better view. Nope. *Two* girls. Of an age with her at least—late twenties or early thirties. The one nearest Esther had short brown hair and a Chinese symbol tattooed on the nape of her neck. The other was blonde, her dark lipstick and eye makeup smudged by last night's festivities. Esther lifted the duvet. Yep. They were all completely naked. Esther avoided looking at the oversized sex toy lying next to a set of glossy black toenails as she lowered the covers again.

Holding her breath, she slipped out gingerly from beneath the blankets. She remembered the brunette from the club now, but not the blonde. And she couldn't recall any names.

She cast her eyes about the room. Shit. No sign of her clothes. With one eye on the sleeping women, she tip-toed quietly from the bedroom.

The sitting room bore all the signs of heavy partying the night before. Standing there, stark naked, Esther was relieved not to discover anybody slumbering on the sofa. She quickly spotted her clothes, mixed up with other female garments scattered on the floor next to the sofa. She picked through the underwear until she found her own.

Among the debris on the glass coffee table were three empty wine bottles and a half-empty bottle of vodka. Esther spotted two giant glass bongs sitting in a corner of the room and said a silent prayer that she hadn't partaken in that, or that if she had there would be no drug tests at work any time soon. She couldn't smell any trace of cannabis smoke in the air, but her nose was unlikely to register anything short of a fire in a plant factory right that minute.

As she tugged on her knickers and snatched up her jeans, Esther told herself for the hundredth time that she had to stop doing this. It was getting worse. Blowing away entire evenings in a blur of alcohol and waking up with strange men—and women, now… It was getting ridiculous. As she looked about the living room, where the Asian themes continued in the form of wall-hangings and ornaments, Esther tried—and failed—to recall any of the drinking or conversing or cavorting that she'd engaged in here last night. She had no idea what part of town she was in or what bloody time it was.

She found her jacket and grungy leather handbag draped across the back of a chair in one corner. Inside the bag she was grateful to find her purse and phone, although her phone's battery was on the verge of dying. Just after eleven a.m., and already the screen showed four missed calls from Jared. *Shit.* This was their late Friday shift. He wouldn't normally be looking for her before two in the afternoon; if he was phoning her this early it meant something serious had happened.

There were two text messages from him.

The first was sent at 10:06. It simply read: *Are you up? Need you in early. Call me.* The second was sent at 10:48. It was an address, and from the postcode she guessed it would be somewhere up in the Norwick hills. The message below it read: *Come straight here. Dead woman. DCI on his way.*

Esther groaned. She needed to hurry. And she didn't even know where the fuck she was.

"Leaving already?"

Esther jumped at the sound of the woman's voice behind her. She turned to see the short-haired brunette standing in the doorway to the bedroom. She hadn't bothered with a robe. She stood, lean, tanned, toned and beautiful, and totally unconcerned by her own nakedness. Esther noticed another string of Asian symbols tattooed in a neat row down one side of her enviably flat tummy. Weirdly, under that sharp blue gaze, Esther felt like *she* was the one who was naked.

"Yeah, uh, work." Esther waved her phone idiotically. "Gotta, um... gotta go."

"Okay." Perhaps the woman sensed Esther's discomfort, because she smiled in amusement. "Might see you around again sometime?"

"Maybe, yeah," Esther replied. *No fucking way,* she thought. "See you around, and thanks for..." *Thanks for what?* Esther wished she could remember just a little bit of what had happened last night. Like what she'd done with the amused-looking lesbian and her blonde friend. If Esther had been absolutely certain that all the events of last night would remain irretrievably lost to her, it might not have been so bad, but she had some experience of drink's treachery; she would gradually recall small pieces over the rest of the day, or week, and these little scraps of memory, while not enough to furnish her with a sufficient story, would invariably make her cringe. The brunette's impish smile seemed to suggest that she already knew all the things Esther would spend the rest of her day cringing about.

"Thanks for last night," Esther finished lamely, wondering if she really ought to be thanking the woman for last night, or whether maybe their antics in the bedroom meant it should be the other way around.

"Thank *you,* Esther," the woman chirped with a cheeky grin. "It was... *memorable.*"

Clearly, she knew Esther couldn't remember her name. *Trish? Tara?* Something beginning with T, Esther was sure. Tanya, maybe...

Esther hurried to the front door. "Okay, see you."

She slipped out quickly, away from the bongs and the empty bottles of booze and the naked woman with the pixie-like smile.

2

ESTHER PULLED UP just short of the police car that was blocking the narrow country road. A uniformed officer had his hand raised, signalling her to stop. Just beyond him, a length of police cordon tape was stretched across the tree-lined roadway. It was mid-October and the leaves had turned. A canopy of red and yellow reached out over the road, and drifts of fallen leaves littered the verges.

Esther spotted her boss standing in the shadow of a tree next to the cordon. Detective Inspector Jared Wilcox was a tall man—over six-two—with broad shoulders, wild white hair, and a permanent coat of stubble on his sagging cheeks. He was smoking and chortling with a portly grey-haired sergeant in uniform. An old buddy, Esther guessed.

She scanned the roadway beyond the police car and saw that the press were corralled behind the far cordon, about a hundred yards away. Esther groaned when she saw the sharply suited black man addressing them. Detective Chief Inspector Warren Porter had beaten her to the crime scene. As she pulled in next to the patrol car and cut the engine, she saw the DCI glance over his shoulder towards her. He couldn't fail to recognise her battered Fiat. Even at a hundred yards, she could feel his baleful glare. *Fuck*. This was not her morning.

Before getting out, Esther angled the rear-view mirror to check her face. A touch of make-up had hidden the worst. She still looked bleary-eyed, and her dark hair was dishevelled, but it was too late to fix that now. She grabbed her notebook and pen and stepped out of the car. There was no discreet way of checking her overall appearance in the reflection of the car window, so she marched with as much confidence as she could muster towards the officers manning the roadblock. As she flashed her warrant card to one of the uniform officers, Jared looked over and saw her. The DI waved goodbye to his sergeant friend and plodded towards her.

"Detective Sergeant Penman," he said dryly. "You made it after all."

"Sorry, Jared," she sighed. "Late night."

"Porter's pissed off," he muttered, with a nod towards the DCI and the press. He lifted the cordon tape for her to duck underneath, and led her up the country road, toward a stately house where white-suited CSIs were shuffling in and out, going to and from a crime scene van with bags of evidence and bits of kit.

Esther swallowed a sarcastic comment as she glanced again towards where DCI Porter was chatting up the reporters, no doubt hoping to see his name in black and white in tomorrow's editions. Probably waiting anxiously for the TV cameras to appear so he could deliver some over-rehearsed soundbite of commiseration and determination to the national populace during the evening news bulletin.

"This is happening too often," Jared said. "He might make me do something about you soon."

Esther was about to reply when she caught a whiff of his breath. *Hypocrite,* she thought.

"You smell like whiskey," she growled.

He shrugged guiltily. "I had a late one too. Wasn't expecting the phone call this morning." He began fishing through his pockets and found a pack of gum. He popped a piece in his mouth and began chewing vigorously.

"Can I get one of those?" she asked.

He handed her the chewing gum.

"So, what are we looking at?" she asked, as she took a piece of gum and handed the packet back.

"Middle-aged woman," he told her. "Doc reckons a blow to the head killed her. Place is ransacked. Looks like a burglary gone wrong. Neighbour found her a short while ago. She's not long dead."

Another line of police tape was stretched between two tall stone pillars, beyond which lay a long, curving pebble driveway. At this inner cordon she and Jared signed the logbook that another uniform officer held out for them. They went to an open equipment box sitting nearby, full of plastic-wrapped kits: white hooded coveralls, masks, gloves, overshoes. The CSIs were still going through the scene, so Esther followed Jared's lead and began suiting up. When they both pulled their hoods up and snapped their masks in place, they looked identical to all the other scene technicians on site.

The house itself was massive, with a grand front

porch and bay windows on the third floor. The garden was expansive, and its broad, well-tended lawn was lined with laurel bushes and willow trees. As they made their way up the drive, Esther spotted several deep divots in the pebble surface, some of which went right down to the dirt in places. She pointed them out to Jared, who shook his head.

"No tyre marks, unfortunately," he told her. "Looks like somebody either pulled away in a hurry or pulled up in a hurry, but the damn gravel was too thick. No treads in the mud under it."

"And that?" Esther pointed to the television lying in a bush on the far side of the driveway.

Jared nodded. "Like I said, burglary gone wrong."

"No CCTV cameras?" she asked, checking the façade.

"Nope."

"Neighbours?"

"Too far away. Nobody heard or saw anything until poor Missus Hamilton came by."

"Missus Hamilton?"

"Nearest neighbour. Found the victim shortly before ten a.m. But you can't even see the Hamilton house from here, so it's no surprise we're struggling for witnesses."

The set of patio doors leading into the house stood open. A CSI came out, carrying a set of fingerprint lifts in an evidence bag. Another was taking photographs just inside the door. Esther and Jared stepped through between shots, into the kitchen.

The dead woman was still sprawled, face up on the floor. A pool of blood had spread out from beneath her. As she studied the scene, Esther noticed that there was blood on the edge of the marble worktop, just above where the woman lay. The red puddle on the floor was itself largely undisturbed; there was only one footprint, and it had the word POLICE stamped across it in tiny lines, showing her where the FMO— the police doctor—had approached to examine the body.

"How many blows to the head did you say?" she asked Jared.

"Just the one, I think."

Esther pointed out the blood on the worktop. "That's where she got the injury, I guess. Hit her head on the way down, cracked her skull."

"Pushed?" Jared wondered aloud.

Esther took in the two broken nails on the woman's right hand. "Well, there was some kind of struggle," she said. She studied the rest of kitchen. "Okay for me to get a little closer?" she asked the photographer, indicating the open drawers and cabinets.

He nodded. "Got that already. Just about to do the living room."

Esther went from one drawer to the next, carefully studying the contents. Disturbed, yes... but as if someone had just reached in and messed everything up. A set of silver cutlery had been scattered about one drawer. Even a drugged-up half-wit of a burglar would know it was worth something, and yet the set looked complete. In another drawer she found a plastic coin bag, imprinted with the logo of a national bank, stuffed full of pound coins. It would have been obvious to anyone searching for cash and valuables. And sitting atop a nearby counter was a top-brand laptop. It was still plugged into the wall, untouched and unnoticed.

The kitchen was linked to a plush living room via a set of wide-open folding doors. The photographer was capturing the damage to a wall there, where the television had been pulled out, the steel mount hanging from broken plaster and the cables dangling loose. Esther took in the rest of the room. Cushions from the sofa lay tossed on the floor. Crystal ornaments were knocked over or smashed.

"The rest of the house look like these two rooms?" she asked Jared.

Jared shook his head. "No. Looks like she disturbed them here, spooked them, they hit her—or pushed her—and she gets killed. They panic. They run. Rest of the house is all in order."

It was Esther's turn to shake her head. "This isn't a burglary gone wrong," she said.

Jared sighed. "Okay. Hit me with it, Sherlock."

"Whoever's done this, they've tried to make it *look* like a burglary, but they've not been looking for anything to steal." She pointed out the money in the drawer and the laptop on the counter. "They've left behind cash and valuables. Even if the woman's death spooked them, that laptop hasn't been touched, and the TV... why take it out and then dump it in the drive?"

"Well, maybe they figured it'd link them to the homicide, and they decided it wasn't worth it and ditched it?" Jared countered.

"Well, then, why smash the crystal?" she asked, and looked at him. "Going by your premise, they went to the sitting room first, and took the TV. They had time to get it out, into a waiting van or whatever, before she disturbed them. Why not take the crystal, instead of toppling it and smashing it? Doesn't make any sense. Why pull cushions from the sofa? This is the work of someone trying to make a place *look* burgled, not someone trying to steal shit."

Between the lining of his mask and the drawstring of his white hood, Esther watched Jared's eyes scan the scene, seeing it all over again. He looked at her. He nodded. "Okay," he said. "I buy that. Good. So why were they here in the first place, if not to burgle?"

Esther turned back to the body. Clothing undisturbed. "No evidence of a sexual assault," she mused. "I take it we have an ID by now? Who is she?" She locked on the wedding ring. "Husband would be top of my list of suspects to start with."

"Her name is Rachel Gorman, fifty-two years. Married to one Charles Gorman. He works as a manager at Belfield Logistics. They're a homegrown firm, but a pretty big one. Land-based freight, mainly. They have depots all over Europe. Haven't managed to do much more digging than that, but neither person has any intel flags on them."

"Any history of domestics?" she asked.

"None."

"The victim's phone? Is it here?"

"Well, there was a phone on the floor near her hand. Already boxed up and tagged. I assume it's hers."

Esther nodded. "And has Mister Charles Gorman been informed yet?" she asked.

Jared shook his head. "I held off sending a uniform crew. Wanted to hear what my star detective would say first."

"Aw shucks, Jared, thanks. Well, I say hold off on

the crew. Let's go ourselves. See how he reacts." She looked up from the dead woman and surveyed the scene one more time. "Yeah. Let's go do that now." She marched back outside without waiting for him.

Jared followed with a sarcastic, "Roger, Sarge."

3

ONCE THEY'D STRIPPED off their white coveralls, Esther drove them to the headquarters of Belfield Logistics, or *Belfield European and International Logistics (UK) Limited,* to give the company its full title. Jared had been chauffeured to the crime scene by a local uniform crew. He ordered the same crew to tail them to the offices as well, in case the bereaved spouse needed a lift to the mortuary, or the local custody suite.

Belfield Logistics was headquartered in one of the countless industrial estates that spread west from the city. En route, Jared used his phone to pull up a picture of Charles Gorman from the company's website. In his early fifties, Gorman looked every inch the middle manager. He was smiling amiably for the camera, his piggish little eyes squinting through his bifocals, his thin blonde hair receding, his jowls and chin falling heavily over collar and tie.

"His bio is as boring as he looks," Jared murmured, using his thumb to scroll through the webpage. "Seems like a pretty regular guy."

"A regular guy who might have killed his wife this morning," Esther quipped.

"A regular guy who might have killed his wife this morning," Jared repeated as he put his phone away.

There was a long pause. "You know the Superintendent Promotion Boards are coming up in a couple of months," he said.

Esther chortled. "I'm a few ranks short of being eligible for those, Jared."

"I mean, you need to be careful with Porter for a little while," he replied. "He's up for promotion and he's pissy with everyone these days. And ever since he arrived, he's seemed to have it in for you."

"That's just because I don't bat my eyes at him and ask him to let me suck his dick like the airheads in the office."

Jared nodded. "Maybe. But he keeps bringing up your punctuality, your reports and your... *attitude.*" He said the last word with a grimace, knowing how it sounded.

"What about my *attitude?*" Esther shot back hotly.

Jared raised his eyebrows.

Esther blushed. "What about my attitude, Inspector?" she asked, in her sweetest tone.

Jared laughed. "Save it for the DCI, Esther."

"And my files are fine," she went on quickly. "How many files have the CPS sent back to you since I started? How many requests for further evidence?"

"Zip," Jared conceded with a sigh. Clearly, he was already regretting having started the discussion.

"Correct," Esther replied. "My files are good."

"I'm not talking about your criminal case files. I'm talking about your end-of-quarter evaluation reports."

"I've no time for that shit, Jared. I have *actual* police-work to do."

"Just..." he sighed again. "Just be careful with him. Try not to give him something to use against you. That's all."

Esther shifted her eyes from the road to her boss. He seemed serious, and worried. After a moment she nodded.

"Okay," she said. "Thanks for the heads-up."

"Don't mention it. What would I do without you? I'd probably have to do some actual police-work of my own."

She smiled.

Traffic around Belfield was still sluggish, and it took them almost half an hour to get to the Southwest Industrial Estate, home to several national and multinational companies. Belfield Logistics had a broad plot all to itself, its sprawling warehouse and truck depot separated from the office block by a small car park. Esther pulled into one of the parking bays marked for visitors.

"Let me do the talking," Jared said, unbuckling his seatbelt.

Esther frowned.

"I want you to watch him while his attention is on me," he told her. "Besides," he quipped, "I'm the sensitive one, remember?"

She snorted. "Yeah right."

The front office of Belfield Logistics had floor-to-ceiling windows and potted plants to either side of the main doors. As they crossed the parking lot, Esther glanced toward the gates to the yard. The patrol car was idling just out of sight. That had been another of Jared's instructions to the crew: be close by, but don't be obvious about it.

Inside, the reception area was unremarkable. A fake palm stood by the windows, next to a couple of leather sofas and a glass coffee table. Generic cityscapes hung in frames along the walls. A tall wooden counter faced the door, the words BELFIELD LOGISTICS affixed to the front in tall chrome letters. All that could be seen of the lone receptionist behind it was the top of her blonde head. She needed her roots done, Esther noted as they approached. The woman's low murmur suggested that the phone call she was on was a personal one.

Jared cleared his throat and the woman looked up, startled, and hurriedly ended the call. Esther sized her up quickly: a bottle-blonde in her mid-forties, weary-eyed and wearing too much make-up in her effort to hide it; she was a working mother, and she was either a single parent or she had a lazy husband at home.

"I've got to go, John. I'll ring you later." She hung up and beamed at them with a bright, professional smile. She spoke in a tone to match her smile. "Hi there, welcome to Belfield Logistics, how may I help you today?"

"We're looking to speak to Charles Gorman," Jared replied brusquely. He pulled out his warrant card and showed it to her. "Name's Jared Wilcox. I'm a Detective Inspector with Belfield CID." He nodded to Esther. "This is my colleague, Detective Sergeant Penman. Is Mister Gorman in this morning?"

Esther grimaced. *Sensitive one indeed.*

The receptionist sputtered for a moment, but she recovered quickly and began flicking through a large hardback notebook in front of her. Esther saw that it was covered with jotted appointments and telephone messages. "He, um, Charlie… yes, he's in. Is everything okay?"

Jared tucked his ID card away. "We need to speak to him privately, ma'am. Would that be possible?"

"Well, yes, of course." She picked up the phone again and hit a button. There was a protracted silence. The receptionist frowned, hung up, and punched another button. Success this time. "Hi, Steve, is Charlie Gorman about? He's not in his office. Oh good, will you tell him there are a couple of police officers down here looking to speak to him? Ta." She hung up and beamed at them as if she'd solved a mystery. "He was just in another office. Someone's fetching him for you now."

"Has he been in the office all morning?" Jared inquired.

The receptionist nodded. "He came in a few minutes after I opened up."

"What time was that?" Esther asked.

"About half eight, twenty to nine?"

Esther pulled out her notebook and jotted the times down.

"And how did he seem this morning? Anything unusual about him?"

"Who, Charlie?" The receptionist frowned. "Fine. Normal. Why?"

Esther just nodded and ignored the question. "And what was your name, sorry?"

"Penelope," the receptionist replied, glancing from Esther to Jared and back as if she might be in trouble herself. "Penelope Newman."

Esther jotted. "Have you worked here long, Ms

Newman?"

"Five years," she replied, and as Esther wrote this down Ms Newman gestured to the leather sofas by the window. "Why don't you have a seat?" she suggested. "Would you like tea? Coffee?"

They both shook their heads and said "No, thanks."

The phone rang. Penelope Newman looked more relieved than apologetic as she excused herself and grabbed it. She ducked behind her computer screen once more, clacking away at her keyboard as she spoke to the client on the other end.

Jared shared a look with Esther as they drifted towards the sofas. "Thought I was doing the talking?"

Esther nodded. "I'm just sweeping up."

Jared harrumphed.

"Arrived as normal," he recapped quietly. "Seemed fine, she says."

Esther nodded. "We'll see for ourselves in a moment."

But Gorman did not appear right away. In fact, the minutes began to tick by as they sat waiting. Esther, feeling restless, stood and started to pace. She stopped in front of one of the framed cityscapes. Paris by night. It was a photograph with a long exposure, turning the traffic into a series of red and yellow streaks. It was fairly banal, and just about right for an office waiting area.

After another few minutes of pacing, Esther glanced at her watch, and then at Jared. He had taken a seat facing Ms Newman, who was now very busy trying to make herself seem busy, and affecting not to notice the DI's deepening frown. Esther was about to approach the woman again to ask her what the delay was, when a flash of movement from the parking lot caught her eye. It was Charles Gorman. Esther recognised him immediately from the photo she'd seen on Jared's phone earlier. Even without that, their suspect would have given himself away by the nervous glances he cast over his shoulder as he scurried across the parking lot.

"Jared!" Esther shouted, as she headed for the doors. "Jared, it's Gorman! He's doing a runner!"

Gorman was already sliding into the driver's seat of a silver Mercedes.

Esther shoved the doors open and took to her heels, darting between the first row of cars. Too late. She heard the engine rev, and she was still several yards from the vehicle when it spun backwards out of the parking bay and gunned forward towards the gates.

But the uniform officers must have seen Esther running; all of a sudden, the patrol car appeared, blue lights flashing, blocking the gate and the only way to the road beyond. The Merc skidded to a halt, the reverse lights came on, and Gorman began backing up.

Esther wasn't far now, Jared only a little way behind her. There was no other access to the car park for motor vehicles. Gorman seemed to realise this too, because suddenly the driver's door flew open and he was out on foot, making for a pedestrian gate in the fence on the other side of the parking lot. A sign over the gate told Esther it led to the railway line that serviced the industrial estates.

"Police! Stop where you are!" she yelled, as she darted between the parked cars and raced after him.

But Gorman kept running.

Esther was glad she'd stuck with her low-heeled boots last night. Of all the officers now giving chase, she was out in front. A uniformed policewoman had jumped from the patrol car, but she was still some distance behind them, and Jared was wheezing as he fell even further back.

It was up to her.

Once through the narrow gate, Gorman scampered down the path to the railway platform. Esther spotted an opportunity to halve the distance between them by hurdling the shrubs and leaping down a grassy bank. But she landed awkwardly on the platform. She stumbled and cut her knee, tearing her jeans in the process. Scrambling quickly to her feet, she took off again, only a handful of yards behind her quarry now.

"Police!" Esther shouted again, a little more out of breath this time. "STOP!"

Startled commuters stepped back and stared in shock as the pair raced by. A young man in an expensive suit, with a satchel over one shoulder and a Kindle in his hand, took half a step forward but then hesitated. Any half-hearted notion the man had of tackling the suspect faded as Gorman reached him. And then both Gorman and Esther were pounding past him and the opportunity was gone.

Gorman was heading for the end of the platform, where a waist-high barrier bore a sign that declared AUTHORISED ACCESS ONLY BEYOND THIS POINT in big, bold lettering. It wasn't designed to stop anyone who chose to ignore it though, and in a surprising show of physical ability, Gorman leapt the barrier and took the steps leading down to the tracks in three clumsy bounds.

Esther followed him. Gorman risked a quick glance over his shoulder. He tried to quicken his pace, but he was a pudgy middle-aged man who had probably not done any meaningful exercise for many years. Esther might not have been to the gym in a while, but she was still much fitter. She was going to catch him. She knew it. He knew it.

They were out onto a wider strip of scrubland now. Warehouses stood behind chain-link fences to either side. The tracks were raised a couple of feet from the ground on a bed of stones.

It was only when Gorman scrambled onto the railway line that Esther noticed the oncoming train. Still some distance away, it was approaching fast, its single white headlight bright even in the daylight.

Esther had a better purchase on the dirt below the tracks than Gorman did running on the loose gravel between the sleepers. She wasn't going to catch him down here, though, and she knew if the train kept coming, he could jump down the other side and make good his escape. He was right between the rails now, running straight for the train and its hazy headlamp.

Fuck it! She scrambled up the gravel bank and onto the railway line proper. She lost a few yards on Gorman in the process, but quickly picked up her pace again, using the concrete sleepers as footing.

The train driver had spotted them at last. Two long blasts of the train's horn were followed by the squeal of metal-on-metal as the locomotive started braking hard.

Esther was close now. Close enough to make a grab for him. But if she got it wrong, stumbled… Brakes or no brakes, that train was bearing down fast...

"Police! Stop!" Esther cried, but her words were lost in the din of the train's rumbling and screeching.

Two more horn blasts. The train was going to hit them if they didn't get off the line. But instead of scrambling down the stony bank to the other side, Gorman just kept running straight down the middle of the tracks.

The fucking idiot is going to kill himself! Esther thought, and then the cold realisation struck her that he might be intending to do just that.

Suddenly Gorman stumbled and Esther saw her chance. It was now or never. If she didn't make a move, she was going to have to jump and leave Gorman to his fate. She'd be writing for weeks...

She dove, caught hold of Gorman's belt and threw her weight to one side, hauling him with her. They both lost their footing, struck the stony bank, and tumbled from the railway line in a tangle of arms and legs.

The train thundered past, brakes screeching, deafening Esther. She could feel the bumps and bruises already, even with the adrenalin in her veins. She ignored the pain in her left elbow and knee as she scrambled to her feet, ready for a fight. But Gorman didn't even try to get up. He just lay on his back, suit rumpled and torn, covered in dust, gasping for air, his face red and coated in sweat.

As Esther stood over him, catching her breath, she watched Charles Gorman heave the air into his lungs and stare blankly at the sky, until the uniform officer arrived at a run and pounced on him. The young PC pulled her handcuffs out and Esther helped her get Gorman restrained. Once the second uniform officer arrived, Esther stood back and let them haul the man to his feet.

Jared arrived last, wheezing worse than any of them.

Esther finally found breath enough to speak. "Charles Gorman, you're under arrest for the murder of your wife Rachel. You do not have to say anything, but I must caution you that if you do not mention, when questioned, something which you later rely on in court it may harm your defence. Anything you do say may be given in evidence."

Gorman was slumped between the two PCs, each of them gripping an arm in case he tried to run again. But as Esther's words registered with him, Gorman straightened and gaped at her. Staring into those startled eyes, Esther realised that Charles Gorman's shocked expression was not feigned.

He hadn't known his wife was dead.

4

THE INTERVIEW ROOM was not a very big place. Four people made it feel crowded. They sat around a small table affixed to one wall, two to either side, facing each other. The chairs were bolted down to prevent any prisoner—unhappy with how proceedings were unfolding, perhaps—from turning them into weapons. The clock high on the back wall was digital, red numbers on black, and screened with Perspex; it displayed the day, date and time in twenty-four-hour layout, the little figure on the right morphing as each second ticked away.

Esther had lost count of the number of people she'd interviewed here, in this windowless cell with its foam-panelled walls. She had spent her whole career in this district, so her very first shoplifter had been in one of these rooms. They hadn't changed much in all those years, apart from the technology—the clocks had had hands and faces when she started, and the digital recorders had been tape decks. Cassette tapes were certainly an invention she was happy to see fall by the wayside.

She and Jared were sitting with their backs to the door. Charles Gorman and his solicitor sat opposite. The lawyer was a man in his fifties, with an unruly mop of grey hair and thick glasses perched on his broad nose. He sat silently, a legal pad resting on one knee.

The interview was ten minutes old, and not at all the straightforward affair her foot chase might have led her to expect. Gorman's attempt to flee had seemed like a vindication of Esther's suspicions at first, but his reaction in the moments after his arrest had made her doubt his guilt. He was so exhausted from the run, it had taken him a few moments to respond.

"Wh-what did you say? Murder?" he stammered.

"The murder of your wife Rachel," Jared repeated sternly, still trying to catch his breath. He hadn't seen the man's reaction to Esther's words.

"Rache..." Gorman sagged. Esther thought he was going to collapse. His face went from red to white. He looked like he'd been struck in the gut. "Rachel... Rachel... I didn't... I..."

"Sir, you're under caution right now," Jared advised him, growing impassive and professional as he recovered from his exertions. "Anything you say now can be used as evidence."

Gorman looked stunned and bewildered as he was led away by the uniformed officers. The two constables practically had to carry him. If the shock at hearing of his wife's demise was an act, Esther would eat her boots.

She watched him now, sitting across the table from her, sipping lukewarm tea from a paper cup. His hands were shaking, his eyes red from crying. He looked broken. Broken and pathetic, in the grey cotton tracksuit the custody officers had given him to replace the clothes they'd seized. He had recovered his wits sufficiently on the journey to the police station to remember his daughter, Charlotte. She was at university in Cambridge. Jared had put through a request to Cambridgeshire Constabulary to have the death message passed, and assured Charles Gorman that news of his arrest would not be shared. Gorman had seemed a little relieved by that, at least.

Esther decided that the latest silence had gone on long enough.

"So, you last saw your wife this morning, before you left for work?" she recapped. "Is that correct?"

He nodded.

"Alive and well?"

He snivelled and nodded.

"Is that a yes, Mister Gorman? I need you to speak up for the tape."

"Yes," he answered, and wiped his nose with the back of his hand. Cleared his throat.

"What time did you leave the house?"

Gorman shook his head. "About half seven. Quarter to eight, maybe?"

"Did Rachel show any signs of concern this morning? Anything odd about her behaviour?"

Gorman shook his head. "No. No, nothing. She just said 'see you…'" He broke down into quiet sobbing again. It was the third or fourth time so far. Esther gave him a moment to pull himself together and carry on. "She said 'See you later' and I left. That's it. Normal. Nothing… there was nothing unusual. She seemed… she seemed fine."

"So why did you run, Mister Gorman?" Jared asked.

Gorman just shrugged and shook his head. Said nothing. They'd asked him the same question earlier in the interview and gotten much the same response.

Esther decided to change tack. "How was your marriage?" she asked.

That got his attention. "Our marriage?"

Unfazed, Esther repeated herself. "How was your marriage? Was it happy? Did she ever cheat on you? Did you ever cheat on her?"

Gorman didn't reply.

"Mister Gorman?"

He took a deep breath. "I had an affair. But it was years ago. She knew about it. We fought at the time. She was upset. As you can imagine. But we got through it. It was years ago. It was behind us."

Esther had her pen poised for the details. "Who was she? Name, address."

"What has this got to do with *her*? It's in the past. It's history."

"Who was she, Mister Gorman?"

Gorman sighed.

"Her name was Lydia. Lydia Fenton." He gave Esther an address, which she noted. "But this has nothing to do with Lydia!"

"Did your wife have any other enemies?"

"Lydia wasn't an enemy!" Gorman snapped. "You make it sound like Lydia was out to get her. This will have nothing to do with Lydia Fenton! The idea is ridiculous!"

"Did your wife have any enemies that you know of? Anyone who might want to hurt her?"

Gorman shook his head.

"What about you? Do you have any enemies, Mister Gorman? Anybody who might want to hurt your wife to get to you?"

Gorman stared at Esther, and she sensed she'd finally hit the mark. She could see in those red-rimmed eyes that he was thinking. Thinking quickly, or trying to. His gaze dropped to the table again. He licked his lips.

"Mister Gorman?"

"I need to speak to my solicitor. Privately."

This announcement seemed to surprise his solicitor as much as anyone else.

"Okay," Esther said, "Interview with Charles Gorman suspended at fourteen forty-two hours." She hit the button and the red light winked out. But as Gorman and his lawyer made to get up, she spoke again. "Remember, please, Mister Gorman, that you are a suspect in the investigation into the murder of your wife." She glanced at the solicitor when she said this, ensuring that he realised that this little speech was as much for his benefit as for his client's. "If you have any information—any information at all—that could lead us to *another* suspect, or prove that you are *not* the man who killed her, then it is most certainly in *your* interest, as well as ours, for you to provide us with that information."

Jared led Gorman and his solicitor out of the interview room and down the corridor to the consultation rooms, where he left them. He joined Esther again at the gaoler's desk, as she signed Gorman's custody log.

"What do you think?" he asked.

"He's into something," she replied, quietly enough that none of the custody staff could overhear and none of the custody microphones would pick her up, "but he didn't kill her. I could see it in his face at the railway line. He didn't know she was dead."

They were interrupted by one of the gaolers approaching. "Inspector, there was a call while you were in interview." The young man handed Jared a post-it with an extension number scribbled on it. "Detective Constable Brian Thornton."

Thornton had been put in charge of the Gormans' house search and door-to-door enquiries. Jared thanked the gaoler and went to one of the telephones on the wall nearby.

"Brian? Jared here. What have you got for us?" Jared fell quiet as he listened. He grunted once or twice in response to something Thornton was saying. Finally, looking at Esther meaningfully as he spoke, he said, "Roughly two-hundred grand, you reckon? Where exactly?" He grunted again. "And the neighbour—is she sure about the timings?" Another pause. "Okay, thank you, Brian. Go ahead and write it up, and get that cash logged and bagged." He hung up with a frown.

"What was that about two hundred grand?" Esther asked, feeling impatient.

"Search team found about two hundred thousand in cash stashed over the rafters in Gorman's shed. Sterling and euro. Bad news is we have a neighbour swears she saw Rachel this morning in the garden, when she drove past, just after eight o'clock. That receptionist—Newman—told us Gorman was at work by about half eight. It would have taken him more than half an hour to get from his house to the industrial estate during rush hour."

Esther shrugged. "Told you. He didn't kill her. But he's into something. Something big. The two hundred grand is proof of that. And I reckon

Gorman has realised now that whatever it is he's into, it just got his wife killed. Question is, is he more scared of prison for life, or the people who did it?"

Jared's gaze shifted over her shoulder as he glanced down the corridor. "Well, it looks like we're about to find out."

Esther turned. Gorman and his solicitor were emerging from the consultation room. The solicitor was clutching his legal pad in one hand, his face set.

"Let's start by asking him about the money," Jared muttered quietly. "See how he responds."

They met halfway down the corridor, Jared confirming with the lawyer that everyone was ready to resume, and then they shuffled back into the interview room one after another. Once they were all settled in the same seats again, Esther hit the record button.

"This is the continuation of the interview of Charles Alistair Gorman," she declared. "I am Detective Sergeant Esther Penman, and with me is Detective Inspector Jared Wilcox of Belfield Central Police Station. Also present is Mr Gorman's solicitor. The time, by the clock on the wall, is fourteen thirty-five hours. Mr Gorman, you've been cautioned for the murder of your wife, Rachel Gorman, and I'd like to remind you that you are still under caution at this time. That means you do not have to say anything, but if you do not mention when questioned something which you later rely on in court it may harm your defence. Anything you do say may be given in evidence."

Before Esther could say any more—before Jared could even mention the money they'd found—the solicitor cleared his throat and produced a page. Both pairs of police eyes fixed on it. "My client is going to maintain his right to silence. I have prepared a few lines that he would like to submit, but he will not be answering any more questions." He began to read: "I, Charles Gorman, would like to state clearly that I had no involvement in my wife's death. I left for work this morning at approximately a quarter to eight and at this time my wife was alive and well and there was no dispute between us. I did not kill her, and I did not arrange to have her killed. Signed, Charles Gorman." The solicitor, looking oddly sheepish, passed the paper across the table for Jared to pick up. Both Esther and Jared scanned the lines and shared a look. Jared folded the paper and put it with his notes.

"Do you confirm that this is your statement?" Jared asked Gorman.

Gorman nodded, but kept his eyes down. "I do."

"The police searching your house found approximately two hundred thousand pounds worth of cash, in sterling and euro, hidden in the rafters of your shed," Jared said.

Esther was watching Gorman. She saw him flinch.

Jared waited, letting the silence linger. After a minute or so the solicitor began to shift in his seat. Before he could ask if there was a question for his client, Jared spoke again. "Would you care to tell us why you have two hundred thousand pounds in cash hidden in the rafters of your shed?"

Gorman shook his head. He still wouldn't look at them.

"You'll need to speak up for the tape, Mister Gorman," Jared pressed.

"No comment," Gorman replied without looking up.

"Where did the money come from, Mister Gorman?"

"No comment."

"Does the money belong to you, or your wife?"

"No comment."

"Was this money acquired legally, Mister Gorman?"

"No comment."

The interview ran for some ten more minutes in this vein, Jared pressing Gorman about the money from different angles, Gorman refusing to comment in reply to any of the questions put. Eventually they moved on to the possibility of Gorman having hired someone to kill his wife. Esther again watched Gorman closely. He continued to reply "no comment", but Esther could see that the accusation was upsetting him. The struggle between following his lawyer's advice by sticking to the "no comment" route and the desire to refute the charges was clear on his face. She was quite sure he had no part in his wife's death. At least, not directly. The money though…

In the end they had no option but to release Gorman on bail. He couldn't leave the borough without notifying police and he would have to surrender his passport. He was advised that the money would be retained, and ultimately His Majesty's Revenue and Customs would interview him before he could get it back. The solicitor made a half-hearted attempt to have him released unconditionally since there was no evidence, but the discovery of the cash in the shed roof took the wind out of his sails somewhat. No doubt Gorman was going to get another quizzing, this time from his lawyer, once they left the police station.

As they were walking to the front doors, Esther approached Gorman one more time.

"Mister Gorman," she said, and he stopped but didn't meet her eyes. "Charles," she said, more softly this time, and at last he looked up from the floor. "If you're in trouble, even if you've done something wrong, we can help you. Somebody killed your wife. If that wasn't you, whoever it was might be looking to go after you next. Or your daughter." She tried to hold his gaze, but it slipped to the floor again. The solicitor opened his mouth, on the verge of protesting, so she added. "Speak with your solicitor about it, Charles. If you didn't kill your wife, I think you have an idea who did. You need to work with us."

"That'll do, detective, thank you," the solicitor muttered, and hustled Gorman out of the station.

Jared joined her as she watched them cross the plaza in front of the station and disappear into the crowds on High Street.

"What do you think?"

Esther shook her head. "Didn't do it. Didn't hire anyone else to do it either."

"And the money?"

"Like I said, he's into something he shouldn't be. And he knows who killed his wife." She turned to him. "He's afraid, Jared. He knows it's a message."

Jared breathed out noisily. "Some fucking message."

Esther nodded. "Yep."

They were interrupted by Calvin Brett, a lickspittle DS from financial crime, who strutted up in his squeaky wingtips, his garish tie hoisted so high and tight that Esther thought his fat round head might pop off and float away at any moment. He ignored Jared and gave her a slimy grin.

"Chief Porter wants to see you in his office, Esther," he said. "And he's not happy." He added that last comment as though he was imparting some sage advice, rather than relishing the opportunity to tell her she was in trouble. "I wouldn't keep him waiting, if I were you."

Esther grimaced and looked at Jared, who shrugged. Nothing he could do. She headed for the stairs.

The DCI's office stood at one end of the large open-plan room shared by all the CID detectives. Floor-to-ceiling windows separated his office from the workers at their desks. His predecessor had kept the vertical blinds pulled and drawn at all times—it was widely rumoured the old guy had slept half the day at his desk—but Porter always kept them open. The rank-and-file detectives muttered that he didn't trust them and liked to keep an eye on them all at their work, but Esther suspected the motive had less to do with seeing than being seen. As she stepped into the office, she was keenly aware of a few curious eyes peeping over monitors to watch. She deliberately left the door wide open as she stepped inside, and stood her ground directly in front of Porter's desk.

Detective Chief Inspector Warren Porter was in his late thirties, a handsome man who kept himself in good shape. His skin was dark black, and his full head of dark hair was cropped short on top and tight at the sides. He sported a thin, neatly trimmed beard that accentuated his jawline. His shirt was silk and tailored to fit. He wore a heavy gold Rolex on his left wrist, and Esther was pretty sure it was no accident that his cufflinks were a matching shade of gold. He glanced up from his paperwork as Esther planted herself in front of him, then tossed down his pen. Even that was gold-plated.

Sitting back in his leather chair, he looked her up and down. "You look like shit," he said. "You were late this morning, and you turned up like some hick who'd rolled out of a barn and into her car."

Esther just stared at the wall above his head. She didn't hear any questions, so she didn't offer any responses.

"You need to dress more professionally, Detective Sergeant Penman."

Esther resisted the urge to look down at herself. She already knew what she was wearing: the outfit she had put on to go to the bar last night—tank top under a loose casual shirt, and blue bootcut jeans over brown leather roper boots. Not very different from her usual attire. Only now she was covered in dust and her jeans had a hole in one knee.

"This is not the LAPD in some trashy American movie," Porter continued. "Office attire from now on. Suits or skirts, whichever you prefer. Understood?"

"Sir."

"Why were you late this morning?"

"Sir?"

"Don't 'sir' me. You were late. Your team was on-call and I got to the crime scene before you did. Maybe Detective Inspector Wilcox doesn't feel the need to address your tardiness, or the state you show up in, but I will not let it slide any longer. This is not the first time I've had to speak to you—or to Jared—about your appearance and your slackness. Jared might think you're some kind of Sherlock Holmes, but you'll find I won't indulge you the way he does. There are rules, and there are codes, and there are service policies. You will follow them, just like everybody else. This is *my* department, and I'll not tolerate you dragging its image through the mud. Am I making myself clear, Miss Penman?"

"Sir."

Porter clenched his jaw. Esther thought she could hear his teeth grinding.

"I've had enough of your attitude, Penman," he growled, his voice low enough so that it wouldn't carry beyond the door. "One more step out of place and I will be sending you straight back to uniform. Don't think I won't."

Esther met his gaze then, and held it. There was fury in his eyes. "Whatever you think, sir."

"And the next time you show up in this state, I will breathalyse you myself. This is your last warning. Now get out."

"Sir." She turned on her heel, listening to him exhale loudly, and strode out.

5

JACK BARRY WAS trembling, but he tried hard not to show it. The boss was pacing slowly back and forth, and frowning as though he was mulling over a maths problem. He was short, the boss was, and if you saw him in the street, you'd think nothing of him. Funny that. If Jack had met him in a bookies or in the pub, he'd just think he was a weird little poof. Small and skinny, he had a girlish kind of face, and a haircut like those upside-down-bowl-cuts the Beatles used to have in the sixties. The round spectacles he wore should've made him look even softer, but they didn't. In fact, it was those funny little glasses that drew your attention to the boss's eyes. And it was his eyes that made you realise he was dangerous. There was a darkness—a hardness—in those eyes that made Jack shiver.

They weren't alone. Buck and Gary were there, and another man that Jack didn't know, all standing behind him as if Jack were a prisoner. He felt like a prisoner all right—a prisoner being interrogated.

He'd been sat down at a table. On the table were some blank pages and a pen, and a bottle of whiskey and two glasses. Jack kept glancing at the whiskey. He wasn't sure why it was there, whether it was for someone else maybe, but he sure would've liked a sup to steady his nerves. Might stop him trembling so much.

"You wiped down all the surfaces?" the boss asked.

"Yes, boss, did that and all," Jack stammered back. "Everywhere I touched, wiped 'em all down, I made sure."

"What about your boots?"

Jack hesitated and looked down at his Doc Martens.

"Are those the same boots you wore across her tiled floor?"

Jack's heart sank. There he was, thinking he'd been clever. He wasn't clever. He was stupid.

"And hairs? Were you wearing the mask?"

He nodded, able to give the right answer to that one at least. "Yes, boss. Wore the balaclava the whole time. Burned it all with the car."

"With the car?"

Jack hesitated, unsure, then nodded. "Yeah. Took the Jeep right up into the mountains and waited till after dark, just like you said. She were properly burning when I left."

"Hmm."

Jack tried to read the boss's expression, but it was hard. It was dark in here, with just a lamp on the table to see by, and it kept catching the boss's glasses now so that all Jack could see were discs of bright light instead of eyes. When he stopped in front of

Jack's chair, the man was just a shadow. Short as he was, he was looming over Jack now.

"Give me your hand, Jack," he said softly. Jack never liked it when the boss spoke softly. It was the same as other men shouting. "Give me your hand."

Reluctantly, Jack held out his right hand. He was shaking worse than before. He couldn't see Buck and Gary and the other guy, but he could feel them watching from behind. They'd have a good laugh at him about this. Maybe that was part of the punishment. If it was, he'd take it. He'd seen what the boss could do when angry. He'd take a bit of ribbing over that any day.

"You're shaking, Jack," the boss pointed out. He put his hand on Jack's shoulder. Jack flinched. "Relax, Jack," he whispered. "Relax."

There was a long, uncomfortable silence as Jack sat there with the boss's hand on his shoulder. And then abruptly the hand was gone, and the boss was pointing to the bottle of whiskey.

"You need to relax, Jack," he repeated more loudly. "Pour yourself a drink."

Jack frowned. He was about to question the order when the boss spoke again.

"It'll help settle your nerves," he said. "I am going to ask you to write something. You can't write with your hand shaking like that. Take a drink and settle yourself down."

Jack nodded. He reached out and took hold of the whiskey bottle and poured himself a generous shot. He swallowed it in one go. The burn felt good. It *did* settle his nerves.

"Take another."

Jack didn't argue. He poured himself an even

more generous measure this time, but sipped this one a little more slowly.

"Now, there's some paper and a pen there, Jack, do you see it?"

Jack nodded dumbly, still concentrating on the sharp comfort of the whiskey warming his insides.

"I want you to write out, fifty times, the line 'I didn't mean to kill her'."

Jack must have given him a puzzled look.

"Didn't you ever have to write out lines at school?" the boss asked.

Jack cleared his throat, "Uh, yeah, I guess."

"Well… this is like that. Write out, fifty times, in your best handwriting, the line 'I didn't mean to kill her'. There," he pointed to the paper and pen on the tabletop. "Off you go. That's your punishment."

Jack hesitated. It seemed too easy.

He caught the boss's frown. "Unless you would like me to come up with something more… physical, perhaps? Did you get caned in school, Jack, or was that before your time?"

Jack shook his head. "Nossir, wasn't caned, but I'll do the lines, if that's what you want." He swallowed back what was left in his glass and set it down, then took up the pen. His best handwriting was by no means great, but he tried his damnedest to keep the lines neat and tidy. With the boss looming over him, he did the lines one by one, rather than columns of words one after another like he would have done back in school. By the third line, he was feeling fuzzy and warm from the whiskey, and was becoming utterly consumed with his task…

*

Peter Darren supervised Jack Barry, peering over the man's shoulder as he scrawled out the line he'd given him, slowly and with intense concentration. He wrote 'didn't' as 'dint', but it would do. By the fifth line, Darren reckoned he had enough. He turned to Buck and Gary and JT, nodded to them, and stepped back.

The three men—huge, burly iron-pumpers, all of them—moved swiftly for men so large. Gary looped the electrical cord around Jack's neck while the other two grabbed an arm each. Jack was stunned, and it took him a moment to react, but by then it was too late. For all his kicking and struggling, he was totally outmatched. Darren moved around to the front of the desk. He liked to look men in the eye when they went. It gave him a thrill. It was almost sexual. No, it was better than sex.

Jack's face was going purple. He was a scruffy man in his early forties, with no family other than a disabled father in a council flat who was simply going to have to learn to cope by himself. Jack would be no great loss to society. He was neither good-looking nor productive. Sending him to Gorman's house had only served to confirm his uselessness and stupidity. It had been a simple task, or so Darren had thought. He had given Jack a chance to prove himself with the job, and the man had failed miserably. Now he was paying the price. His bulging bloodshot eyes met Darren's, and Darren just shook his head sadly, like a teacher showing his disappointment to a pupil.

Eventually Jack's frantic kicking became intermittent jerks of his legs, and then he stopped moving altogether. Darren sighed as the light in Jack's eyes went out. Gary held the cord tight for a moment more to be sure.

Darren straightened. "Tie it using the knot I showed you," he directed. "Do it now, while it's on his neck—don't take it off first."

Gary did as he was told. One end of the cord trailed along the floor, at least eight feet in length. They would need every inch of it if they were going to hang Jack Barry from the branch of a tree.

While the three men worked at fixing Jack's noose, Darren donned a pair of rubber gloves. He lifted the pen by one end and the page bearing the scribbled lines by a corner and placed both of them in the pocket of Jack's coat. Carefully taking hold of the whiskey bottle just above its base, he left the room and walked the few feet down the corridor to his small kitchenette. The back rooms of his art gallery were cramped and dingy. It was not the ideal place to manage this kind of business, but this was where Jack always came when Darren had jobs for him. Suggesting anywhere else might have made the man suspicious.

Darren poured half of the remaining whiskey down the sink and placed the bottle into a plastic bag. When he emerged back into the corridor, Buck and JT were already carrying the body towards the yard and the waiting van. He handed the plastic bag with the bottle in it to Gary.

"Remember: not too high. Bend his knees as if he's just let himself hang. Leave the bottle in the grass near his feet. Keep your gloves on and handle it near the base only. You remember the place? You'll find it okay?"

Gary nodded. "Yeah, not a problem, boss. We'll find it." He turned and followed the others to the van.

The yard was dark. Darren had been careful to knock the lights off earlier, just in case. He watched them load the late Jack Barry into the back of the white panel van and slam the doors. *Such a hearse,* he thought. Somehow, those three big lads squeezed into the front seat together. Then the van fired up, brakes momentarily washing the yard in a harsh red light, and it pulled away.

Darren closed the back door and bolted it. He was already moving on to his next problem: Charles Gorman.

*

Esther sat in her leather armchair, watching the traffic slide up and down Temple Street three storeys below. Her apartment was close to the centre of the city, only half a mile from Belfield's shopping plaza and City Hall, and it commanded an impressive view of the south side of the city and the river docks beyond. The Norwick Mountains rose above the blanket of urban lights to the north, blacker shapes against the night sky. The room was gloomy, half-lit by the streetlamps below and the moon above. It hadn't been dark when she sat down, but Esther had so far failed to summon the energy to get up and turn on the lights, or the television set. She simply sat, watching the night fall, with a glass of vodka in one hand.

She glanced at the clock on the wall. She should go to bed, get an early night. Especially after Porter's warning. But she didn't go to bed. Instead, she poured herself another half-glass by the half-light.

Neat. It was a long time since she'd felt the need to mix her vodka.

Just one more half-glass—she'd been limiting herself to half-glasses all evening—and then she'd go to bed.

6

MORNING SUNLIGHT FILLED Esther's living room. Low and blinding, it roused her from her slumber, and she squinted and groaned as she sat up. There was a thump as the empty glass tumbler she'd been holding hit the carpet. She was still sitting in her armchair, overlooking Temple Street, only now the four lanes were jammed with slow-moving traffic, and the occasional bleat of a horn drifted up from below.

She grunted as she struggled out of the armchair. She had slept awkwardly, and her neck was stiff. She could feel the headache starting already. She glanced at the vodka bottle on the floor next to her chair; it was empty, but it had barely been a quarter full to begin with, so that wasn't so bad.

A glance over her shoulder at the clock on her kitchen wall made her curse. She was going to be late again. She needed to move. Aspirin and a shower.

She dialled Jared's number quickly. It went straight to voicemail.

"Jared, sorry, I'm running a bit late this morning. I

know Porter's going to nail my ass to a wall if I'm late again. Any chance you could pop out and meet me in town and we'll do some outside enquiries? I'll be at the Coffee House on Chester Street at ten, if that's okay. Thanks. And again—sorry! See you shortly!"

She hung up. She needed to get herself organised. Aspirin first, then shower. She would have to pick an outfit from her courtroom selection to keep Porter off her back. Impractical, but fuck it—if it kept her away from uniform duty and off nightshifts, she would just have to suck it up.

She flicked on the bathroom light and stripped off quickly. The hot water sluiced away the aches and pains, or maybe it was just the aspirin starting to kick in.

After drying herself, she tied a small towel around her hair and padded into the bedroom. She stopped in front of the stand mirror and examined her naked body. Her legs and crotch needed a shave. She turned and studied herself side-on. There was more of a bulge around her middle these days for sure, but she was by no means fat. Her tits still pointed the right way, but her ass was definitely getting wider. She'd stopped going to the gym about six months ago. Screwing that hot young fitness instructor had seemed like a good idea at the time, but his girlfriend the manager hadn't agreed. Another stellar Esther Penman move. She moved away from the mirror and the shitty memories she was stirring. She needed to start running again, maybe start swimming. A different health club of course. Soon. Maybe next week.

She dressed quickly. She might not be as trim as she used to be, but she could still pull off her tight court outfits with only a little sucking in. She chose grey trousers and a cream silk blouse, with black strappy two-inch heels and a black three-quarter-length coat over the top. She scraped her hair back into a ponytail—no time to blow-dry it—and gave herself a quick once-over in the mirror by the door. Then she left the apartment. She had five minutes to get to the Coffee House. Not gonna happen. She thumbed a quick text to Jared to say she was going to be five to ten minutes late, and then hastened her step.

*

Jared spotted Esther dodging between the lorries and street trams of Chester Street as he sat on the bonnet of his old Volvo. She was dressed like she was on her way to Crown Court rather than heading out to do enquiries. He took a drag of the cigarette in one hand and a sip from his take-out coffee in the other. As she approached, he indicated to the second take-out coffee sitting on the bonnet next to him.

"Hey, sorry I'm late," she said. "Is that for me? Ta." She took the cup and sipped. "Mmm. Thanks, Jared. You're a star."

He looked her up and down. "You trying to impress someone?"

Esther stuck out her tongue at him. "DCI's orders. Office attire."

Jared sniggered. "You can take the girl out of the streets…"

"Oh fuck off, Lord Wilcox, like you're one to talk. Boy from the estates made good."

He laughed. "I don't come from an estate."

"Talk like you do."

Jared chortled but had no comeback. "C'mon," he said. "I have to call by the house quickly before we do anything else." Just the thought of it made the laughter die in his throat; he pulled open the driver door and climbed in quickly, hoping she wouldn't ask why. "You're lucky," he went on as she sat into the passenger seat. He supped his coffee before sticking it in the holder and pulling on his seat belt. "Porter was in a meeting this morning. He sent me an email yesterday. I'm to discipline you and make him aware of every late appearance."

Esther shook her head. "He's such a fucking prick."

Jared nodded. "Yes, he is a prick, but that prick is our boss, Esther, and I'd rather make it to retirement."

"Understood, Inspector. I'll do better. Promise."

"Thank you."

He pulled out into the slow-moving traffic and left the conversation at that. Esther was a great detective, but she was a bloody mess too. Problem was, Jared Wilcox was in no position to talk to *anyone* about their drinking, and Esther knew it. If he even broached the subject, he knew she'd be perfectly justified in shooting him down with some retaliatory observations of her own. He couldn't fight that fight right now. He had other problems to deal with. Like what he was going to say to Samantha when he got to the house. He'd rather have gone home alone, and off-duty, but he couldn't make himself wait. Daniel would be at Tech and he needed to get this sorted. He needed to see her. They'd been married for thirty-four years for Christ's sake! You don't just walk away from that!

"So, have you had any ideas about the Gorman case?" he asked, hoping to derail his train of thought.

"I want to put a rush on the examination of Rachel Gorman's phone," Esther replied, sipping her coffee. "I know we're fishing, but if there's something significant there I want to know, and if not, we need to rule it out as a line of enquiry sooner rather than later. And I want to put in a warrant application for Gorman's phone records as soon as possible. I think we could maybe push for one for Belfield Logistics too, what do you think? No idea if a judge would grant it—might say we're reaching a bit—but if you don't ask you don't get, right? And, given the money we found, I'm thinking Charles Gorman's job is a factor in all this. It's a transport firm, for fuck's sake—clearly, he's neck-deep in some kind of smuggling or trafficking operation. Then there's the boot prints CSI lifted from the crime scene…"

Jared made noises of agreement as Esther rattled through her plans, but he couldn't focus on her words. His mind was already on the task in front of him. Less than twenty minutes later, he was pulling up in front of his house.

"I'll just be a few minutes," he told Esther, as he unbuckled and opened his door.

"Sure," she replied. She already had her phone out, flicking through her emails.

Jared stepped from the car and took a deep breath. As he approached the house, he saw that the lock on the front door was different, and he wasn't really all that surprised when his key didn't work.

He rang the bell and waited. There was movement inside, barely visible through the frosted glass panel in the door. He rang the bell again and rapped on the glass. No answer, and no movement this time.

He glanced about at the neighbours' houses to see if anyone was watching him, then leaned down and opened the letter box. "Samantha? Samantha, just give me a couple of minutes. Please. Talk to me."

Nothing. No response. He glanced around again. Esther had lifted her head from her phone and was watching him with a curious frown. He just shook his head for her to stay put, then quickly slipped around the side of the house.

*

Esther watched Jared slip around the side of his own house like a burglar. Samantha must have kicked him out, she guessed. Her mobile phone, sitting in the palm of her hand, began to chirp with an incoming call. It was the office. She tapped the green icon.

"Hello. DS Penman."

"Sarge, it's Andy in the office." It took her a moment to put a face to the voice. He was a new guy. Young. Cute, but short and a bit too preppy for her taste.

"Hey, Andy, what's up?"

"Sarge, there's been a sudden death up in Norwick Forest," he said hesitantly. "Guy found hanging."

"Okay. Is it suspicious?"

"Looks like suicide."

"Okay," Esther repeated, trying not to sound impatient. "And what's it got to do with us? If it's a suicide, it stays with uniform."

"There's a note with the body," he told her. "Might be linked to the Rachel Gorman killing."

Esther pulled out her notebook and pen. "Give me directions to the scene. Tell Despatch that I'll attend directly and DI Wilcox will attend with me. And let the duty sergeant know we're on our way. Where is it?"

She began scribbling down directions.

*

Jared was becoming exasperated. The door between the kitchen and the hall lay open, and he could see a shape moving in the reflection of the oven door.

"For God's sake, Samantha, I can see you! You're hiding behind the kitchen door. Open up. Be reasonable!"

She didn't come out of hiding, but she did shout. "Go away, Jared. I don't want to see you. The solicitor said you're not supposed to be here."

"I just want to talk. Five minutes. After thirty-four years you can give me five minutes."

"I've given you too many years of my bloody life, Jared Wilcox. Now clear off before I call the police."

"Samantha, please, just be reasonable. I only want to talk."

"Go away!" It was almost a shriek.

Esther must have heard that because the Volvo's horn sounded out in the street. Jared turned. Esther was still frowning at him. She had moved into the driver's seat. He heard her start the engine. She tossed her head at him, indicating that he needed to return to the car. He looked back into the house. *His* house. His house that he couldn't even walk into anymore. Samantha was still hiding just out of view. With a sigh he turned and trudged back to the car.

As he sat into the passenger seat, Esther pulled away from the kerb and moved quickly towards the main road. She filled him in on the phone call as she drove.

He nodded. "Okay," he replied. "Let's go see what they've got."

They drove in silence for a time, but Esther's surreptitious sideways glances started to grate on his nerves. "If you want to say something, spit it out," he snapped.

"Who was she?"

"What?"

"Your wife's kicked you out. Clearly you were fucking someone else. Who was she?"

"You jealous?"

"Just nosey."

When he didn't say anything for a moment, she took her hand off the gear stick and poked him in the side. "Who was she?"

"Oh, for God's sake, Esther," he said. Hesitated. "Helen Simmons," he mumbled.

"Helen Simmons?"

"It was just the once," Jared replied defensively.

"But *Helen Simmons?* That squeaky little girl from Neighbourhood? Are you serious, Jared? She's, what, eighteen?"

"She's twenty-nine," he replied dryly, "as you well know."

"She's half your age is what she is. And that voice." Esther gave a dramatic shiver. "I remember when we were in the Emergency Response Unit together. God, that voice on the radio could make your eardrums bleed."

"She's not that bad."

"Does she squeak in bed too?"

Jared didn't answer. He just shook his head, trying and failing to keep the smile from his face.

"She squeak when you fuck her?"

He burst out laughing. He couldn't help it.

"For God's sake!" he exclaimed, in a failed attempt at disgust.

"I can just imagine her," Esther said with a grin. "Squeak... squeak... squeak-squeak-squeak-squeak..."

"Get your mind out of the gutter, Penman."

"Squeak-squeak-squeaksqueaksqueaksqueak... SQUEAK!"

They laughed, and then fell silent. After a moment, Esther spoke again. Softly this time. "Apologise profusely, beg forgiveness, buy her something nice, and Samantha will come around," she said. "You'll see. Just give her time."

Jared sighed. "I don't know, Esther. I hope you're right, but I just don't know."

They drove on in silence.

7

NORWICK FOREST WAS a riot of autumnal colour, the ground between the trees soft with fallen foliage. *So much for tracks,* Esther thought as she kicked at a drift of leaves. She looked up towards where a couple of officers were cutting the body down from the limb of a chestnut tree. They were on the side of a long hill, deep in the heart of Norwick's woodlands, police tape strung from tree-trunk to tree-trunk, creating an arbitrary scene amidst the wilderness. Esther hadn't bothered suiting up this time. What was the point? No tracks, and a scene open to the elements. The CSIs had already photographed and bagged the whiskey bottle and the suicide note. Jared had made a comment about the cheap whiskey, and the fact that the deceased—Jack Barry, according to the driving licence in his pocket—had left behind a couple of twenty-pound notes.

"Enough to splash out on a single malt, surely?" Jared had murmured. "Might have given him second thoughts. Drinking that shit would only encourage a man to throw up the rope!"

"Maybe that's what did it, Jared," Esther had replied dryly, losing patience because there was something wrong here and she couldn't quite put her finger on it. Everything pointed to suicide. The note read like a confession—a confession that would work nicely to tie up the only murder of a woman in Belfield in the last three years—and when Carl, the senior CSI at the scene, had pointed out that Barry's boots looked like a match for those impressions lifted from the kitchen floor in the Gorman house, it seemed to wrap the thing up. They had a matching Jack Barry on the police database with plenty of priors for burglary. So the immediate working theory was that he had killed Rachel Gorman during yet another burglary, one that had gone badly wrong, and he'd been driven to suicide by the guilt. Case closed.

But something was niggling at Esther. The reason Carl had been able to make his observation about Barry's boots so quickly was because they were spotless. Not spotless, exactly, but certainly too clean for having trekked through the forest. Even if there was no mud in the immediate vicinity, mulch and bits of leaves were sticking to everyone else's feet. Why not Jack Barry's?

She watched as the portly old police doctor finished his examination of the body, snapping off his gloves and gathering his things. He began stumping his way down the slope towards her. His bulging medical bag made him list to one side as he walked. Esther was afraid the old boy might topple at any moment. But he made it to her without incident.

"Well, Doc?" she asked. "Still dead?"

The doctor nodded. "Still dead. And I would

hazard that the cord around his neck's what done it," he quipped.

"Timeline?"

"Rigor mortis well-established, but the local wildlife hasn't really had a go at the poor bugger yet. Been dead about twelve hours, I'd say."

Esther nodded. "Anything unusual? Something about this doesn't feel right to me."

The doctor frowned. "Actually, yes. You'll need to wait for the postmortem results to be sure, but there are faint bruises on his arms, which may or may not be bruises from finger grips. And the settlement of the blood suggests… well, the body may have changed position post mortem."

She knew it! "He's been moved?"

The doctor raised his free hand in a sign of non-committal. "Whoa, I don't know that. These are just visual observations. There may be other explanations. Most of the blood has settled in his feet as you would expect. The discoloration to his back could be something entirely different. And the bruises could be anything. But…"

"But?"

"I would keep an open mind until you get the pathologist's report."

"It could be murder."

"He might have been moved after he died," the doctor stated carefully. *"Might* have been."

Esther knew he wouldn't give her anything more definitive, so she thanked him and marched off towards where Jared was talking on his phone nearby.

"Yes, sir," Jared was saying. "Yes, I understand. I'll brief the duty officer myself… Yes, sir… Okay. Bye." He hung up and put away his phone.

"I think we may have a murder on our hands here," Esther announced without preamble.

Jared frowned. "That was the chief. I've just briefed him about the preliminary findings. He wants these cases linked and closed ASAP—murder cleared; suicide written up."

Esther shook her head. "Doctor reckons the body's been moved after death."

Jared winced. "He said that?"

"Well, he said *might* have been," she admitted. "We'll need to wait for the PM results."

Jared let out a heavy breath. In his younger days, when hip-flasks were part of a detective's kit, he would have been reaching for his. Instead, he fished out his cigarettes and lit one up. "Porter won't like it," he grumbled. "Wants this closed. Clearances. It's all he's interested in these days."

"But if it comes back from the PM that Jack Barry *was* moved, it'll be you and me for the chopping block," Esther pointed out, "and guess who'll be first to swing the axe?"

"I know, I know." He sighed again. "I'll ring him back." He pulled out his phone and started dialling.

While Jared sucked furiously on his cigarette and paced away with the phone to his ear, Esther decided to have another poke around. She turned a slow circle, taking in the woodland that stretched away in every direction. They were within line of sight of two popular woodland paths here, both of which lay downhill from where Esther stood. She could see the yellow-coated police officers standing guard there, turning walkers away from the scene. One of those paths was wide enough for the forestry service vehicles. It was lined with police cars now, and it was the route the first responders had taken when the call came in. Here, among the foothills of the Norwick Mountains, there was still good access to most areas of the forest, with tracks and walkways criss-crossing the woodlands. If Jack Barry had committed suicide, it was not unreasonable that he might have trudged the hundred yards or so uphill to this spot. On the other hand, had he been killed and brought here... Esther turned to look in a direction that no one was paying much attention to. She had watched the two police officers struggle with Jack Barry's body as they cut him down. He would not have been an insignificant burden. With a weight like that to carry, would a killer really want to move uphill? She began trudging upslope of the crime scene.

As she walked, the sounds of human activity faded behind her, replaced by the twittering of the birds overhead and the steady swish of her shoes through the leaves. She had to watch her step in her courtroom heels. She'd almost turned an ankle earlier, and she quietly cursed Porter for his stupid directions. She decided that she would begin to work her way back into her normal attire from the *feet up*. Suit pants might look odd with her brown ropers, but these heels were completely impractical for police work. Porter could kiss her ass.

She was just wondering whether she'd be better off taking her shoes off altogether and going barefoot when something caught her eye. About twenty or thirty yards away to her left was a muddy track. Making her way towards it slowly, she studied the nearby undergrowth. Her tottering continued, but her shoe dilemma was momentarily forgotten; she was seeing freshly broken twigs, and green briar leaves that had fallen in the mud.

And then she spotted them. Tyre tracks. She stopped short of the muddy patch that bore the recent imprints of a vehicle. The clearing appeared to be a dead-end branch-off from a wider roadway, just at the point where it grew too narrow for a vehicle to continue up into the hills. The far end veered west towards the main road.

Esther picked her way carefully around the patch of mud, scanning the earth for any sign of footprints or fallen clues. It didn't take her long to spot something, lying on a patch of grass halfway along the narrow track. A shard of amber plastic, glinting in a thin beam of sunlight that cut through the canopy of leaves. Pulling on her gloves, Esther knelt and plucked it from the tangled grass. It was a piece of the amber casing used for motor vehicle indicators. Clean and dry, it had not been lying long. A glance around showed her the cause of the damage. A shoulder of mossy rock jutted from the ferns that verged the track nearby. Esther could see a line of freshly-scraped moss along the side of the rock, and there were tiny amber sparkles glittering in the raw grooves. As she studied the tracks and the shard of indicator, Esther knew that they belonged to the same vehicle, and that there was more than an outside chance that it was the vehicle that had brought Jack Barry here last night.

She straightened and stared downhill at the crime scene. She could see the white figures moving among the trees, two hundred yards away at most. A natural clearway through the wood, the one she had followed uphill, led directly to Jack Barry's chestnut tree.

She walked a little way on towards the road, but

the path grew more solid and there were no signs of further tracks or vehicle damage. She returned to the muddy turning circle, and from there she worked her way slowly back downhill towards the crime scene, eyes scanning the carpet of leaves and the trees around her for any further clues. She fancied that if she squinted as she looked at the ground between her and the crime scene, she could just make out a couple of lines, runs of darker disturbance through the bed of leaves towards that chestnut tree. But there was nothing more tangible than that. No bits of clothing snagged on low branches, no footprints, no lost identity cards providing her the name and address of her suspect...

She found Jared standing in the same spot where she'd left him. He was watching the CSIs lift the markers and bag their evidence while he puffed industriously on another cigarette.

"We need to send someone up to get pictures and a cast of some tyre tracks," Esther blurted as she stomped up to him, a little out of breath from her hike. "Up at the top of that ridge," she indicated, "there are tyre tracks and I found this"—she showed him the piece of amber plastic—"not far away. If we get a mapper up there too, I'll be able to log where I found it."

Jared didn't turn to her, or reply. He was watching two crime scene investigators carefully assist the coronial morticians bag and tag the body of the late Jack Barry.

"Jared?"

"Chief wants this closed up, Esther," he mumbled. "He's been pretty emphatic. Unless the PM provides us with conclusive evidence that there was foul play, it's to be closed as suicide, and Barry is to be recorded as the perpetrator in the Gorman murder—which will let him close that too."

Esther shook her head. "Pathologists are *never* conclusive," she snapped. "He'll give us some report which will leave enough wriggle room for us to take it either way. The only conclusive thing he'll tell us is that this fucker died because of the electrical cord around his neck."

"Lower your voice, Esther, for Christ's sake," Jared replied. "Let's just wait and see. I'll get the CSIs to gather your evidence, but don't get too into this."

"I'm sorry, *what?* You're letting Porter kill a murder investigation because it'll help him get his clearance figures up for his next promotion board?"

Jared spun around and fixed her with a hot glare. "Keep your fucking voice down," he hissed. "I am following the instruction I have been given by a senior officer. If there is evidence to move it forward, we will. Just…" He softened his tone, and his stare. "Just let's take it one step at a time. Okay?"

Esther shook her head.

"Am I clear, Esther?" his tone was growing firm again.

"Yes, Inspector," she replied, searching his eyes for some inkling that this was a joke. But Jared just looked tired. She suddenly wondered how long he'd looked like this without her noticing—a tired old man.

"I'm going to go and bag this," she muttered, waving the indicator shard about. She stomped off to find an evidence bag and left him standing there.

8

ESTHER SHIFTED IN her seat as she watched DCI Porter's eyes scan the pathologist's report. It was a summary of the findings from Jack Barry's autopsy. The Rachel Gorman report was there too, sitting on the desk to one side. Clearly the chief inspector was prepared for this meeting, despite his show of studying the pages in his hand. She already knew where this was going. Jared had pretty much spelled it out the other day at the crime scene. The superintendent promotion boards were coming up and DCI Warren Porter was a hotly tipped candidate to get one of the coveted positions. Two murders on his patch in the space of a week would *not* go down well at those interviews, unless he had some results to show or some answers to give.

Esther adjusted her position again as the silence stretched. She could never get comfortable in these horrible little seats. She strongly suspected Porter had deliberately selected the most uncomfortable chairs to put in front of his desk, to make those he summoned squirm while he reclined in that giant leather contraption of his. Jared, sitting next to her, hardly moved, although Esther suspected his mind was elsewhere. Even if it was trouble of his own making, she couldn't help feeling a little sorry for Jared. She'd only met his wife Samantha a couple of times—on the rare occasion when a work function invited wives and partners to attend—and the woman had always struck her as a waspish old bat. Or maybe it was just that Samantha found it hard to hide the fact that she resented Esther spending so much time with her husband. She couldn't be sure.

By the time the crime scene in Norwick Forest was closed on Monday, both Jared and Esther had cooled off enough to offer muttered apologies to one another. The pressure was getting to him: Samantha, retirement, Porter breathing down his neck, et cetera, et cetera. She was right to chase the leads, he conceded. Just doing her job. That's why she was his best detective. And so on. She'd bought them both coffees on the way back to the office and by the time they'd returned to the police station they were back to their usual comradely banter. That was the way of it with Esther and Jared, and to be honest Esther wasn't sure how she would manage whenever he *did* retire, and she had to work with a new boss. Theirs was a relationship that had mutual benefits—she relished the freedom he afforded her, and he relied heavily on her doing the detective-work. It's what she was good at, and it's what she loved. Other teams just dished out tasks and had endless reviews and meetings. Esther would suffocate in an environment like that. She felt guilty for suddenly wondering if Jared's marital breakdown might lead to him staying on a few more years.

The crackle of paper brought her back to the present. Porter folded the report and set it down. He cleared his throat.

"Okay, well, it seems fairly straightforward to me," he stated. "We have confirmed prints from the boots Barry was wearing at the scene of the Gorman murder. We have his clear-cut suicide note—a confession when you put it with the footprints. I have considered DS Penman's points, in that the pathologist has highlighted some marks on the deceased's arms. However, if we run with the most obvious hypothesis—that Jack Barry killed Rachel Gorman in a burglary gone wrong and subsequently killed himself because of the guilt he was feeling—then we could attribute the bruises to Rachel Gorman. She may have inflicted them during a struggle. Or they could be something else altogether—nothing to do with either murder or suicide. The pathologist can't put a time on those bruises. And we cannot confirm how they were caused."

"Bullshit," Esther blurted, unable to stop herself. "Those are marks by strong fingers, strong hands. A man's hands. Rachel Gorman couldn't have done that. And what about the discoloration to his back? He was moved after he died!"

Porter fixed her with an icy stare. Jared finally shifted in his seat, but remained silent.

"Detective Sergeant Penman," Porter said, "I will have you watch your tone and your language when addressing me. You are already on a warning. I should not have to remind you of that. The discoloration and the bruises are not conclusive indications of foul-play. The pathologist has said himself that the blood was found in the feet and lower legs, as we would expect, and the possibility of the body having been moved is one of several possible reasons for the discoloration on the back. The deceased's activity and position before death, a slight change in position during hanging, the weather."

"The *weather?*" Esther scoffed, and before Porter could speak, added, "I do not think the weather is a reasonable explanation, sir."

Porter bit down on whatever he had been about to say. His face was a storm, but he kept his voice level. "Nevertheless, there is no conclusive evidence that this is anything other than a suicide, and it will be closed as such."

"But the tyre marks and the piece of indicator—"

"Might have been sitting there for days and are unlikely to have anything to do with this case."

Esther took a deep breath to keep from shouting. When she spoke, she infused her tone with as much respect and deference as she could muster. It wasn't much. "Sir, with all due respect, those marks were fresh, and the indicator was dry and recently broken. The mottled coloration to the deceased's back is a strong indication that the body was moved *post* mortem, and the marks to his forearms suggest a *strong* grip on his arms—as though he was struggling or resisting against someone holding him."

Instead of replying to Esther, Porter switched his gaze to Jared. "Detective Inspector Wilcox, I have provided my review of the evidence. The murder-suicide scenario is the one that the evidence points to. Do you concur?"

Jared hesitated. Esther turned and glared at him, but he didn't look at her. He was staring at his hands. Esther wasn't sure he'd heard the question, but then he nodded.

"Sir, if that is your assessment, then I'll write it up."

Porter nodded. "Thank you, Jared. Send the report to central stats straight away. Don't forget the quarterly review meeting. Upstairs conference room at three p.m. sharp. I want updates on all ongoing investigations ready before then. And I think you need to speak with your DS here. I've already had a chat with her about her frequent tardiness and general attitude, but I think it would be most helpful if she was to receive a talk from you as her direct line manager."

Esther almost exploded. A tiny hand gesture from Jared, just out of sight of the DCI, was the only thing that forestalled a very messy, and potentially career-altering, outburst. She held her tongue, but she was sure that Porter saw the anger in her expression. He didn't smirk exactly, but there was a light of victory in his eyes that only stoked her rage. *I will get you back, you cocksucker!* She tried to communicate the thought with her eyes. But Porter was already turning to other work on his computer screen as he dismissed them. Jared got straight to his feet with a mumbled "Sir". He plucked at Esther's shirt to get her to follow him, perhaps afraid that she might sit there and glare at the DCI until he looked up again. Slowly, Esther stood and followed Jared out of the office. She didn't bother pulling the door closed behind her. Petty, but even that little rebellion took the edge off her anger.

Jared gestured for her to follow him into his office.

Before she could make some smart-ass remark, he closed the door behind them and spoke first. "I know you're angry, Esther, and I know you're disappointed with the result of the review."

"You're potentially letting someone get away with murder here, Jared," she replied, as annoyed by Jared's lethargy as the chief's arrogant posturing.

He fixed her with a level look. "Do you think Jack Barry killed Rachel Gorman?"

Esther frowned, then nodded reluctantly.

"And then someone killed him?"

Esther nodded. "Yes. Or the people who helped him kill her killed him. Who knows? He might have been coming to us to confess. They shut him up. We found two hundred grand in Gorman's shed, Jared. There's more going on here. There are other people involved."

"Do you think Charles Gorman killed Jack Barry?"

Esther frowned again and shook her head. "No. That man hasn't the stomach for it."

"So, Barry was done in by accomplices."

Esther nodded again. "I think so. Barry knew about the cash. Others knew about it. Maybe it's what they were after when they broke in. Gorman has got that cash by doing something he shouldn't, which is why he was so cagey in interview. It's why he ran—not because he killed his wife, but because he's involved in something else. I'm guessing it's something serious. Organised crime. He's up to his neck in it, and it's the link to Jack Barry. We should not be closing this case, Jared."

Jared bobbed his head, a half nod. "You might be right. But that's not your call. That's the call that Detective Chief Inspector Porter gets to make. And he's made his call. I will be writing my report to include your concerns and outline, very clearly, *his* rationale for why the case is being closed the way it is."

"He'll not let you put it all on him," Esther replied. "You know that, right? He'll want your backing in the report."

"And maybe I'll give it."

"So, you don't care that Barry's killer gets away with it?"

"I wouldn't say that exactly," Jared replied with a frown. "I'm just tired of fighting the top brass. The politics of this place wears you down. You're young, Esther, but the politics will wear you down too. I've had enough. Barry was a scumbag, and he's not worth this hassle. The drugs guys, the intel unit, they have the info about the cash in Gorman's shed. Let them piece it together. We'll get the rest of the gang in the long grass and sweep up whoever did this to Barry in the process." Jared heaved a sigh. "Just let this one go, Esther. Porter has it in for you. You give him any excuse and he'll send you back to uniform. Nightshifts. Drunken bar-room brawls and road traffic accidents to fill your days. You really want to go back to that?"

Esther really didn't. But she said nothing.

Jared sighed. "Just do me a favour and let it go. Work on your updates for Porter's meeting later. With any luck, he'll get promoted and fuck off somewhere far away." He rubbed a hand over his face. "I need a coffee. You want a coffee?"

Esther shook her head.

"A coffee and a smoke," Jared mumbled as he opened the door to his office and wandered off.

Esther watched his big, broad frame, looking somehow smaller now, slope down the corridor towards the canteen. Then she went to her own office. *Fucking up-their-own-holes bosses! Fucking stats!* She ignored the wary looks her colleagues gave her as she stomped between their desks to the office she shared with two other detective sergeants. Both were either out or off duty. She slammed the door, went to her desk, and fell into her swivel chair. Porter was a self-interested prick. In her experience bosses came in two categories: disinterested or ambitious. The disinterested ones were lazy, indecisive, and wanted you to do all the work for them, but they were far better than the ambitious ones, who were ruthless and utterly selfish. Porter was one of the latter. *Fucking prick.*

After a moment of scowling at the empty room and stewing in her own anger, she pulled open the bottom drawer of her desk. She stared for a long moment at the shoulder of vodka peeping out from behind a box of pens. A glance towards the closed door. Who'd know? She stared at it for a long time, then shook her head and instead reached forward and pulled out the forensic bag with the piece of amber indicator casing. She studied it for a moment, then lifted her phone and dialled switchboard.

"CSI main office," she told the woman who answered.

The phone rang once. A gruff male voice answered "CSI" like he was challenging the caller to insist they had the right department.

"Carl, is that you?"

Slightly less gruff: "Who's this?"

"It's Esther Penman."

"Esther," Carl said, and the gruffness was gone. "What can I do you for, my dear?"

"The scene in Norwick Forest on Monday. I need to have the suicide note sent to Fingerprint Branch."

"Sure, no problem. Will you get the mortuary to fire over the elimination prints from the deceased? I take it you *are* looking for fingerprints *other* than his?"

"You take it right," Esther replied. "Yeah, I'll give them a ring now. Also… could you send me anything you have on those tyre tracks? Pictures, and any tread analysis?"

"Yeah, I can email you the pictures, and I can tell you now that they were Michelin two-oh-fives."

"That means nothing to me, Carl."

He laughed. "Used on mid-size panel vans."

"Perfect, thank you."

After she hung up, Esther rang the mortuary and left instructions to have Jack Barry's prints sent to Fingerprint Branch. She woke up her computer with a tap of the keyboard, logged in and looked up Jack Barry. She was greeted by a number of mugshots going back to when Barry was a kid. It was eerie to see a man's life recorded over time as a series of snapshots from his visits to custody. He had quite a rap sheet, but it was all petty stuff apart from an armed robbery ten years ago. Barry was caught but two others were never traced. He was sentenced to four years—which meant he did two—and that appeared to be the longest stint. The rest were all fines, community service and suspended sentences.

Esther pulled a sheet from her block of sticky notes and jotted down Barry's address. It was a flat in one of the high-rises off the Drakehill Estate—a real shit-hole—where, according to the records, he had lived with his father. Stuffing the evidence bag with the shard of indicator into her pocket, Esther grabbed her coat and headed for the door.

She passed Jared on his way back from the canteen, a steaming cup of coffee in one hand, the reek of tobacco smoke preceding him up the corridor.

"Where are you going?" he asked with a frown.

"Just a quick enquiry," she announced, without slowing or stopping.

"What about the review?" he said to her retreating back. "You got your updates done?"

"I'll get them to you by three," she called back over her shoulder, "don't worry."

And then she slipped through the doors to the stairwell and made good her escape.

*

Charles Gorman stared at the message on his phone. He was at work, sitting at his desk with the door to his office firmly closed, the phone clutched in one hand. His secret phone. The one he *really* didn't want the police to find. It was a cheap, old-fashioned Nokia, with actual plastic buttons and a screen that was just a screen. Phone calls and text messages. No internet and no fancy displays. 'Burners', the guy who delivered them—a new one each month—called them. Charles had thought about chucking it in the river after he'd left the police station the other day, but hadn't had the courage to return to the office and retrieve it. Now here he was. And here was the message.

His mind flitted from one possibility to another, each one worse than the last. From the moment the police had showed up at his work his whole world had slipped its orbit, spinning faster and faster out of control. His wife murdered. Him accused of it, arrested, and put in a cell. And his money—the funds that he'd been saving to escape all this shit—seized! Over one hundred and ninety-eight thousand in cash. Gone. He would never be able to explain it to Revenue, no matter how hard he tried. It was too much, his debts too great, to explain away.

And Rachel… He had been ready to take his stash of dirty money and vanish. Part of the pleasure of his long-term plan would have been to leave her saddled with a raft of maxed-out credit cards and a mortgage it would take three lifetimes to clear. That's how cold and sour their relationship had become. But now that she was gone, he missed her. Odd that. Maybe it wouldn't have been as easy to cut-and-run as he had imagined. Rachel dead. Murdered. In moments of rage he might have wished her dead, and that sent a shiver through him now. Their marriage had been full of love once. A long time ago. Back when Charlotte was small. Charlotte. He wouldn't have left Charlotte with nothing. He'd have left her a bag full of cash on his way to sunny anonymity. He'd have sent her letters. He'd have explained.

Not now. Now he had nothing. Nothing but his dead-end job, his mountainous debts, and the man at the other end of this phone. That man was the reason he was here, back in work, a week after his wife met her bloody end, locked in his office having run the gauntlet of curious gazes on the way in. No one had spoken to him. The offices and hallways had fallen silent as he'd moved through the building, like he was a muffler of sound—Muffleman, arch-villain—stifling all chatter as he proceeded down the corridors, leaving only whispers and hushed murmurs in his wake. They were whispering about him even now. Especially that fat cow Bertha from accounts, staring at him so coldly with her powdered jowls and her painted face. Gossipy bitch. He knew what they were thinking. What they were saying. Even though the police hadn't charged him, he had run. Why had he run? The pressure had been getting too much. He'd panicked. He'd seen the police and decided it was time to cut and run. *Stupid, stupid, stupid.*

When the board of directors had learned of his stunt on the railway line there had been talk of unpaid leave, but his solicitor had quashed that notion on the grounds that no charges had been filed. Union reps had got involved. It seemed that the board of Belfield Logistics were loath to pay a man to stay at home indefinitely, or to run the risk of being sued. Rajesh Patel, Charles's direct line manager, seemed to have been lumbered with the task of keeping a closer eye on him. And so here Charles was, back in his office the week after Rachel's death, and desperately grateful for it.

The main phone on his desk rang. He ignored it and looked instead at the Nokia in his hand. As he re-read the message on the tiny screen for the hundredth time, a familiar range of emotions tumbled through him: anger, sorrow, wrath, loss, fear.

Mostly fear.

QUARRY. TONIGHT 10PM. MAKE SURE YOU ARE NOT FOLLOWED.

It was a summons, and Charles Gorman knew he

had no choice but to answer it.

9

A TARMAC YARD stretched between the four high-rise tower blocks. At some point, someone had had aspirations for this place. You could just make out the faint lines of a basketball court on the broken, weed-mottled surface below. And the concrete plateau to one side of it still bore the scars of a torn-out playground; there were holes and sawn-off steel tubes where swings and slides used to stand.

Esther was on the eleventh floor of the northern tower block, ambitiously entitled 'Mountain View'. From her vantage on the open walkway, she could make out a lone boy kicking a ball against one of the tower walls. The thump of the ball was thin at this height, echoing up between the brutal concrete structures. Further away, on a path that led through the litter-strewn belts of grass towards town, a woman was pushing a pram and calling to a small girl running across the grass, her voice distant and faint.

All the ground-floor flats had boarded-up windows and layers of graffiti. At least a quarter of the cars in the parking lot were abandoned stoleys, or scrappers that had been left to rot, with smashed windows and concrete blocks in place of wheels. Belfield Towers was a depressing ghetto, there was no doubt about it. Back during her days in uniform, Esther would never have come here without at least one other callsign to back her up. She probably shouldn't be here on her own now either, plain clothes or not, but she needed to get out of the office. Needed to be alone, to clear her head.

She turned away from the grim vista and moved down the grey concrete walkway. How had anyone ever thought so much concrete would ever look anything but hideous?

She was cautiously hoping this little enquiry would prove more productive than her visit to Lydia Fenton. She and Jared had called in on the woman during the week, and what a waste of time it had proved to be. At least they could rule Charles Gorman's ex-lover out of the picture when it came to Rachel's death. The girl was not what Esther had expected in an illicit girlfriend; she might have been half Gorman's age, but she was easily twice his weight—soft and weepy and utterly *doughy*-looking. Her wet eyes had popped at their questions, and it had taken them no time at all to conclude she was telling the truth when she said she hadn't seen 'Charlie' in years. Well, it was one line of enquiry closed, anyway—although if Porter had his way, they were all closed now, and this little trip to the ghetto was another waste of her time.

She found flat 11F and rapped loudly on the door. Ten seconds passed with no answer. She knocked again.

The occupant of flat 11H opened her door and

shuffled out onto the walkway. She was a haggard-looking woman in her middle years, her pink dressing gown hanging open to reveal a stained nightshirt with a picture of Betty Boop on the front. A cigarette was clamped between her thin lips, and she squinted at Esther through the smoke.

"Is he in, do you know?" Esther asked, indicating the door to 11F.

The woman shrugged. She wrapped the pink nightgown around herself and leaned back against her doorframe. She took a long drag of her cigarette and plucked it from her mouth. Still, she said nothing. Just watched.

Esther gave the woman her best 'fuck-you-too' glare and knocked on the door to 11F again.

A gruff voice came from within, telling her to hold her horses, followed by the sound of door-chains being undone and bolts being slid back.

The door opened to reveal a man in his late sixties. He too was in his dressing gown, a dark blue flannel, left hanging open like his neighbour's, but underneath his robe were no Betty Boop motifs, just a simple string vest and grey cotton track bottoms, both of them grubby and stained. One of the old man's hands rested on the handle of an oxygen tank on wheels, a couple of clear tubes feeding the contents directly up his nose.

Despite the shorter stature and the grey beard—stained yellow by nicotine around his mouth and nose—and despite the lack of hair, Esther could see the similarity between this man and his son. They had the same eyes.

"Mister Barry?" she enquired.

"Who wants to know?" the old man grunted.

"My name is Esther Penman," she replied. "I'm a detective with Belfield CID."

The man's face darkened. "I been speaking with you lot already this mornin'. The young fella in uniform said you couldn't let us have Jack yet to bury him."

"I'm sorry for your loss, Mister Barry," Esther said quietly, conscious of the neighbour staring at her from two doors down. "I'll get that confirmed with the coroner as soon as I get back to the office and I'll let you know. There shouldn't be any delay now that the autopsy has been done. But first, would you mind if I asked you a few questions about Jack?"

"He weren't no killer," Barry growled. "He did some bad things, mostly just stupid. Yeah, a stupid boy sometimes, but he never killed no one. Didn't kill that woman like you lot are saying. Maybe one of his mates did, but he couldn't have. Weren't in him."

Esther nodded, brow wrinkled, doing her best to portray empathy. She cut a glance towards the smoking woman again, and lowered her voice. "Do you think we could go inside and speak privately? I promise I won't take up too much of your time, and I'll give you a call when I get back to the station and let you know about getting Jack released for you."

The old man followed her glance towards the neighbour, then nodded brusquely and shuffled back into the flat, pulling his oxygen tank with him. Esther stepped in after him and closed the door behind her. She was immediately struck by the stench of must and stale cigarette smoke. Barry Senior led her past a darkened bedroom that looked like the aftermath of an explosion in a launderette, and the kitchen clearly hadn't been cleaned in years—every surface was covered in some kind of container or box, and the sink was piled high with rotting crockery.

"You want a cup of tea?"

"No, thank you," Esther replied quickly.

For some reason his slippers made no noise as he led her down the narrow hall to the living room; her own shoes seemed to stick to the cheap lino with every step.

The living room was the best of a bad lot, as far as the tour of the flat went. The dusty sofa was piled high with old copies of The Racing Post and other tabloids. Some were so old that Esther caught a glimpse of an old Page Three Model peeking out from under one pile on the floor, her giant breasts on full display. The chipped coffee table held an assortment of stained mugs, empty liquor bottles and two overflowing ashtrays. In stark contrast to the rest of the ancient furnishings, a shiny sixty-five-inch HD TV stood proudly in one corner, complete with Blu-ray Player and satellite box. A premiership match was on playback, the sound turned down. There was a story behind the acquisition of that thing, Esther thought, probably involving Jack, but now was not the time...

Barry settled himself into an armchair positioned directly across from the television, within easy reach of the coffee table. It was clearly the only chair to see regular use. Esther perched herself on the edge of a sofa cushion. Barry pulled a near-empty bag of rolling tobacco from his dressing gown pocket and began to roll a cigarette, pushing the oxygen lines aside and tucking them under one arm in order to do so.

"Jack's death weren't no suicide either," he said,

sounding much less combative than he had at the door. "Not that you'll be hearing me shout about that. Just saying, Jack didn't kill hisself. No more than he killed that woman. Maybe he was there, I don't know, but he weren't the killing kind, Jack."

Esther fought the urge to pull her notebook out. She didn't want to deter him from talking; she could always jot her notes down in the car after.

"You think Jack was killed?" she probed. "Who do you think killed him?"

Barry grimaced and gave her a flat look, eyebrows arched sceptically. "Them he was involved with. The usual sort. You know what I mean."

"Organised crime," Esther said. "Jack was involved with a gang?"

"Aye, low level stuff. He weren't the brightest, Jack. Just a quiet lad, got involved with the wrong sort when he was a teenager. Drugs and that. But he weren't no junkie. I'd have known. Enough of the dirty bastards hanging about these towers to know a junkie when I sees one."

"Can you tell me any more? Names? Nicknames, even?"

Barry licked the gum on his roll-up and sealed it. He shook his head as he fished in his pocket for a lighter. His first drag brought on a fit of coughing so violent that Esther stood to assist, only for him to wave her back into her seat. When the coughing subsided, and he'd finished hocking and swallowing, Barry shook his head. "Jack never said any names. He weren't bright, but he weren't *that* stupid." The man's eyes were streaming, and his face had gone a worrisome shade of red. He produced a dirty hankie and spat into it.

"The thing is, Mister Barry, I don't think he committed suicide either," Esther told him. "There is some evidence to link him to Missus Gorman's death, so I do believe he was *there,* but I don't think he killed himself. And I don't think he wrote that note."

Barry continued smoking, stifling small coughs every now and again, though nothing as alarming as after that first drag. At last, he made a face. "They wouldn't show me the note," he said quietly. "Did it mention anything about me?"

Esther shook her head. "But, again, I don't think he wrote it. Or he wrote it under duress. And I don't think he killed himself," she repeated. "Problem is, I'm having trouble convincing my bosses of this."

Barry gave her a mirthless smile. "Of course you are. As handy for the Old Bill as it is for them un's, wrapping it all up in a bow. You're probably causing a bit of bother yourself, missy, digging around for the truth. I'd just leave it if I were you. You look like a smart young lass, but I been around a mite longer'n you, so take it from me—if I ain't kicking up a stink about them killing my boy, you probably shouldn't do either. They'll win in the end. Old Bill thinks they always win in the end, but that ain't really the way it is. Not to put you off your job or nothin'. Jack knew what he was into, and he knew the risks. Them's the risks."

Esther wasn't sure how to respond to that. Barry puffed on his cigarette and glanced towards the football on the TV. When the silence grew lengthy, he spoke again without looking at her.

"I know that might seem a little strange to you," he said quietly. "But I grew up in these towers. I know who runs the town. It ain't the mayor, and it ain't you lot. Jack shouldn't a' got killed. He were a crim, but he weren't a bad crim, if you get my meaning. What's that saying about dying by the sword? Well, that's just the way it is." He cut a glance her way. "And you ain't goin' changing this old dog's attitude now."

Esther nodded. "Okay, Mister Barry. But I'm going to keep digging. I want to know who killed your son."

He shrugged, depressingly blasé about it all. "It's your funeral, missy," he wheezed and turned back to the telly.

She knew she wasn't going to get any more out of him. There was nothing left but to give him another reassurance that she would make enquiries with the coroner and the mortuary, and let him know about the release of the body. Then she bade him good day and showed herself out. Before she got to the front door of the flat, he'd unmuted the television. She shut the door behind her on a din of football chanting and the clichéd prattle of the commentators.

The nosy neighbour had gone back inside. All the other doors along the row were closed too, some boarded up with metal sheeting like the ground floor flats.

Her phone rang. She took it out and answered.

"Penman."

"Esther, it's Carl."

"Hey, that was quick."

"I put a rush on the print job. Suicide letter has to go to the coroner if the DCI is ruling it not suspicious." He paused for emphasis. "You didn't tell me he was ruling it not suspicious."

Esther winced. "Sorry, Carl." She began making

her way down the stairwell to the ground. The lift had made some unsettling noises on her way up. That, and the fact that it smelled of piss, was reason enough to brave the concrete steps. "If you'd known, would you have done it?"

"Of course!" he sounded offended. "For you, my dear, anything. Anyway, doesn't matter. Got the results back and the paper is covered in Barry's prints—that's palm heel prints in the right places as well as fingerprints—which would all indicate he wrote the note."

"Nothing else?" Esther asked. Her disappointment was checked by growing noise from the stairwell below her.

"Well… I didn't say that…"

A group of five teens in tracksuits and baseball caps were hollering and playacting on the landing below her. Esther kept her head down and did her best to ignore them. She continued trotting down the steps as if they weren't there.

"Oi, nice phone!" came a shout.

"Well, what did they find?" Esther asked, ignoring the cocky kid who had shouted at her. She strode through the group and onto the next flight of steps.

"Where are you?" Carl asked. "Sounds rowdy."

"Belfield Towers," Esther replied. "Just kids. What else did they find?"

"Looks like glove marks," Carl told her. "But whoever was handling it wasn't careful enough. There's a partial print on one edge. Half smudged, possibly by the gloves. Doesn't match any of Barry's. They've put it against the database, but nothing comes back. Could be innocent, or it could be the glove-wearer forgot they'd touched the paper before they put gloves on."

"Oi, pretty lady, you deaf?" The kid was following her down the steps. By the sounds of the chortling, his mates were coming after him.

"That's great, Carl. Thank you for that. I really appreciate it. Sorry. I gotta go. Do us a favour and ring Despatch and get a patrol car to Mountain View Tower above Drakehill. I might need a little assistance." She hung up before he could say anything more. Popping her phone into her pocket, she touched the pepper spray that was in there too, and spun around to confront the yob. He pulled up short, looking a bit stunned by her sudden stop. He was no more than fourteen, with spots on his face and a wisp of fluff on his upper lip. He was dressed in the usual scumbag uniform: tracksuit and trainers, with not a hint of them being put to any athletic purpose.

"If I was deaf, I wouldn't be talking on a phone now, would I, dickhead?" she snapped.

The youth stared at her as if she had sprouted a second head. But then his mates erupted in laughter, hooting and repeating the word 'dickhead', and the cocky kid's expression grew dark.

"Gimme the phone, bitch, and gimme your fucking money and all."

Esther considered the spray, but left it where it was. A quick glance at his mates told her they wouldn't get involved, at least not straight away. They were onlookers for the moment. If she gave them enough reason to keep their distance, or kept them amused, they wouldn't help their friend just yet.

She held her would-be mugger's gaze for a moment. Just long enough for him to grow unsure, but not long enough to let him come up with another quip or say something that might get his comrades involved. She stepped forward. "You want my phone?"

He scowled. "Yeah, give it to me or I'll fucking stick you."

His hands were empty.

"You want to stick me, you need something to stick me with," she replied.

Fifty-fifty this kid had a knife on him. When he didn't go for it straight away, Esther decided to take those odds. She reached forward, quick as a flash, grabbed him by the right wrist, pulled and twisted. He was nowhere near ready for her sudden attack. Caught off balance, he pivoted as she twisted his hand up his back so he was facing his mates. He cried out as she bent his hand back and put the pain on. His mates all looked stunned.

"Surprise," she said quietly. "Police." She turned her attention to the four watching. "So far, I have one coming with me for attempted robbery. I have a second car waiting downstairs at the doors, which means room for two more. Any of you about to help this young man in his little endeavour?"

A couple of heads shook. Somebody muttered 'fucking copper'.

"Well, I wonder how I'm going to remember the whole incident, traumatised as I am? Maybe you all surrounded me and demanded my things? A bit unfair? Okay, I'll tell you what—anybody who has disappeared by the time I count to five will be considered an innocent bystander. A witness who left before I could get their details. One..."

Two of the four were already climbing the steps

and getting out of sight fast—the two with bail conditions or prison sentences hanging over their heads, no doubt. One in a blue tracksuit, the youngest, looked unsure. He was watching the boy Esther had a hold of. He looked concerned. Younger brother, maybe. The oldest-looking one of the pack, in his late teens with a scar on one cheek, looked like he wanted to go for her. There was hatred in his eyes. His hands twitched, and Esther immediately knew that he *was* carrying a knife. But she had positioned herself with her back to the wall, just next to a flight of steps. He couldn't get to her easily, not with her holding his mate hostage in front of her.

"Two…"

There was a distant sound of sirens, growing louder. *Good on you, Carl,* Esther thought. That seemed to decide the older boy. But he didn't want to seem cowed, wasn't going to tuck tail and run like the others.

"Three…"

"Where you taking him?" he asked in a surly tone. At least his hands weren't hovering at his waistband anymore.

"Custody. Belfield Central. Four…"

He nodded, then turned to the younger boy. "Come on." He climbed the steps slowly, the youngest one glancing back until they were out of view.

"Right, my lad, let's back down these steps slowly, because if we take a tumble, I'm going to add assault on police to your charges and I am also going to beat the living shit out of you. Are we on the same page?"

The kid nodded, and did his best to take the steps

carefully as she sidled down the stairs with her back to the wall, glancing up every now and again for any sign of her prisoner's mates reappearing. None of them did.

"By the way, in case you didn't figure it out, you're under arrest for attempted robbery. You do not have to say anything…" Esther almost lost her footing as she cautioned the boy, but steadied herself. She felt him tense, but when she applied a little more pressure to his wrist he grunted and became compliant again.

The sirens were loud now. They cut off, signalling the arrival of the patrol car, and by the time Esther got down to the fourth floor two uniform officers were running up to meet her. Two big burly lads, she was happy to see. She handed over her prisoner, and they put him in handcuffs and searched him while Esther gave them a brief. She was dismayed when one of the officers pulled a small flick-knife from the boy's sock. *Fifty-fifty…*

As she walked with the two PCs back down to their car, Esther glanced at her watch. *Shit!* She was going to be late for Porter's quarterly review meeting. No way she was going to make this trip to custody and get to his stupid meeting on time. She tried ringing Jared's phone, but it just rang out. She wondered momentarily whether there was any chance the chief might understand, given that she had a live arrest. Unlikely. He had it in for her and would use any opportunity to give her another bollocking.

She sighed. There was no way around it. She would have to book this kid in and organise an interview.

And risk the chief's wrath again, for the second time today.

10

Two hours later, Esther hurried up the back stairwell of Belfield Central Police Station to the CID floor. Custody had been mercifully quiet, but she was still over half an hour late. She'd left a message on Jared's phone. Hopefully that had been enough.

She stuck her head into the DCI's secretary's office. Georgia was a pinhead, but Esther got on okay with her, considering how frosty her relationship was with the woman's boss.

"Hey, Gee, what's happening? Is the meeting still going?"

Georgia gave her an apologetic look and nodded. That didn't bode well.

"Is he really pissed?"

Georgia just nodded again.

Esther heaved a deep sigh and went to fetch her files from her desk. With a pile of paper folders under her arm she made her way to the upstairs conference room. When she got there, she put her ear to the door. Porter was talking, but she couldn't make out the words. She eased the door open and tried to slip in as discreetly as possible. No good. Porter stopped speaking mid-sentence. All heads turned. Every eye followed her progress to the only empty chair at the table. That prick Calvin Brett was smirking as she took her seat.

"Sorry, sir, I had an arrest and—"

"Yes, Miss Penman, I've been informed. I'll speak with you after."

Jared gave Esther an exasperated look. Esther's heart sank. So much for understanding. This wasn't going to be good. She tried to sound contrite, although it was a struggle for her...

"I've got my files, sir, but to be honest—"

"I'll stop you there, Sergeant Penman," Porter cut in sharply. "You've not had a chance to summarise them, I know. Because you don't follow instruction. You prefer to do your own thing. That's why you've spent the last couple of hours down in the basement dealing with some punk kid when you should be doing your work for *this* department." He stopped, although it looked like it took some effort. There was a moment of silence as he frowned at his own notes. "Detective Inspector Wilcox updated me with regard to your investigations as best he could." He looked around the room: "I think we've covered everything for this quarter, folks. Detective Constable Smyth will forward a copy of the minutes and actions. Make a note of your deadlines for those actions and send updates by email directly to me. Okay, that'll be all, thank you." He turned to Esther. "Sergeant Penman, my office please."

"Sir—" Jared began, but Porter cut him off.

"No, Jared, I will deal with Miss Penman myself,

since you seem incapable of doing so."

With that, he stood and strode from the room, leaving a hush in his wake. Nobody moved. Everyone was staring at Esther. She tried to catch Jared's eye, but he kept his head down and began gathering his papers together, his face red. She felt a wave of guilt for having caused him such embarrassment. There was nothing for it; she stood and followed Porter from the room. With Jared still sitting there, the room remained silent as she left.

DCI Porter strode briskly to the stairwell. Esther deliberately kept her pace slow and even. Porter held the door to the stairwell open for her and they made their way downstairs to his office together. Having to wait for her seemed to piss him off even more, but she would be damned if she'd let anyone see her scurry after this arsehole.

"Close the door behind you, please," he said when they reached his office. Esther did so and then moved to stand in front of his desk. She had a feeling she was not going to be invited to take a seat.

"You made an arrest at Belfield Towers, I hear?" he said, tipping his chair back and studying her over steepled fingers.

"Yes, sir, I was making some enquiries when a group of youths confronted me in the stairwell of one of the tower blocks."

"Who did you go there with?"

"No one, sir."

"You went to the tower blocks alone?"

"Yessir."

He paused. Looked her up and down. "Have you been drinking today, Penman?"

"No, sir!" Esther replied sharply. Perhaps the

indignation with which she invested the words convinced him; whatever the reason, he accepted her answer.

"And what *enquiries* were you conducting, on your own, at Belfield Towers?"

Esther swallowed. There was nothing for it but to go ahead and come clean. "I was speaking with Jack Barry's father."

"Why?"

"I wanted to know what his thoughts were on his son's suicide."

"You were going against my instructions, you mean? Trying to convince an old man to make a complaint, maybe?"

"No, sir, that was not the way of it. Mister Barry is not one bit interested in making a complaint. But he knows his son was killed. He just thinks he'll be in danger from the men who killed Jack if he makes any noise about it."

Porter sat forward, scowling. "Jack Barry committed suicide. That is the finding of the investigation. And that is the end of the matter." He sighed, closed his eyes, and shook his head. "But I'm tired of repeating myself. You are clearly incapable of taking direction. You'd rather gallivant around on your own, doing your own thing, making low-level volume-crime arrests on the streets. Well, I can help you out there. Clear your desk and dust off your uniform, because I'm sending you back to Uniform Response. Monday, twenty-two hundred hours, you are to report to Inspector Livingston at Yorkgate Station. I've already spoken to the District Commander about it. From Monday you'll be Yorkgate's night duty sergeant."

Esther felt like she'd been punched in the gut. He couldn't... *But he had.* And he'd already had it cleared by the chief superintendent. He'd done it. Why had she thought he wouldn't? Because she was good at what she did? No. Why would he give a shit about something like that?

She opened her mouth to protest, but no words came out. If Porter garnered any satisfaction from her obvious shock, he didn't show it. In fact, his expression grew darker as he growled, "Now get out of my sight before I consider taking your stripes too."

Esther had no choice but to turn and leave. She was glad he had believed her about the drinking because she practically staggered from his office, and the added humiliation of being breathalysed in front of the entire department—and he would do that, the bastard—would have been too much.

When she got to her office, she realised that she wouldn't be taking any of her investigations with her. It would be up to Jared to dish them out to her replacement. That left very little to pack up: just some stationery, her bottle of vodka and a silly little bobble-head clown, with eyes that rolled around when it shook, and the slogan 'you don't have to be mad to work here, but it helps' splashed across its weighted stand. No framed photos of family. No colourful childish drawings. Nothing like that. This job was all she had. Esther was not a woman who cried easily, but she was close now. She grabbed her bag and the bobble-head, and did her best to transfer the vodka bottle from the desk drawer to her bag without anyone seeing.

When she turned, Jared was standing in the doorway. He looked apologetic and disappointed in her all at once.

"I'm sorry, Jared," she said. "I've let you down. I just… If it hadn't been for that little punk, I'd have made it back on time."

Jared shook his head. "It doesn't matter, Esther," he mumbled. "We are where we are. You're going to have to learn to keep your head down and do what you're told. You'll make it back to CID, don't worry."

"The fucker has put me on nightshifts," Esther said, her laugh mirthless and clearly a front for potential tears. "Duty sergeant in Yorkgate, of all fucking places! Maybe he wants me patrolling those fucking towers every night as a punishment."

Jared took a couple of quick steps towards her and put his hands on her shoulders. "You'll be fine, Esther. You're a crazy bitch sometimes, but I'll be damned if you're not the best copper I know."

Esther cleared her throat and nodded. "Thanks, Jared."

He put his arms around her. They stood there for a long moment, and Esther didn't care if anyone looked in and saw them.

At last, she heaved a sigh and pushed away from him. She gave him a level look. "How about a drink?"

Jared smiled. "Sounds like a plan."

11

"I'M SORRY, ESTHER, I shoulda stood up to him," Jared said, for the umpteenth time. His words were slurring now, five pints later. His tie was loose and he was in his shirtsleeves, sleeves rolled up and baring his hairy forearms. He was staring into the dark murk of his bitter.

They were in the Crown and Lion, an upmarket high street pub, with stonework on the walls, lots of brass fittings, stained glass in the windows and polished wooden floors. It was early evening and the place was already filling with office workers getting a head-start on the weekend. Pop music was being piped from speakers somewhere in the ceiling, but the noise of chat and laughter was loud enough to match the tinny beats. Esther and Jared sat across from one another in a high-backed booth.

"Stop apologising, Jared," Esther said. She'd had at least as many vodka tonics as he'd had pints of bitter—neat shots of vodka not being the most sociable of drinks—but she fancied her words were still sharper. "Porter had it in for me. We both know it. He's just a prick. Same as all of them. No cop left in him. He's all politician. All ego. Besides, there's no point in giving him an excuse to bin both of us. Not when you're only a year from retirement. No, I'm the one who's sorry. Sorry for letting him make you look like a dick in front of everyone."

Jared blinked, and grimaced. "Fuck. I forgot about that." He swallowed a mouthful of beer. "Thanks."

"Sorry," Esther repeated. "I just... How can we let this go? Barry was murdered. You don't just ignore shit like that because it's convenient. Good cops don't do that."

"Politicians do," Jared rumbled. He looked at her and shook his head. His eyes weren't quite as focused as they'd been three hours ago. "S'why I shoulda stood up to him. I've known you a long time, Esther. I know how good a detective you are. I shoulda told him. I shoulda..."

"What?" Esther asked. She was growing weary of talking round in circles. She wasn't quite in the same zone as Jared. She wondered if the fuckers who ran this place watered down the vodka. "What could you possibly do, Jared? Same thing I did? I went against him and look at me. I'm back to doing nightshifts in the ghetto, for fuck's sake!"

"I know, I know, I know," Jared replied, frowning at his drink and nodding fervently. Abruptly his nodding became headshaking. "I just feel like a bit of a spineless shit. He's got me by the balls, Esther. And with Samantha and me..." He trailed off.

"What's happening with you and her?" Esther asked carefully, eager to change the subject. "Has she let you back into the house yet?"

Jared was silent for a long time. Esther wondered if he'd heard her over the growing noise of the bar's patrons, but at last he gave a slight shake of his head. "No. Now the boys have found out about the whole thing. Andrew's threatening to come back from London. It was all I could do to convince him that everything was fine and to concentrate on his studies. Fuck knows what she's told them."

"Where are you staying?"

"B and B out in Springhill."

"What? Why didn't you say? You can stay with me. My couch is a fold-out. Why are you wasting your money on a bed-and-breakfast? You should've said!"

Jared shook his head again. "No. As long as I'm paying for a B and B it feels temporary. Moving in with friends would be a step closer to giving up. I'm not ready for that."

She reached out and placed her hand on his. "Samantha will come round, Jared," Esther told him, investing the words with all the assurance she could muster. Truth was, she had no idea if Samantha would come around, but she hated seeing him so despondent. "She will. You'll see. You guys have been together so long… she'll come around. Don't worry."

Jared grunted, a neutral sound that gave Esther no indication as to whether her words had helped, and then drained his glass.

She tapped his arm. "My round," she chirped. "You could do with a whiskey, I think." She grabbed her purse and slid out of the booth.

"No, Esther, I've had enough," Jared replied

quickly, reaching for his jacket.

"Don't be ridiculous," Esther replied, heart dipping. She wanted to stay out longer. She wanted to keep drinking. "It's not even eight o'clock yet."

Jared had to steady himself as he stood. Pulling on his jacket was more of an effort than it would have been sober. "No, I've had enough. Not a young man anymore. You should go home too. We can share a cab. Your place is on the way to Springhill." He shrugged into his overcoat.

Esther shook her head. "Maisie from cybercrime division said she'd come out to meet me after work," she lied. Maisie had texted an hour ago to say she had other plans, as had several others. Nobody seemed to want to go out anymore.

Jared nodded. "Fair enough. Tell Maisie I said hi." He probably had no idea who Maisie was. "Enjoy yourselves." He checked his pockets for his keys and phone and wallet. Then he paused and gave her a thoughtful look. "Be careful, Esther. In Yorkgate, I mean. On your nightshifts. It won't be forever. Just say a few prayers that Porter gets his promotion. Chances are he'll get shipped off to another department. And then I'll get you back. Even if I have to hang on an extra couple of months to do it." He smiled weakly.

Esther smiled back. "Thanks, Jared."

He winked at her and reached out to give her shoulder an affectionate squeeze. "I'll give you a call tomorrow," he promised. Then he turned and walked out, a lot less steadily than he'd walked in.

As he disappeared through the doors into the twilit street, Esther turned and made her way to the bar. She almost lost her balance once, but it was just her legs, weak from sitting down too long. She took out her purse and studied the other patrons along the length of the bar. There was a hot guy at the far end. Dark hair and bronzed skin, chiselled jaw and stubble. She stared at him, willing him to look up from his drink. It was only when a blonde with long legs and big boobs sat down next to him that she noticed there were two drinks in front of him.

She sighed and looked the other way. Someone at the other end of the bar had noticed *her*. Unfortunately, the guy checking her out was far too ugly, with those gaunt cheeks and protruding frog-like eyes. She turned her attention to the approaching bartender instead and flashed a smile. He was cute, and clearly a gym-junkie from the way his shirt stretched around his upper arms and chest.

"Double vodka tonic, please," she ordered, her words only a little slurred.

Her smile had little effect. "Ma'am, I think perhaps you've had enough?" the bartender replied, eyes hard and jaw set as he regarded her coldly.

Esther was affronted. She considered protesting, but her head was fuzzy, and she realised that she had reached the point of the evening where she was definitely *not* too drunk to reasonably be denied another drink, but still too drunk to argue the point and win. She gave the bartender a hard stare of her own. Then she turned on her heel and, with as much dignity as she could muster, grabbed her bag and jacket from the booth and strode from the bar. It was spoiled only once by the slightest of wobbles.

The fresh evening air struck her like a slap in the face. The streetlamps were alight, the evening sky fading from deep purple to black. Jared was already gone.

A short stroll around town and she would be okay to go to another bar, she decided. She set off in a random direction, concentrating on walking steadily and standing straight...

*

Charles Gorman muttered a curse as his precious Mercedes struck another pothole. The last crater he'd hit must have caused damage, given the thump it made.

He could understand the man's desire for caution, but he'd always found the instructions for attending these meetings to be excessive. Nevertheless, he had done as he was told and checked his mirrors at least once every five minutes since leaving the house; he'd driven ten miles out along the motorway and back again, before wending his way up the mountains to this disused narrow track. There had been no sign he was being followed.

His headlamps dipped and bobbed across overgrown verges and endless lines of spruce trees, their trunks fading like rows of ghostly pillars into the darkness on all sides. He could hear the brambles scraping against the paintwork of his car. It was going to look a total mess. But not once did he entertain the idea of turning around, or not showing up. This was not the kind of summons you declined...

Eventually the trees fell back and the lane broadened into a clearing of mud and stones. There were just as many potholes, but at least there were no brambles. Beyond the clearing stood a rusted chain-link fence, a fence that would do little to stop anyone getting onto the site of the abandoned quarry—with its stagnant black lake and towering man-made cliffs—had anyone the inclination to trek this far. No one did. It was too far from town. It was too far from anything.

There were two vehicles parked up there already. A white van and a black pickup. Three men stood in the darkness near the tree line, and Charles had no doubt he'd passed others further back along the trail, watchers hidden behind the trees. As Charles's headlamps swept across the scene, the passenger door of the pickup opened and out stepped Mister Darren. Charles had no idea if Peter Darren was his real name. But it was the name he knew him by. Peter Darren. The Art Merchant.

He pulled up twenty yards short of the other vehicles and studied the scene for a moment. Like something out of a crime movie. Men meeting in the dead of night at a disused quarry. It was in scenes like this that characters got killed off and dumped in stagnant black lakes. He felt himself break out in a cold sweat. No. Darren needed him still. That, after all, was the whole problem…

Charles switched off the engine and killed his lights. He stepped out. There was a chill in the air, and his breath turned to fog in front of his face. He wiped his damp brow quickly, pulled his coat about himself and trudged over to the man who was more his boss now than Mr Patel back at the firm.

Darren and one of his goons stood in the darkness between the vehicles. Both sets of headlamps were pointed at Charles as he approached, making him squint. He had only covered half the distance to

Darren before the command came.

"Stop there, Charlie, there's a good fellow."

Charles stopped, squinting and blinking into the light. He raised an arm to try and shield his eyes. All he could make out were the shapes of the two men facing him. Then Darren's henchman stepped forward and frisked him. Made him lift his shirt and turn around so he could check for a wire. Charles suffered the indignity without protest. When the search was complete, the man stepped to one side, slightly behind Charles, but close enough to intervene if he made any sudden moves towards the boss.

"You're quite sure you weren't followed?" Darren asked.

"Yes, sure as I can be," Charles replied. "I took all the usual precautions."

There was a long pause. Then all the lights went out and the engines were cut.

Silence, incredibly thick and heavy, rolled in around them.

After several seconds had passed, Charles's vision began to adjust. He could make out Darren standing there, his head cocked to one side as he studied Charles.

"I—"

Darren cut Charles short by raising one finger. The silence stretched. Only after what seemed to Charles like an inordinately long time did Darren nod to himself and step forward.

"Helicopters are easy to hear, Charlie, but drones... drones can be a little harder to detect." Charles could see him smile by the light of the moon. He couldn't tell whether the smile reached his eyes. "Now, let me start by professing my condolences.

Your wife..." He sighed. "Well, I'm sorry for your loss. There was no need for it, and I wish it hadn't happened. I want you to know that the man who did it... he is no longer with us. That is better justice than the police will ever give you, don't you agree?"

Charles nodded dumbly.

"It was an unfortunate mistake, your wife. But there are associates of mine who are not happy with the delay your foot-dragging is causing. And there are only so many acts of justice I can carry out, you understand. We need that new route sorted. Your company does runs to Belgrade. We need one of our men on that route, Charlie. In fact, we needed our driver doing that route two months ago. You understand how serious this is, I hope? We lost millions because we couldn't get those goods lifted. Millions, Charlie. When certain people lose out on millions of pounds, well... other people die."

Charles felt that cold sweat popping out on his forehead again. His heart was hammering so hard he was surprised all six of them couldn't hear it echoing off the nearby quarry walls. He licked his lips, about to say he understood, but Darren went on.

"I want you to know that these associates of mine, they are not patient like me, Charlie. They have no appreciation for the efforts you've gone to in the past. They have no concern for your difficulties getting access to these routes. I've tried convincing them, but... let's just say, I can only do so much. You need to do something to help both of us out here, Charlie. You need to get our man on the Belgrade route. This month. Not next month, not the month after, but by the end of this month."

To Charles, those words seemed to bring with

them a weight, like someone had loaded rocks onto his shoulders. He heard himself whimper, and it was all he could do to force the words out.

"I can't," he half-sobbed. "It was all I could do to keep the Warsaw line running. I had to completely falsify all the quarterly reports to keep that route open. It's only a matter of time before somebody figures it out! I'll be fired. Or jailed. If they don't try and pin my wife's murder on me before then!" He was crying now. He felt ashamed, but he couldn't stop. It was all becoming too much. Those rocks became boulders, and he was sucking in air. His chest felt tight. No shooting pains yet. That would be just perfect. If he had a heart attack here and now, he wasn't wholly convinced these men would take him to a hospital. He wasn't sure his necessity to them stretched all that far. He might possibly end up in the black waters of the quarry after all. He tried to slow his breathing. Tried to find some calm.

That's when he noticed it. He thought he'd seen it before, the last time they'd met and Darren was pressuring him. He wasn't sure at the time that it was related to their little chat, but now here it was again. Darren's left eye twitched. The man sighed softly, but his eye twitched again as he spoke.

"You will be taken care of, Charlie," he said quietly. "Haven't I always taken care of you? I will keep taking care of you. But I need you to help me. My associates are not reasonable people. I need that route, Charlie. I need it. Help me to help you. Help me to keep you safe."

More eye-twitching, as Darren frowned thoughtfully at the ground.

"I can protect you if you help me, Charlie. I'm

relatively confident that my friends don't know about Charlotte or that she's in Cambridge. In fact, I'm not sure if they know you have a daughter at all. So I think she's okay. For the moment. But help me to keep them from coming after *you,* Charlie. Get me that route."

Charles tried to take another deep breath, but the sound of this man saying his daughter's name was too much. His deep breath turned into a coughing sob.

He shook his head. "I can't... I can't get that route," he choked. "The firm's downsizing *everything.*" He had thought about this. He'd come up with something else since the text arrived that morning. Now Charlotte's life as well as his own relied on him selling the idea to Darren, here and now. "But I've thought of a way... something that might help."

Darren raised one eyebrow questioningly. "Oh?"

"If you can get your hands on a truck, I can get you a set of company curtains and do up fake transit papers."

Darren shook his head. "Hiring an articulated truck is going to draw attention I don't want."

Charles licked his lips. "I might be able to get a truck from the maintenance yard. But I'll have to pay off the night guard and the chief mechanic."

Darren frowned. "How much?"

"Three grand should do it."

"It will come out of your fee, Charlie."

Leaving him to take all these risks for next to nothing, Charles thought, but he had anticipated as much, and he didn't care. It wouldn't solve anything in the long run, the way business was going at Belfield Logistics, but it would keep Darren off his back for a month or two at least. Time to come up with a way out of the godawful mess he was in.

He nodded. "Okay," he said. "Leave it with me. I'll get you a date and time next week to have one of your guys pick it up from the depot. I might need... an advance for the guard."

Darren studied him coldly for a long moment. His eye twitched again. "When you have an arrangement let me know. I'll put one thousand in an envelope and leave it on the counter at the gallery. It will be a simple brown envelope marked with your initials. You can stop in and pick it up and leave the transit papers off. Do it discreetly. And don't loiter at the till. Make sure you look at a painting or two before you pick up the envelope, and browse in the other shops along the street too. Just in case you're being watched." Twitch. "Don't let me down this time, Charlie. Don't let Charlotte down."

With that, Darren turned and got into the pickup. The rest of his men climbed into both vehicles and the engines rumbled to life. The pickup drove off first, followed by the white van, and Charles was left alone in the cold darkness. As the sound of the engines faded into the trees, he sank to his knees and cried. Charlotte. His beautiful, talented daughter. Oblivious to the danger her stupid, greedy father had put her in. And he was helpless to protect her. He had to keep doing what Darren wanted. He dreaded jail, but in some ways, he realised, he was a prisoner already. A prisoner of circumstance. A slave to the darkness he had dabbled in. How he wished he could undo it all. Go back in time and tell that stupid self not to do it, not to get involved. Bank debts were more manageable than this hell. Too late now. Now he was trapped. And he had no choice but to follow through with his plan. And hope to God that the supervisor of the maintenance yard was as corrupt and greedy as Charles had been…

*

Three and a half hours later, Esther found herself kissing a random bloke at the door to his apartment in downtown Belfield, while he struggled to get the key into the lock. She'd been turned away from two more bars before finally getting into that seedy biker joint and meeting… she couldn't remember his name. He was not much to speak of, skinny and young and nervous-looking in his thick specs. But he had a nice, kind face. Did he say he was an IT consultant or something? Something computery, she was sure.

With a muttered curse, Mister Computer-man pulled himself away from her so he could work the key into the hole. Finally, the door swung open.

The dark corridor was spinning ever so slowly as Esther half-dragged the man—shit, what was his name again? Fred? Frank?—into his own apartment. She wrapped her arms around him and kissed him hard on the lips, their tongues wrestling as he struggled to kick the door closed behind him. His hands squeezed her backside, his clumsy fingers moving round to try to fiddle her trousers open. She pushed him away abruptly and dropped to her knees, already tugging at his belt. She got belt and trouser buttons undone rapidly, perhaps betraying a practised ease. She smiled up at him. He looked a little startled but didn't make any move to stop her, although he touched her awkwardly on the cheek and said, "You don't have to."

"I want to," she replied breathily. She heard the slur in her own words and tried to speak clearly. "I want a big fat cock in my mouth right now. I hope you have a big fat one for me." Christ, did she just say that?

Fred—or Frank, or whatever his name was—looked at her wide-eyed. To stifle her embarrassment, she concentrated on tugging off his pants.

Shit. Not big at all. Short and stubby.

A disappointed sigh escaped her lips before she could stop it, and the poor man must have noticed her reaction and sudden hesitancy. His diminutive manhood, such as it was, began to bow before her eyes. Unable to crush his self-esteem completely, and not knowing what else to do, Esther went down on him anyway. She fancied that she was something of an expert at nursing men back to life...

It must have been the shock of feeling the soft little thing jerk slightly and gush, or the sudden unexpected taste of the sticky liquid filling her mouth, but the premature ejaculation brought on a sudden, violent wave of nausea in her. The world began to spin rapidly and before Esther could stop herself she was throwing up all over the poor guy's junk. She pulled back. But there was more, and she ended up throwing up all over his shoes too.

"Oh God," she gasped and coughed. "Oh God, I'm so sorry. I'm so sorry."

Computer-guy, probably paralysed by combination of orgasm and getting puked on, just stared. Esther managed to quell another heave as she struggled to her feet.

"Sorry," she blubbered. "I'm sorry!"

To give IT man some credit, he recovered remarkably. In a gentlemanly fashion—as if he wasn't standing there with his trousers around his ankles, his cock covered in her vomit—he said, "It's okay, it's okay. Are you okay? The bathroom's just at the end of the corridor. I'll get you some water."

Esther shook her head. "No, I gotta go. I'm so sorry."

Swallowing another urge to throw up, she turned, pulled the door open and ran from the apartment without a backward glance. She heard him call out "Wait!", followed by a thump and a curse as he tripped on his trousers—or slipped in the puke—and fell to the floor.

Esther kept going, as if she could outrun both the nausea and the shame if she moved fast enough.

12

SHE WAS WOKEN by the sound of her ringtone. She lay still for a long moment, eyes closed, feeling the tilt and turn of a world bobbing on a tide of alcohol. Here she was again. She recognised the queasy feeling that came with being hungover and drunk at the same time.

She opened her eyes. The room spun wildly in two different directions for a moment before the images slowly merged and steadied into a nauseating drift. She fought the urge to throw up.

At least she was waking up in her own bedroom, she thought, as she took in the familiar scenery. With some considerable effort, she turned her head. *And* she was alone. Even better. Propping herself up carefully on her elbows, she found that she was sprawled atop her bedcovers and still fully dressed.

Then it all came back to her. The meeting with Porter. The demotion.

The ringing from her phone stopped, then started up again a moment later. *Persistent caller.* Maybe

Porter had changed his mind, she thought, struggling to sit up. Another wave of nausea hit her as she swung her legs to the floor. She followed the ringtone to where the contents of her handbag lay spilled in the doorway, the handbag itself lying on the carpet nearby. Snatching up the phone, she answered quickly.

"Hello, DS Penman," she said, before she realised that she was no longer a DS as of yesterday. She was back to plain old Sergeant Penman.

"E-Esther?" The woman's voice on the other end was tentative and vaguely familiar.

"Yes? This is Esther Penman."

"Esther, it's Jean," the woman said. "Your Aunt Jean."

Esther opened her mouth, but no words came. *Auntie Jean.* Had she not still been half-drunk she might have recognised the voice first time round.

The silence lengthened. "Hello?" Jean asked awkwardly. "Esther? Are you still there?"

Esther cleared her throat. "Yes. Sorry... Auntie Jean. How are you? It's been... it's been a while." Esther silently congratulated herself on the understatement of the year.

"I'm fine, dear. Fine. But... I'm ringing about your mum. I know you two... you two fell out... but... Hannah's not well, Esther. She's not well and she'd like to see you."

She said the last in a rush, as though eager to get the message delivered and worried about what sort of reception it would get. And not without cause. A million thoughts crashed through Esther's mind. Or not thoughts exactly, but memories with emotions attached. Emotions like anger and bitterness.

Emotions like hatred.

She thought of the last time she'd seen her mother. She was sixteen years old and, like so many memories she had of Hannah, they were screaming at each other. Trading fists too. Hannah had been wasted at the time. But then, her mother had been wasted most of the time during Esther's high school years. How many times had they had blow-outs like that? How many times had neighbours had to call the police? How many visits from social services? Poor Esther and her drunken mother. Domestic Central. Hannah could never remember any of it when she was sober and apologetic, but there was generally some physical evidence about the house. Smashed crockery, broken windows. All that shit.

But that last argument… *that* had been the worst one of all. Esther had walked out of the house and never returned. She had not spoken to her mother since. Fifteen years had passed without a word between them.

It had taken Esther a long time to move on, and to put all thoughts of her mother and her shitty childhood behind her. She never thought about Hannah anymore. Or even Jean, although her aunt had been good to her.

"E-Esther?" A pause. She could hear Jean take a deep, shaky breath. "Esther, Hannah has cancer. It's… very advanced. She's in hospital. She doesn't have long. Please come."

Esther couldn't speak. She was surprised to find she'd welled up, and only noticed when a tear escaped and the salty taste of it hitting her lips brought her to herself. She cleared her throat again.

"Where is she?"

"Belfield City Hospital. Ward Eight North. Room Eight-Two-Two."

Esther wondered how long her mother had been in Belfield without her knowing, and whether it was Esther's presence that had brought her back to the city, or something else. Someone else. If she'd come looking for Big Mike, she'd come back too late. Maybe they'd both been drawn separately to the place that had been their home the longest. The place they'd kept returning to throughout Esther's early years. Belfield was where Jean and Hannah had grown up. Esther had been eleven and Hannah had been on the wagon for almost a year when they'd moved back for the last time together, for their brief couple of years of happiness, during what proved to be her mother's longest stint of sobriety ever. She'd met Big Mike shortly after they'd moved here. He was their local neighbourhood police inspector, and a real change for Hannah. He was friendly and generous and easy-going, not like the creeps and druggies and winos she usually dragged home. Esther had loved Big Mike. He had been good to her, and the only father-figure she'd ever known. He'd made a bigger impact on her than anyone else, even Jean. Of course, her mother couldn't stay sober and she'd fucked it up, like everything else, and away they'd gone again, disappearing in the middle of the night for yet another city and leaving debts and burnt bridges in their wake. That was the beginning of the end as far as Esther's relationship with her mother went. She'd gotten used to bouncing from town to town, but it was running out on Big Mike that hurt the most. It set the scene for some turbulent teenage years. When she'd come back to join the police,

Esther had been saddened to learn that Mike had died only a few years after she and Hannah had left for... where had they gone next? Birmingham maybe.

"Di-did you get that? Do you want it again?"

Esther had to work some moisture into her mouth to reply. "No. Sorry. Thanks, Jean. I got it."

Esther jotted the ward and room number on a notepad on her bedside dresser, and Jean promised to send her a message with the visiting hours. After she hung up, Esther sat on the end of her bed and stared at the wall, phone clutched tight in one hand. Her eyes were still leaking, but it wasn't proper crying. She was just tired. Tired and emotional. It was the vodka.

The phone began to ring again. Blinking away the tears, she glanced down and recognised the number immediately. Police switchboard. She cleared her throat for a third time and sniffed away the tears. She tried putting on her most professional, most sober-sounding, voice.

"Hello?"

"Sergeant Penman?"

"Speaking."

"Inspector John Livingston here. I'm the station inspector at Yorkgate police station. I understand you're starting with us on Monday. I just wanted to ring and let you know that I'll expect you here for a quick briefing on how things operate in our division before you start duty. DCI Porter has spoken to me already about your transfer, and I want you to know right from the off that I run a tight ship here. I will not tolerate lateness or absenteeism. This is Uniform Response. Briefings are on time, patrols are out on the ground within half an hour of duty, and I expect my sergeants to lead by good example. So I want you here early on Monday to let me take you through the procedures. Twenty-one thirty hours at my office. In uniform, of course. I take it you still have your uniform?"

Again, Esther found herself lost for words. Another wave of nausea hit. She stood quickly and headed for the bathroom. The world tilted and spun again.

"Hello? Sergeant Penman? Can you hear me?"

Esther swallowed a burp and replied in a rush: "Yessir. Twenty-one thirty hours. Your office. Yes, yes—all received." She hit the end-call button and tossed the phone onto the bathmat as she reached the toilet, not caring if he thought she was taking the piss.

She was just in time. As she dropped to her knees and grabbed hold of the toilet bowl, up came everything that was left in her stomach.

*

He had been an idiot to think it would be that easy. He'd arrived expecting to get a chance to talk to her, but as soon as he pulled up he'd spotted the suitcases and boxes on the lawn. Not flung about, to be fair, but stacked neatly under the eaves. She could at least have told him to bring a van. He might get all this stuff squashed into his old Volvo estate, but it wouldn't be easy.

There was no sign of life inside the house. He had been sitting in his car chain-smoking for five minutes now, staring at the suitcases and watching the windows. Her car was not in the drive and the house had an unoccupied air about it. The upstairs hallway light was on, even though it was mid-morning. It had been his habit, when the boys were younger and they went on holidays, to leave a light on to make it look like someone was home. It must have rubbed off on her.

As Jared sat and stared, he felt like he was saying goodbye to a part of his life. He couldn't shrug the horrible, sinking feeling that this was it. The sliver of hope that Samantha might forgive him was disappearing fast.

Well, he couldn't put it off any longer. The sky was grey and overcast as usual, but there were dark purple patches drifting among the paler cloud. He might as well get his stuff loaded before it rained. With a sigh, he pushed open the door and hoisted himself out of the car.

Popping open the boot, he shuffled up the path. He decided to try the doorbell, just in case. He listened to the familiar chime and waited. No movement, no further sound. The side gate was locked. He wasn't sure what he was looking for. What was he going to do? Burgle his own house? All his stuff was already outside and waiting for him. With another sigh, he set to work.

He had piled about half the boxes into the car when he saw Mrs Tedford from next door picking her way carefully down her garden path with her little tartan shopping trolley rattling along behind her. He reckoned she was about eighty now, and a widow these last ten years.

"Missus Tedford?" he called, and then louder: "Missus Tedford?"

The old woman looked up.

He made his way over to her.

"Have you seen Samantha today?" he asked. "She sent me a message earlier, but she doesn't seem to be home."

For eighty years of age, Mrs. Tedford was still sharp enough. She eyed the suitcases sitting in his front garden and the half-packed Volvo.

"I saw her leave early this morning with a bag packed," she said carefully.

Jared frowned at his feet, cleared his throat and forced the next question out. "Was she… was she with anyone?"

Mrs Tedford tutted loudly. "I don't believe *that* was the issue, Mister Wilcox," she replied acerbically, and then turned and rattled away towards the nearest bus stop.

Jared watched her disappear around the corner, feeling even more wretched than before. He went to get the rest of his things.

*

The arrival of his daughter had put Charles even more on edge. Not that the sight of her—or having her fling her arms around him in a fierce hug the moment she saw him—was not welcome. It was. It was desperately needed. Charlotte's presence—her unfaltering loyalty, her belief in him and his innocence—was the emotional sustenance he'd been craving.

But it was bittersweet. He couldn't get Peter Darren's words out of his head. He found himself stealing guilty glances at Charlotte when she wasn't looking, his mind churning through one plan after another to keep her safe, and ultimately discarding them all. There was nothing he could do now. He was out of options. And without a bounty of stowed cash and the fantasies of freedom and sunny anonymity it brought with it, he had nothing to distract him from the prospect of his daughter learning about all his dirty dealings. It made him realise how much he didn't want her to know about any of it. The thought of disappointing her was suddenly more than he could bear, and he wondered at how little he had considered it up to now.

Charlotte's belief in him was in stark contrast to the attitudes of almost everyone else here. The service for Rachel had been a short and simple affair. An Anglican priest had given a blessing and a short eulogy. This was something Rachel's parents had insisted on, even though everyone knew Rachel had had little time for church or religion. She'd been cremated after the service; he and Charlotte planned to bury her ashes under the oak tree in the back garden, the one she sat under in the summer to read those awful romance novels she liked so much. Charlotte had suggested it, but even her neglectful and distant husband had known that was her favourite spot. Charles was looking forward to the quiet closure it would bring, just him and Charlotte saying goodbye when the sun began to set.

First though, he was going to have to suffer through the rest of this event. At least the service was over; what that shuttled-in Anglican speaker's sermon had lacked in intimacy and warmth was made up for by Charlotte's eloquent words. Charles had felt his grief conquered by pride as he listened to his daughter address the gathering. She was such a good speaker. So confident and charismatic. Where had she got that? Not from him. Not from Rachel.

He'd had to say a few words too, obviously, but he had kept his contribution short—the heat of everyone's eyes on him making him glad he had not opted for a longer speech. Some of the mourners looked accusing—certainly Rachel's parents did, and they had not spoken to him before or since the service—while most just failed to hide those *considering* glances, wondering if he *had* in fact killed her, despite the fact the police had let him go.

A few people had been generous enough to commiserate with him, adding with fervent sympathy that going straight for the husband was just what the police did when things like this happened. Lazy police work, that's all it was. Chin up, don't dwell on it, et cetera, et cetera.

He had withdrawn from the crowd now, his stance and expression warding off even the well-wishers. Most people were happy to avoid him. Avoid the awkwardness of feigning sympathy while hiding their suspicion. He watched Charlotte, talking with her grandparents in the far corner. They'd rented a function room at a local hotel, it seeming a little ghoulish to host a funeral gathering in the home where the dearly departed had been murdered. Rachel's mother and father were all hugs and kisses with their granddaughter. A direct contrast to the icy distance they were maintaining from Charles.

He took a swig of his whiskey as he watched them. He was slipping into his dark place again. It was happening more and more since Rachel's death, though it had happened before, whenever the gravity of what he was involved in blindsided him and threatened to overwhelm him; it was an icy dread that crept over him like a cloak, bringing with it fear and disorientation. It would pass, as it always did, but it seemed that the feeling lingered longer and longer each time…

"Dad?"

Charles blinked. He'd been staring into space, and he saw that Charlotte was standing in front of him now with a small plate of sandwiches in one hand, her brow furrowed with concern. The crowd seemed to have thinned out. Rachel's parents were gone.

"Are you okay?" Charlotte asked.

He nodded, and tried to force a smile. "Just tired, love."

Charlotte set the plate down, indicating to the little triangles of white bread filled with cucumber and ham and cheese. "You should eat something, Dad. You need to look after yourself." She glanced at the empty whiskey glass, but kept her expression neutral and her tone soft. "You want me to get you some tea?"

He shook his head, then picked up one of the sandwiches and took a half-hearted bite. He smiled at her again.

"I don't know how you can stay in that house alone now, after…" Charlotte trailed off. "I wish you'd come with me back to Cambridge."

Charles took her hand and gave it a quick squeeze. "Thank you. But I'm fine, love. I'll manage."

"The counsellor at the university told me I can take as much time as I need. We could go somewhere for a spell, if you'd like?"

Charles shook his head. "I can't… work, you see… there's just so much…"

"I'm sure they'll let you take some time off, Dad."

"That's not it. Not really." He sighed. "Wouldn't you rather have something to occupy your mind, rather than sit around and think about it all day?"

Charlotte conceded the point with a shrug. She had avoided the kitchen as much as possible since her arrival home, but she'd stayed at the house despite her misgivings. He had heard her crying in her room at night, but during the day she was a beacon of stoicism and courage. She whirled about trying to organise everything for him, constantly checking on him. He loved her for it, but he wanted her as far from here and the men who had killed Rachel as he could send her, and as soon as possible too. He had already batted off her suggestion that she come home for a while. With her squeamish avoidance of the kitchen, that had been easier than expected. As for her suggestion that he go to Cambridge with her... If he ran out on the Art Merchant now, she'd be in danger, and he'd be looking over his shoulder every day for the rest of his life.

"I'll tell you what," he conceded. "Let me think about it. It helps me get through the day, having my work, but if things change maybe I'll come down and join you for a little while."

Charlotte nodded. "Anytime, Dad." She put her arms around him and gave him a quick hug.

"You sure you don't want a cuppa?" she asked as she stepped back again.

"I think I just need a little air," he said. He picked up another sandwich, gave her a grateful smile, and headed for the back doors. *Air, and a way out of this mess!*

*

The security guard was watching her suspiciously. She wasn't imagining it. A second security guard had materialized to patrol the foyer about five minutes ago, and he kept glancing at Esther too.

She shouldn't have had the vodka. She'd realised this as soon as she started drinking it, but she'd kept on all the same. One more little sip at a time, until it was gone. The bottle had still been half full when she'd dropped it next to her bed last night. She might have only just chucked her guts up but that hadn't stopped her taking those first couple of sips, telling herself she needed to wash away the taste of vomit, and help her process the morning's news.

She thought she'd left Hannah behind. In the horrible past, where she belonged. But you didn't leave bad parents behind, did you? They stayed with you, like permanent scars, or wounds that wouldn't heal. Wounds that dragged you to a hospital on a Saturday afternoon to be scrutinized by a pair of apes in security uniforms.

She'd been standing here too long. Maybe almost half an hour now. Staring up at a dozen storeys of glass reflecting the dull grey clouds that hung low over the city.

She was up there somewhere. Dying.

Hannah.

Her mother.

Esther lost her balance as she squinted up at the tower of windows. She stumbled, and only just kept herself from landing on her ass. When she looked down at the front entrance again, she saw that both of the guards were standing outside now, staring at her. One was talking on his radio.

Fuck. She knew she was too drunk to go in. Too drunk to ask directions to the ward and the room. But at least she wasn't too drunk to know it. She needed to go home and get sober.

She turned and staggered away.

13

ESTHER TRIED NOT to stare at the massive backside waddling along in front of her as she followed Yorkgate's station sergeant through the grim corridors of the dilapidated Victorian-era building. Yorkgate was the district's oldest police station and the evidence of this distinction was everywhere, from the cracked tile floors to the small barred windows that let in little or no light. Pipework ran along the walls at the corners of the ceiling, where upgrades to plumbing and heating post-dated the walls of the building, and a lingering smell of must hung everywhere. Esther wrinkled her nose.

She'd managed to stay off the booze for almost twenty-four hours now, helped by the fact that she'd drunk every last drop of alcohol in her apartment yesterday. But the hangover was still strong. A binge of painkillers and coffee was seeing her through the final throes of it, or so she hoped.

The station sergeant, Daniella, a very fat little woman who looked like she spent all eight hours of her working day sitting at her desk eating biscuits—which was how Esther found her fifteen minutes earlier—prattled on as she led Esther around the station, giving her the guided tour. Esther trudged along behind her with a sports bag full of uniform over one shoulder and a cardboard box under one arm. It had been a happy discovery to learn that her old uniform still fit her. She might need to order new trousers soon—they were a bit tight around the bum—but she was secretly delighted with having been able to squeeze into them at all. Small victories. She realised she was staring at Daniella's arse again and forced herself to look away.

Daniella finally led her through a set of double-doors at the end of a corridor on the second floor. A labyrinth of seven-foot-high lockers greeted them on the other side, the woman negotiating the maze a bit too quickly for Esther, who lost track of where the doors were after the fifth turn. They stopped in front of a locker that was lying open. Daniella pulled a big white sticker from a roll she was wearing on her wrist like a bracelet and slapped it onto the locker door. Pulling a black marker from her shirt pocket, she held the door steady and used her teeth to uncap the marker. She wrote SGT PINMAN on the white label in big bold letters. Esther considered correcting her, then decided she couldn't be bothered.

"There," the little round woman announced proudly, as she put away the marker, "Welcome to the station, Esther. I'll speak with the other sergeants and we'll have a desk cleared for you on Monday night. Sorry it's not available yet, but you know how they do things in the police!" She chuckled. "If you need anything else, you know where my office is. Just give us a tinkle." And then she bustled off. Esther made a note of which way she turned at the end of the row of lockers, then began unloading her bag.

As she set about hanging up her shirts and trousers, she felt defeated. Being sent back to uniform was a punishment, and an open-ended one at that. She had no idea what the DCI had said to the district commander, or whether she was here for a long haul or a short stint. She suspected the former. She pulled her belt rig from the bag and loaded her equipment onto it. She had become accustomed to her covert little pouches for her cuffs and pepper spray. She was going to have to get used to loading up like a commando again. A soldier in bright shiny yellow.

As she checked the velcro straps on her hi-vis stab vest, she hesitated. The DCI had dumped her from CID and suspended her detective status, but that didn't mean she couldn't keep digging. She was still a cop. And if nightshifts in Yorkgate turned out to be the chaotic drunken bloodbaths of old, there was nothing to stop her from looking into Charles Gorman in her own time. Well, nothing apart from a few pesky surveillance laws. But fuck the warrants and the by-the-book shit-heels in headquarters— Esther decided she wasn't letting this one go. She was going to get to the bottom of it all and find out what Gorman was involved in. Warrants and audit logs be damned.

Full of a sudden urge to do something, she pulled her pepper spray back out of its uniform holster and slipped it into her coat pocket again. She padlocked her new locker and set off, only needing to double-back twice on her way out of the locker room.

Less than an hour later, she pulled her little Fiat up outside Gorman's house. There was no sign of his silver Mercedes, but there *was* a shiny red Mini, and the glimpses Esther had of a blonde pony-tail bobbing past an upstairs window suggested Charles Gorman's daughter was at home alone. Detectives from Cambridgeshire Constabulary had attended the girl's flat in the university town to deliver the death message the day of Gorman's arrest; at Jared's request they had asked some subtly-put questions about the nature of the relationship between her mother and father. Nothing in the report back had raised any eyebrows, and Porter had used that to add further weight to his conclusions.

Esther was considering approaching the house to speak with the daughter—Charlotte, she thought her name was—when abruptly the lights on the Mini flashed and the girl appeared in the driveway, lugging a small travel case. Esther was sure then that Gorman wasn't home. And her conspicuous little Fiat would be spotted in this neighbourhood of high-class cars if she lingered any longer. She was here for Gorman, not the daughter. She stuck her car into gear and pulled out.

Next stop, Belfield Logistics. It was the last place Esther expected to find him on a Sunday afternoon, but she didn't have too many other ideas.

When she got to the industrial estate, she found the gates to Belfield Logistics lying open. And there was Gorman's Mercedes, parked right out front next to the main doors.

Esther pulled up outside the gate and watched for a moment. There was no movement in the reception area, and no lights on in any of the windows above.

But she couldn't idle here or she'd be seen. She glanced around. Everywhere else in the complex was closed. The whole industrial estate was like a ghost town, all shuttered units and empty parking lots. There was one carpark bordered by short hedges about two hundred yards away. A couple of vans had been left parked up in it. It would be far enough away to give her a bit of concealment and still provide a direct view of the Belfield Logistics front office. She drove over and pulled in behind one of the vans. Then she killed her engine and waited.

After ten minutes she began to regret the morning's coffee binge and her lack of foresight. But despite the growing pressure on her bladder, she was determined to sit tight and wait for Gorman to come out. When it started to rain—big fat raindrops trickling down her windscreen—she gritted her teeth, tapped the wipers, and turned up the radio.

Five more minutes passed, and Esther was trying hard not to think of how much she needed to pee. She was seriously debating the wisdom of the whole escapade when her phone rang. She pulled it from her pocket. *Aunt Jean.* Newly added to her contact list. She stared at the screen for a long moment, then flicked the mute switch and put the phone away again. It continued to buzz for a few seconds more, then went silent.

A memory came to her, unbidden: her mother screaming at her, face red, tears in her eyes. Esther would have been crying too, she was sure, but she couldn't recall the details of that. Or the words that had been hurled back and forth between them. Hurtful, cutting words. No, all she could remember was Hannah's face. A memory she had used to sustain her anger for months after she'd walked out. A memory that had fed her resentment for fifteen years. Nothing can make that go away overnight. Not even cancer.

She waited a moment, then checked her phone. No urgent texts, no voicemail messages. She decided that if her aunt rang again, she would answer it. If not, Esther would make herself go to the hospital soon. Just not today.

The rain stopped as abruptly as it had started. Esther tapped the wipers again, and as the water was swept away she caught sight of movement at Belfield Logistics. Charles Gorman. He was dressed in casual clothes—beige slacks, a quilted green raincoat and a tweed flat cap. He came scuttling out of the office with a white envelope clutched in one hand. As he locked up the office, he glanced about. Esther slid lower in her seat. Gorman's behaviour was furtive, but he seemed either too distracted or too impatient to notice her. He drove through the gates, then stopped and hopped out to close them before jumping back into his car and driving quickly away.

Esther waited a few seconds, then pulled out and followed. She had no training in tailing people like this. She kept well back at first, keeping a full block behind him as they made their way through the empty industrial complex. When they moved onto the main roads, she drew a bit closer. The Sunday afternoon traffic was light, but there were enough cars to stay one or two vehicles behind him and not lose sight.

Very quickly, Esther realised he was not heading home. He was moving towards the centre of town. Traffic grew heavier, and she almost lost him when he slipped through a set of traffic lights on amber. She watched him disappear down the next street, muttering curses as she tapped the steering wheel impatiently. When the lights turned green again, she nipped quickly down the street after him, hazarded a guess that he was still bound for the city centre, and caught up with him waiting at another red. Her heart was hammering at this stage, and the excitement of her self-imposed mission had temporarily chased away thoughts of her straining bladder.

At last Gorman pulled into an on-street parking bay, the only vacant space on the street. Esther rolled past him and turned into a barrier-controlled parking lot further down the block. She pulled a ticket from the machine, quietly cursing the greedy bastards who charged full price for parking on a Sunday, then did a quick U-turn so that she could grab one of the last spaces in front of the low perimeter wall. As she pulled in, she saw that Gorman was already out. He was strolling down the street, back the way they'd come. She grabbed her dark Yankees baseball cap from the passenger seat and hurried after him, tugging her hair through the gap in the back of the cap and pulling the peak low over her eyes as she went.

Although she kept to the other side of the street, she could still see the white envelope sticking out of Gorman's coat pocket. Every now and again he would reach down and touch it, as though worried it might get stolen. He clearly had a destination in mind, the way he took one turn after another, moving briskly and without hesitation. Only when he reached Marigate Street did he slow. They were in a run-down quarter of the city centre now, where one out of every three premises was permanently shut with 'To Let' signs overhead and graffiti all over the shutters. The remainder were made up of charity stores, tattoo parlours and sex shops.

Suddenly Gorman stopped and glanced about again. It was all Esther could do not to freeze on the spot. She snapped her eyes front and kept walking without missing a beat. She was a good fifty yards back on the opposite side of the road, and with the cars moving between them and several other shoppers about, she didn't think he noticed her. He ducked into a charity store on the corner.

Esther hesitated, unsure what to do. If she went in after him he'd see her for sure. There was a coffee shop across the street from the charity store. Esther hurried towards it and slipped inside.

The café was full at this hour on a Sunday, alive with the clink of crockery and the buzz of conversation. She stood just inside the door, staring back across the street. In less than a minute Gorman was out of the charity shop. Esther watched him duck into the pawn shop next door to it.

"Everything okay, ma'am?"

Esther turned. A very attractive young man who couldn't have been more than twenty or twenty-one was smiling at her from behind the counter. His hair was gelled to look carefully unkempt, and his stubble was clearly deliberate, but he had the brightest blue eyes she had ever seen and dimples that made her smile right back.

"Yeah, um…" She looked up at the list of drinks chalked on the blackboard over his head. "Can I get a latté to go?"

"No problem. What size?"

"I like mine large," she replied, holding his gaze.

He chuckled and blushed a little at the obvious

innuendo, which just made him cuter as far as Esther was concerned. She paid, and he went to prepare her order.

Out of the corner of her eye she spotted movement. She turned to see Gorman scuttle out of the pawn shop and go straight into the next store—an art gallery. What the hell was he doing? Marigate Street curved gently at this end, and she had a clear view through the art gallery's large front window from where she stood at the café counter. There was only one other person inside—an elderly woman studying some watercolours. Gorman shuffled about the empty gallery floor for a moment. He glanced a couple of times at the old woman, then at the door, before moving to the counter. There was no one staffing it. With another quick glance at the old woman, who had her back to him, Gorman pulled the white envelope from his pocket. He set it down next to the till and lifted a brown envelope that had been lying there. Another glance at the woman, and then he hurried out into the street and back the way he'd come. He pulled out his phone and appeared to tap a quick message, before scurrying on again, around the corner and out of view.

Back at the art gallery the door behind the counter opened. A man stepped out of a back office. Short and skinny, he wore small round spectacles and had a mop of thick brown hair cut in a style that made Esther think of an early John Lennon. He wore a navy turtleneck sweater and a pair of brown corduroys. He spoke briefly to the old woman, who smiled and shook her head at whatever he'd said before turning back to the watercolour. The man then lifted the white envelope Gorman had left and disappeared back through the door behind the counter.

Gorman was gone by now, and Esther decided that she couldn't put it off any longer—she really, *really* needed to pee. Stakeouts and foot-follows were clearly not her thing. She got directions from the hot young barista and hurried toward the restrooms at the back. When she returned, her coffee was waiting for her, complete with the name 'Dale' and a phone number scribbled on the side of the paper cup.

"Thank you, Dale," she said.

"Hot and large as ordered, ma'am," he replied with a cheeky grin.

She chortled, and stepped outside, sipping her coffee. She would ponder what it might be like to fuck a boy ten years her junior later. Right now, she needed to focus on the task at hand. She studied the sign above the gallery. MARIGATE ART GALLERY. *Original.* In line with the banality of its name, there was nothing noteworthy about the place out front, so Esther decided to take a stroll around the back.

A weed-choked alley paved with cracked and crumbling concrete linked Marigate Street with Fortuna Street beyond. It ran behind the terraced buildings to either side, ending in a pair of steel-barred gates. They stood open. Behind the gates was a yard that appeared to be shared by several premises. There were a couple of dumpsters, four metal-plated back doors and one car, a black Audi A4, parked in the yard. The premises were all joined together, like they were at the front, so the only access to any of the stores was via the front doors or this yard. Moving close enough to jot down the number plate on the black Audi, she noted only one CCTV camera, covering yard and gate. She realised she would be captured on any footage it was recording now, so she moved quickly back up the alleyway.

When she returned to the street, she glanced through the art gallery's window as she strolled by. The John Lennon wannabe was out front now, chatting with two new customers—a younger couple—and gesturing to a garish abstract painting hanging near the door. She needed to run the plate from that Audi and find out who this guy was. And what had been in the envelope Gorman had left, and the one he had collected. Unfortunately, she couldn't direct police to stop him; she doubted that either item would be enough to pull the investigation back off the shelf, and she'd have Porter and her new inspector on her ass for it, and probably be disciplined for tailing Gorman without appropriate authority. Still, she knew instinctively that whatever was going on with Gorman and that art dealer, it had something to do with the deaths of Rachel Gorman and Jack Barry.

She sipped her coffee as she made her way back towards her car, turning her discoveries over in her head as she wended her way slowly between the crowds of Sunday shoppers. The day's rain had left the cobbled streets damp and the sun was already low in the sky, but the streets were still busy. Her hangover had faded, and Esther took her time.

When she got back to the street where she and Gorman had parked half an hour earlier, she saw that his car was gone. But she'd got far more from her foray than she ought to have expected. Stakeouts could go days without results. Either she was lucky, or recent events had put Gorman and his cohorts under pressure.

She paid her ticket with the last of the change in her pocket. Only when she was halfway back to Yorkgate police station did she realise that she had forgotten all about Dale and his cute dimples, and had already dumped the cup with his phone number in a trash can back in town.

14

DUSK WAS FALLING and the street lamps winking to life as Esther drove the last block to Yorkgate station, where she went straight to the sergeants' office to find a spare computer.

There was a sergeant on duty, a young man with blonde hair and a cockney accent who introduced himself as Terry. Perhaps it was the combination of youth and rank, but there was an arrogance about Terry that made Esther instantly dislike him. Not half as attractive as young Dale from earlier, Terry clearly thought he was God's gift, leering at her as he showed her around her new office. He pointed out the desk that was soon to be hers, once 'Old Barney' finally got around to clearing it out. Apparently Barney had been stationed here for almost twenty years, an amiable chap who was going to be sorely missed when he retired. Terry couldn't see what all the fuss was about. Old guy spent half his shift snoozing, as far as he could see, and it would be good to have some fresh blood about the place. Listening to

Terry's description of 'Old Barney', Esther realised she was going to have her work cut out for her when she took over his team. There was likely to be a great deal of suspicion and resentment. Teams with lazy sergeants could go two ways—they either became lazy and demotivated themselves, or they became savvy at self-management. Which way Barney's team had gone under his lax oversight would have to be seen, and both produced their own kind of challenge for a new supervisor.

Esther was doing her best to give Terry the coolly polite-but-not-interested-in-talking routine as she settled herself at Barney's desk and logged in to her account on the computer. It took about five minutes, but Terry eventually got the message and fucked off back to his own desk. Esther clicked on the icon for the police database.

She ran the number plate of the Audi from the art gallery. The first result came from the Motor Insurance Database, telling Esther that the car was insured in the name of the company, *Marigate Art Ltd.* A little further digging unearthed a driver, stopped for a minor traffic offence two years back.

Peter Darren.

She ran his details next. She got that same traffic ticket from two years ago in the results, and nothing else. No other reported incidents, no linked associates and no intelligence reports. Esther didn't buy the clean image. That envelope trade was a clear indication to her that whatever Gorman was up to with Darren, it was dodgy as hell. Dodgy enough to get two people killed. Most detectives would chide her for making leaps. Textbook police-work was based on the emotionless, neutral analysis of objective facts. But that was not how humans worked, and it certainly wasn't how Esther worked. Emotions motivated. Opinions formed. For Esther, her hunches and gut-instincts made her follow the leaps, and she tended to be right in the end far more often than not. Jared would have attested to that. But Jared wouldn't be around to back her up anymore. Not at Yorkgate.

A tap at the door made both her and Terry look up from their screens. As if her thoughts had been a summons, there stood Jared in the doorway.

"Surprise," he announced as he strolled over to her, giving Terry an amiable nod in passing. "You said you were moving today, so I thought I'd come see how you were doing. This your new digs?"

Esther nodded. "Once my desk gets cleared it will be." She didn't want to talk in front of Terry, so she logged off the computer and stood. "Come on," she said. "I'll show you around. We can grab a coffee in the canteen."

"This station has a canteen?" Jared asked in a surprised tone.

She led him down the corridors, pointing out the workrooms and the tiny closet they called a gym, until they reached the old canteen on the ground floor. It had been a fully-functioning cafeteria at one time, before the budget cuts. The evidence still stood at one end, where a set of waist-high steel tray-rails ran along the front of permanently-locked shutters. The disused kitchen on the other side was awaiting an injection of funds to turn it into a usable night-kitchen for the troops. Or so station sergeant Daniella had told her during her orientation. The wait had stretched to three years though, so no one was holding their breath. For now, all they had was this old dining room and some vending machines in the far corner. One of the machines offered instant coffee.

It was late evening and, Yorkgate district being what it was, with the Drakehill Estate and river-dock pubs not far away, the radio was already busy with calls for units to attend domestics and drunken fights. There was only one crew in on their break, a man and woman, eating from lunchboxes at the far end of the room. The BBC's 24-hour news channel was running on a muted television set in the far corner. The two uniform cops looked up when she and Jared stepped into the dining hall, then put their heads down again and continued to talk quietly to one another. Esther fed the coffee machine some coins. It rattled noisily. Jared found them a table far enough away from the two other officers to allow a little privacy.

As Esther set their coffees down and took a seat, she asked, "What brings you down here, Jared? You checking up on me? Or you thinking of slumming it for a while too?"

"Wanted to see your new place," he replied. "And tell you I miss you already. Porter has no immediate replacement for you, and I've got detectives hounding me for all sorts of shit, and it's not even Monday."

"You're finally having to do some work?" Esther quipped.

Jared nodded glumly. "Can't say I like it much."

"Don't worry. You'll soon have a new DS to take care of all your shit again."

"Won't be as good as you."

"Of course not," she replied with a smile.

They both looked up at the sound of chairs

scraping across tiles. The two uniform police were on their feet, snatching up their half-eaten meals as they headed for the door. The woman spoke into her radio. "Despatch from Bravo Yankee One-Oh-One, all received. We're responding from base." And they ran out the door.

Jared nodded to the doors as they swung shut after the pair. "At least you'll get a bit of the action down here. A taste of the good old days."

Esther snorted. "Bollocks. I'll get to read about other people getting a bit of the action. Do you not remember your duty sergeant days? It's all paperwork and reports and... boring as fuck if you're not actually out doing it."

"Maybe you'll get out and about a bit."

Esther shrugged but didn't say anything. She blew on her coffee. "How about you and Samantha? She talking to you again?"

"Got a text from her yesterday," he began.

"Oh yeah?" Esther asked, brightening.

"Yeah, to come by the house and pick up my stuff."

"Oh," she said, less brightly.

"All my clothes stuffed into bags, my things packed into boxes, sitting outside the house waiting for me."

"Sorry."

Jared shrugged. "She'll come around. Isn't that what you said?"

"I'm sorry, Jared," Esther repeated. "Wasn't me who shagged Helen Simmons though."

"True."

She frowned. "Are you still staying at the B and B?"

He nodded.

"You should come and stay with me for a while. It's not the Hilton but it'll save you a fortune. Just until you get things sorted."

Jared shrugged. "Thanks. Maybe. Let me think about it." He sighed. "Anyway. Enough about my troubles. How are you managing with your... relocation?"

"I'll take it one day at a time," she replied wryly.

"Won't be forever," he said.

Esther sipped her coffee. The silence stretched.

"I got a call from my aunt yesterday morning," she murmured finally.

"Your aunt?"

Esther nodded. "My mum's in hospital. She's got cancer. Not long left."

Jared's face dropped. "Shit, Esther, I'm so sorry."

She shrugged and frowned hard at her coffee.

Jared caught the mood. "Given that you don't seem hugely cut-up about it, and the fact that—now I come to think of it—I've never once heard you mention your parents in any conversation, I'm guessing you two are not close?"

Esther picked at a splintered groove in the table edge. "You could say that."

She took a deep breath and realised sadly that if she couldn't open up to Jared, she couldn't open up to anyone. She glanced around to confirm they were still alone in the canteen before she started talking again.

"I don't remember my father. Don't even know his name. He ran out on us because he didn't want me. At least, that's what my mother always said. She was a nasty drunk, my mother. She had a lot of boyfriends when I was growing up. She'd have dry spells—I do remember some good times, when she'd kick the booze and go steady with a decent guy for a bit—but they never lasted. Mostly she liked bad boys. Bikers and thugs. Junkies. And the occasional real sleazy creep. Those guys hit on me sometimes, when Mum was wasted and unconscious. Freaked me out when I was younger, but I grew used to ignoring them.

"Then there was Jason. Jason was an artist. Liked smoking pot. A lot. I guess he was mid-twenties when it happened. He was about ten years younger than my mother, about ten years older than me. I was only sixteen. My mother was helping him grow cannabis in our attic. He'd wired the house up so that we would get free electricity while we helped out. He was a thieving little shitbag, now that I think back, but at the time he seemed cute and clever and funny as hell."

She heaved a sigh.

"Then one evening, while my mother was out with one of her friends, he stopped by. I told him Mum was out, but he suggested he wait for her. He had a six-pack of beers. When he offered me one and sat down to talk, I felt... special. Of course. Hot older guy wants to talk to angst-ridden teenager. What a fucking cliché, eh? We finished the beers. And then we were on the couch, and he kissed me... right as my mother walked in. She completely flipped out. We had a huge fight. It wasn't just verbal either. Jason tried to get between us but my mother just lit into him. I was drunk and crying, and shouting all sorts of abuse. Every nasty thing I could think of. She called me a whore, and I asked her what else would I be, when that was all I'd ever seen from her? 'My mother the drunken whore' I screamed, and I stormed out. I never went back. Stayed at a mate's house for a few weeks while I finished my GCSEs—I was a determined little bitch, even back then, not that my results were anything to write home about. Then moved to London and got a job. Sixteen years old and working a deli counter in Soho.

"My mother the drunken whore," she repeated. "Those were my last words to her. Haven't spoken to her since. That's fifteen years ago now."

Jared shook his head, a look of disbelief on his face.

"What? You gonna guilt-trip me?" she asked. "You can't believe I would say that to my own mother?"

"I can't believe you're only thirty-one," he replied, feigning shock.

She sniggered in spite of herself. "Fuck off, you dick."

He smiled and she smiled back.

Then her smile faded. "She always blamed me," she went on, "for my dad leaving us. For men always running out on her."

"Sounds to me like it was her your dad was running from, not you," Jared said, and there was a sadness in his voice. She understood; a shift of blame didn't change the tragedy of her shitty upbringing.

Jared sat back, brow creased, and breathed out noisily. He hesitated before he spoke again, all serious now. "You know, Esther, it sounds like your mum was a real bitch when you were growing up. But people change. If you haven't seen her in fifteen years... you don't know what's happened in that time.

Apart from the cancer." He waited until he caught her eye again, before saying, "Take some advice from an old man who's said goodbye to both his parents: when they're gone, they're gone. Whatever you want to say to her, good or bad, soon you won't be able to."

Esther nodded. "I know. I'm just not sure what I'll do when I see her. What I'll say."

Jared reached out and placed his hand gently on hers. "You might not have to say anything."

Esther gave him a grateful smile.

"Besides," he said, "you have bigger problems to deal with. If this is the only coffee you can get on your nightshifts," he said, making a face as he examined the remaining contents of his plastic cup, "you're never going to make it through."

Esther chortled. "There's a twenty-four-hour Tim Horton's on the far side of the river," she retorted. "The civilised side of town isn't so far away. I'll be okay."

He stood. "Come on, then. Let me get you a decent coffee. Even one of your fancy cappafrappylatty things has got to be better than this shit."

Esther followed him from the canteen. "Well, if you're buying, Inspector Wilcox, then by all means."

"My treat," he confirmed as he dumped his cup in the nearest bin. "Soon enough you'll be spending enough of your own money on caffeine trying to get through nightshifts. Least I can do."

"Jeez, thanks for the pep talk," she countered.

"You'll be alright," he replied as he held the door for her. "Change is as good as a rest, isn't that what they say? Who knows, you might even like it here."

Esther grunted, unconvinced by what she'd seen so far. "We'll see…"

Jared grinned. "Just be sure to bring your own coffee."

15

FOR ONCE, ESTHER'S tiredness had nothing to do with alcohol. Getting used to shift work again was already taking its toll on her. She'd slept badly, before waking shortly after midday, unable to sleep any longer despite her exhaustion. Last night had been busy, the radio non-stop with emergency calls, and she hadn't collapsed into her bed until nine a.m.

She'd gone in early, as instructed, and suffered through the requisite introductory speech by Inspector Livingston, a joyless, moustachioed man who seemed to be made entirely from shades of grey, as if he'd stepped out of a black-and-white film. He looked like he'd have been far more comfortable in an old-fashioned police tunic too. He had repeated all the things he'd told her over the phone, only at much greater length. Esther had bit her tongue, nodded at all the right places, and left without having said more than a dozen words altogether. *Head down, mouth shut, get through it*—that was her mantra now.

The elevator chimed, the doors slid open, and

Esther stepped out into a broad corridor that seemed serene after the chaos of the Emergency Department below. The wall opposite declared her to be on the Eighth Floor, and there was a panel of colourful signs pointing in both directions. Esther followed the arrow that pointed the way to Oncology and the North Ward.

There weren't many other visitors about. Crossing corridors led away to various other wards and departments. One side of the corridor had floor-to-ceiling windows at intervals, which looked out over the older parts of the hospital building, with its flat roofs and giant ventilation ducts. Hardly the most inspiring vista for cancer patients on their way to treatment, Esther thought.

Hannah's ward was at the very end of the corridor. A young black nurse sat at the desk inside the doors. She had a bright smile, but the bags under her eyes reminded Esther that she wasn't the only one struggling with the demands of shift work. Tired or not, she greeted Esther with professional friendliness.

"Can I help you, ma'am?" she asked, her Brummie accent thick enough to cut with a knife.

"I'm here to see Hannah Penman," Esther replied falteringly.

"Are you family?" the nurse asked. "It's just that her sister's already in with her, and it's not *technically* visiting hours. Family only at the moment." She looked apologetic.

"I'm her daughter."

That caught the nurse off guard. "Oh. Is this…" Clearly she sensed the delicacy of the situation. "First time on the ward?"

Esther nodded.

"Room eight-two-two," the nurse told her, offering another friendly smile. Esther could see she was curious, though she was trying hard to appear casual. "Halfway along on the left."

"Thank you."

As Esther moved off down the corridor, she could feel the woman watching her. She stopped at Room 822. The door was open. She tapped lightly, before stepping inside.

Jean was sitting at the bedside. She looked up.

The years had been good to Jean. She was the opposite of her sister in many ways, not least in style of life. A yoga instructor and health-food-fanatic, Jean had often been a source of strength for Esther as a child. And despite Hannah's self-destructive attitude, Esther remembered Jean coming to their rescue time and time again when she was growing up. It was her aunt and not Hannah who had tracked Esther down in London after she discovered what had happened between them. Her aunt, and not her mother, who'd learned that Esther was fending for herself, and who'd tried and failed to convince Esther to come home and stay with her for a while. It had been Jean who had tried to keep everyone together, and it had been Esther who had put all the effort into leaving them both behind.

"Auntie Jean," Esther said, and was shocked at how those old, oft-spoken syllables made her feel like a child again.

"Hiya, Esther, love," Jean replied, coming over to give Esther a fierce hug. Esther hugged her back without hesitation. It felt good.

Then they both turned to the woman propped up in the hospital bed.

Esther stared. The woman lying there was barely recognisable. Pale and skinny, her cheeks hollow and her eyes sunken, she wore a skull-and-crossbones bandana and a faded Guns 'n' Roses T-shirt. Apart from the clothes, Hannah looked nothing like Esther remembered. The cancer, or the treatment, had done its damage. There was almost nothing left of her.

"Mum?" Esther's breath caught. She wasn't crying, but she was close to it.

Hannah stared at her as if she was seeing a ghost, a ghost that had come to usher her into the afterlife.

"I called her, Hannah," Jean told her sister, to break the lengthening silence as mother and daughter stared wordlessly at one another. "I know you wanted to see her. And I know you were too afraid to call her. Afraid she wouldn't answer, or wouldn't come. Well... she came, Hannah. Here she is."

Hannah's mouth worked but no words came out. A single tear rolled down her cheek. She raised one bony arm towards Esther, as if trying to reach her from across the room.

Esther stood frozen to the spot.

Once again, as the silence stretched, Jean came to the rescue.

"Here, Esther, take my seat," she said, steering her niece towards the plastic chair next to the bed. "I'll run downstairs to the cafeteria and get us some juices. They have a good juice bar here, not like hospitals used to be. I'll let you two catch up." She said the last so matter-of-factly, as if they were no more than a pair of old friends who hadn't seen each other for a few years. She sat Esther into the chair and then slipped out without another word.

Hannah was still staring at Esther, eyes wet, mouth

open as if she couldn't really believe it.

"Jean told me," Esther said, clearing her throat and blinking away the moisture in her own eyes. "She said it was cancer. How... what have the doctors said?"

Hannah just stared for another long moment, before she suddenly gasped like she was struggling for breath. Esther straightened instinctively, ready to call for help, as her mother sucked at the air. And that was when Esther realised her mother was crying. Her voice, when she spoke, was cracked and broken, but it was her mother's voice.

"I'm so sorry, Esther," she sobbed. "I'm so sorry." She reached out with one hand, tears rolling down her cheeks. "For everything. I'm so, so sorry."

Esther stared at the offered hand for a moment before she realised that she too was crying now. Slowly she reached out and took her mother's hand. She couldn't speak. Her throat felt stung and swollen. It was all she could do not to break down too, as her mother put every ounce of what little strength she had left into squeezing her daughter's hand.

They were still crying and clutching one another when Jean returned with the juices ten minutes later.

Jean took the seat on the other side of the bed, directly across from Esther. Mother and daughter both finally managed to pull themselves together.

Hannah kept crying and apologizing, until Esther ordered her to stop saying sorry. After years of nursing a resentment that bordered on hatred, Esther suddenly found herself feeling nothing but pity and remorse.

Once they'd both recovered, and Jean distributed the juices she'd bought, Hannah began to tell Esther about the fifteen years since they'd last seen one another. Her drinking had only become worse with her daughter's sudden departure, until one day she woke up covered in bruises and missing a tooth, and she realised she couldn't remember a damn thing that had happened the previous day. She'd phoned Jean, poor suffering Jean—she gave her sister a grateful smile as she said it—who came through for her yet again. Jean had dragged her to rehab. Hannah did well for a while. She started going to AA meetings. She got her life together and stayed off the booze for years. But, of course, a key part of the rehab program involved reaching out to those friends and family members who'd suffered as a result of your addiction. The people you had hurt the most. Hannah had realised it was time to find her daughter. Her drinking had ruined *both* their lives.

It was six years ago, but she remembered the day clearly.

"I tracked you down," Hannah said. "I was surprised to find out you were back here, back in Belfield. I was sitting at a bus shelter across from the police station."

"Six years ago? I was still in uniform at Belfield Central."

Hannah nodded. "I waited an hour. More. And then you finally came out. In your police uniform. I remember just staring at you. I could hardly believe it was you. You looked so different. And I couldn't move. As proud as I was of you, I felt my own shame ten times over. I couldn't move, couldn't speak, just watched you trot down those steps and hop into one of the police cars. I stood there and watched you drive away. I'd never felt so wretched in all my life. How I'd treated you all those years… you were just a girl, just a child…" She began sobbing again. Esther put a hand on her arm and Hannah composed herself quickly, determined to go on. She gave Esther a grateful smile. "Sorry." She heaved a deep breath. "So, what did I do? I went to the nearest bar, of course."

"Oh, Mum."

Hannah nodded, frowning at the crumpled tissue in her hand. "Yeah. That was me again. Another two years on the bottle. And then, once I realised I was sick—whatever the doctors said at the start, I knew in my heart it was bad, I just knew—I was off the drink then for good. Onto the drugs. The hard stuff. All prescribed and above board." She laughed mirthlessly. "And then the chemo… and now… well, they've tried everything. Three to six months, they say, but it could be less."

Esther squeezed her hand gently. Hannah met her eyes. "I was a terrible bitch," she said, flat and matter-of-fact this time. "I was the one person in the whole world above everyone else who should have been there for you and protected you, and I failed. I was a terrible mother to you."

Esther couldn't argue. She said nothing.

Hannah's lip trembled. "Can you ever forgive me?"

Esther nodded. "Of course, Mum. Of course." And she realised she really meant it.

"Thank you," Hannah whispered, dissolving into tears once more. It set Esther off again too, and this time Jean wasn't spared. The three of them sat there, every one of them a blubbering mess, and the juices sat forgotten on the bedside table.

16

IT WAS ONE a.m. The radio was blessedly silent after a hectic first few hours. Esther had worried she was in for another crazy night of domestic stabbings and bar room glassings. This was the third night of her new job, and the first two had been shifts from hell. At first, she thought that she had simply forgotten how manic response policing could be, but the exhausted looks on the faces of her team told her this was not normal. And then the comments had found their way back to her via the other sergeants. She was a jinx, apparently. The crews had linked her sudden appearance with the sudden upsurge in night-time violence... Ridiculous, but coppers could be a superstitious bunch. Like when she wished them a quiet shift at the end of last night's briefing and was met with groans and head shakes. Jamie—the senior constable at forty-five years, but a fairly dashing guy nonetheless, and one Esther was already sure was favouring her with a special attention—had laughed and told her that she couldn't use the 'Q-word'. It was bad luck. Meant they were going to have a crap night. Esther had tutted and rolled her eyes at the stupidity of it… and then they'd all had what could only be described as a *really* crap night.

Now that things had calmed down, Esther was staring at the pile of paperwork the last two nights had generated. She'd spent the last four hours reading reports about traffic accidents, dead-end burglaries and over a dozen domestic assaults. She couldn't read another badly-written police statement. She couldn't look at another shitty road collision sketch. And it was so much harder to stare at a computer screen in the small hours of the morning and get anything done.

Having spent the last two nights sitting by the radio, coordinating her resources and giving instructions to one crew after another as the calls came in, she had only managed to get out to one crime scene: the home of a woman who had taken an eight-inch breadknife to her abusive drunk of a husband and sliced him badly enough to warrant an arrest for attempted murder and a crime scene at the house for the rest of the night. Other than that, she had been shackled to her desk, next to the radio mic and the telephone. She'd thought her head was going to explode when people called her on the radio while every phone in the office rang—officers looking for advice, or despatchers wanting to update her on a new call coming in—and she wondered how the fuck any of the other sergeants stationed here had managed this for so long without going insane…

Now the screen was nearly empty of calls—just a couple of anti-social behaviour reports and a complaint about a noisy party—and the radio had stopped chirping. Esther looked up from the mountain of paper in her in-tray to the cabinet on the wall across the room, where the keys for the patrol cars were kept.

It didn't take much time to decide. She was out of her seat and grabbing the key to an unmarked squad car before her computer had finished processing her log-out command. She shrugged into her hi-vis stab vest, POLICE emblazoned in white on blue across the back, and strapped on her kit belt, checking that she had all the essentials—torch, baton, pepper spray, first aid pouch, handcuffs, pen and notebook—and then she was heading for the door, fitting the radio earpiece into her ear as she made her way to the yard.

The unmarked car was a silver Ford with blue lights hidden under the grill and a camera on the dash. Esther sat in and adjusted the driver's seat. She flicked on the blue lights and gave the siren an experimental tweak to make sure everything was working, then rolled out of the station car park and onto the main drag of Yorkgate Avenue.

She had stopped by the hospital again today before work. Hannah had been sleeping, but Esther had left a note, promising to call by once her shift was done. Jean made the trip from neighbouring Sarsbury every day. Despite all the mixed emotions that thoughts of her mother brought up, Esther was determined to make a real effort at putting the past behind them. Hannah had carried her guilt for years. And Esther had been far from the perfect daughter. They would salvage what little they could of their relationship, and take what little time was left to them.

Esther wiped a tear from her cheek and chastised herself for going all mushy again. She'd been emotionally delicate since that first visit to the hospital two days ago. But she was at work now. Pushing thoughts of her mother aside, she focused instead on the handful of vehicles passing her on the night-shrouded streets. She cruised slowly past shuttered shopfronts, noting with bemusement how many homeless people she passed, huddled in their sleeping bags in the doorways. There seemed to be a lot more than she remembered from her early years of night patrol.

She found herself drifting towards the centre of town. It was a weeknight and there were only a few stragglers making their way home from late-licence pubs and clubs. The fast-food joint near Westland Avenue was the busiest place in town at this hour, but as Esther rolled onto the flagstone streets of the pedestrian quarter she noted, with a touch of satisfaction, that two of her patrol cars were already idling nearby, waiting for trouble.

The further from the hub of nightlife she drove, the less people there were on the streets, apart from the bundled-up homeless in their doorways. Esther kept her car at a steady ten to fifteen miles per hour and prowled on.

Eventually she turned onto the patchy tarmac of Marigate Street. It was empty. But as Esther pulled up alongside the Marigate Art Gallery, she hit the brakes. There was a light on in the rear of the premises. She checked the clock on her dashboard. 02:24. Odd. There were shadows moving in the back office. The old-fashioned accordion-style lattice grill that served as a flimsy shutter was pulled across the front and padlocked. Whoever was in there had gone in via the back yard. Could be a burglary in progress,

Esther thought, but she knew she was just looking for an excuse to be nosey. She left the radio alone and quietly rolled the car down the street, pulling in ten yards shy of the alleyway that led around back. As she killed the engine and stepped out, she shrugged into her black police windbreaker, zipping it up to hide her hi-vis stab vest.

The alley was dark, but there was a security light on in the yard. Two vehicles. One was the black Audi, parked in the same spot as last time, and the second was a white panel van. As she drew closer, Esther spotted something that made her breath catch—damage to the van's front offside indicator. Even in the half-light she could see that the shard of amber plastic sitting in her desk drawer back at the station would fit perfectly into the gap. She pulled out her phone and took pictures of the broken indicator, the licence plate, and the tyre treads on all four wheels. She shone her torch onto the tyre walls and made a note of the make, model and sizes, not at all surprised to see that they were Michelin 205s. She tried the van doors, but found them locked.

Suddenly she heard voices. Gruff male voices growing louder. They were coming from behind the steel-plated door to the art gallery.

Esther darted back to the alleyway. There was a dumpster wedged up against one mossy brick wall. It sat in a pool of darkness just beyond the gates. Esther tucked herself in behind it and watched as three men emerged. One was the skinny John-Lennon-lookalike. Peter Darren, she assumed. Not a burglary in progress then. The other two men were burly meatheads. They looked like bouncers, in their black bomber jackets and jeans, one with a shaved head that glinted in the light, the other with a dark woollen cap around his ears and a black goatee that left his upper lip bare.

Darren said nothing as the two men went to the van, he just glanced around the yard. Esther ducked back instinctively, though there was no way he would be able to see her where she was, in amongst the shadows. Then Darren disappeared, pulling the door to the gallery closed after him as the van's indicators flashed and the locks clicked open. Both heavies climbed into the front.

Esther tried to wedge herself between wall and dumpster as the van rumbled to life and headlights lit up the alleyway. She hoped the driver didn't glance out his side window as he negotiated his way, but she needn't have worried: the van took off at speed, zipping past her, faster than she would have driven in such a narrow space. These guys were used to driving here, and in the dark.

She peered around the back of the dumpster as the van reached the end of the alley, its brake lights washing the walls red. As soon as those lights went out and the van began to turn, Esther was up on her feet and running.

She scrambled into her patrol car as the van took a right at the end of Marigate Street. Pulling out fast, she sped towards the intersection. There was no other traffic, and as she reached the junction she caught sight of the van turning left. It was heading north.

She weighed her options. She could pull them over at any time for that broken indicator, but she didn't want to do that. Not yet. First, she wanted to see where they might lead her, and find out what these two bruisers might be up to at this hour of the morning…

She muttered a quiet curse as they turned onto the slip-road for the motorway, forcing her to reassess. If they were headed any distance at all she would probably end up having to let them go. Either that or pull them over before they left the borough. And, strictly speaking, this was the traffic unit's territory. But Esther was in an unmarked car, so she decided to follow them for a little bit longer.

They continued north, keeping slightly below the seventy miles-per-hour speed limit and staying in the inside lane throughout, except when overtaking slow-moving trucks.

Five minutes into their journey, Esther caught a break. Bright signage for a service station stood tall against the dark night sky up ahead, and the van indicated to take the exit. She slowed, extending the distance between her and her quarry before she moved onto the slip road after them.

There was a truckers' rest behind the service station. Esther slowed as the van drove straight past the forecourt and out into the truckers' lot. There were about half a dozen articulated lorries, all with long trailers attached, parked up in the darkness. Esther pulled up short, knocking off her lights as she eased into a parking space next to the service station building. She watched from behind the cover of a fenced-off kids' play area, locked and cloaked in shadow at this hour, as the van moved slowly between the trucks. Scanning the scene, she spotted their destination straight away: a truck at the far end with BELFIELD LOGISTICS emblazoned along the side of its trailer. Esther felt that heady rush she got when she knew she'd made a break in a case, even before the van pulled up alongside the Belfield truck's cab and the trucker climbed down to greet them.

The speed of the exchange she witnessed next told Esther this was a regular activity. The trucker lifted the side curtain of the trailer and passed one blocky package after another to the baldy goon, who passed it to the goatee goon, who stashed it in the back of the panel van. The packages were big enough that the men needed both hands to carry them, and they were all identically wrapped in black plastic. Esther counted half a dozen in all. And in less than a minute the van doors were closed, the truck curtain fastened in place again, and the trucker was climbing back into his cab. At this distance, she couldn't make out any of the truck-driver's features. He was thinner than the other two, and had a grey baseball cap pulled low over his face.

Esther watched as Baldy and Goatee got back into their van and drove away. But she couldn't go straight after them. The trucker would see her from his cab. No doubt he was keeping an eye out. She cursed silently as she watched the white van pick up speed along the slip road and disappear out onto the motorway again. How long could she give it and still hope to catch up to them? A moment later, a customer emerged from the shop and sat into a blue sedan on the forecourt. As he pulled away from the pump and towards the exit, Esther decided to take a chance and follow. If she waited any longer she'd lose the van completely. She was in an unmarked car, and her police vest was still hidden under her black windbreaker. There was a good chance the trucker wouldn't notice her. Keeping low in her seat, she followed the sedan, and as soon as she hit the motorway she overtook it and put her foot to the floor.

About a mile up the road she came across a convoy of HGVs. She switched to the outside lane and pushed the car to ninety, cursing as she came up behind an SUV doing sixty-five in the overtaking lane. It looked like the asshole was going to stay there and try to overtake the whole convoy. Impatiently, Esther flashed her lights. He didn't move. There was no sign of the van up ahead, so she took a chance and flashed her blues. She didn't want to use the siren, worried that the sound might travel. Fortunately, she didn't have to. The SUV driver pulled in, and Esther gunned her car up to ninety again.

As she left the convoy behind and the road cleared, she saw no sign of the white van. She pushed harder. A glance at the dash. Touching a hundred miles per hour. The road straightened. Still nothing. The motorway was empty apart from another artic lorry half a mile ahead of her.

And then she caught sight of a flash of white on a bridge up ahead. Signalling quickly, she made it onto the off-ramp leading to the overpass just in time. It had been a white van, she was certain. How many white vans would be trundling about the motorway at this hour? She didn't want to consider the answer to that question right now. She broke the red lights at the end of the slip-road—there being no other traffic about to see her do it—and glanced down at the motorway again as she sped across the bridge. There, to the south, back the way she had come—a white panel van. She could see the roof clearly as it headed for Belfield.

She sped up again as she hit the southbound side of the motorway. A sign flashed past telling her Belfield was twenty-three miles away. She was shading a hundred miles an hour in the overtaking lane again when the van came into view up ahead. Esther slowed. She didn't want to spook them. She pulled into the inside lane and closed the distance slowly. A red sports car shot past her, doing well over a hundred, she was sure. As it raced past the van, Esther used the opportunity to push closer. Close enough to read the first few characters on the number plate and confirm it was Goatee and Baldy. She fell back a bit. She was confident that they were headed back to Belfield, so she decided she would pull them over when they got off the motorway. At least she would have backup on her radio channel then, should she need it. Fuck knew where the nearest traffic patrol car was out here.

As predicted, the van took the exit for Belfield North. Esther followed. They stopped at a red light at the end of the slip road. Esther pulled in behind them, close enough so that she was out of view of the van's wing mirrors.

She tapped the steering wheel nervously as she weighed up her options. They could be headed back to the art gallery. Or they could be headed to somewhere with a lot more muscle-heads like them. Either way, if they got onto a premises she would need a warrant. That would take time, paperwork, and a judge's signature, and she hadn't quite figured out how to fix her story. She couldn't say she was tailing them. Without a surveillance warrant the whole thing would be binned. No, better to give the van a tug for the broken light, out here on the street while they were in transit, and take it from there. As for tying Belfield Logistics to it… she'd figure that out later.

The lights turned green, and the van pulled away again. Esther let herself fall back a few car lengths before picking up the radio.

"Despatch from Bravo Yankee Two-two."

"Bravo Yankee Two-two from Despatch, send your message. Over."

"I'm about to make a traffic stop on—" she glanced at the street sign as she came to the end of the block and the van turned left "—Millwell Street and North Way. White van…" She read out the plate number. "Two up, both IC-one males. Any units close by to assist? Over."

"Bravo Yankee Two-two from Bravo Yankee One-Oh-Four, we're ten minutes out from that location. We'll head your way. Keep us updated. Over."

"Roger." Esther took a deep breath, then hit the blue lights. They were in a residential area. The street furniture flashed blue as her grill lights came on.

The van didn't stop. It continued without even slowing. Esther gripped the wheel. Maybe they were panicking. Trying to decide what to do. No way they hadn't seen the lights. The whole street was flickering. She hit the siren—two quick yelps. The van slowed, indicated to pull over, then rolled slowly to a stop.

Esther muttered an update into her radio as she got out of the car. "Bravo Yankee Two-two, that's a stop-stop on Millwell Street." She left her engine running in case they decided to make a break for it.

She was alone. No other vehicles or pedestrians about that she could see. She decided her best course of action was to play dumb and keep them sweet until the backup arrived. Approaching the driver's door as casually as she could, she forced an easy smile, and discreetly touched the pepper spray at her belt for reassurance.

"Hi there," she chirped as she reached the driver door and the window came down.

Goatee gave her a nervous smile. "Morning, officer. What's up?"

"Did you know one of your indicators is broken?"

Goatee shook his head. "Sorry, no I didn't. Work van, you see."

"You got your driver's licence with you?"

Goatee shook his head. "No, sorry. Not with me."

"Anything with your name on it?"

Goatee gave her a sharp, impatient look. "Is this really necessary? For a broken light? I'll get it fixed. You can run the plates. The van belongs to my boss."

Esther nodded. "I'll do that. Who's your boss? It's kinda late. You doing overnight deliveries or something?"

Goatee didn't answer. He turned away from her and glanced at Baldy. Esther quietly cursed herself for not running the plates already. If the plates were bogus, they might try to cut and run.

"Who do you work for?" Esther asked again. "You got any ID at all on you?"

Goatee was clenching his jaw now, not looking at her.

"Okay, sir, tell you what. Do me a favour and knock the engine off for me, will you?"

Goatee turned to his friend Baldy again. And then

the passenger door opened, and Baldy was climbing out. Esther craned her neck. "Excuse me, passenger? Get back in the van for me. Get back in the vehicle *now.*"

Baldy wasn't listening. He was moving around the front of the van towards her. Esther tried to make a transmission, but Baldy was moving too quickly. It was all she could do to hit the emergency button before she had to let go of her radio and snatch her pepper spray from her belt.

She aimed the canister at Baldy, arm straight out so he could see it clearly, and shouted: "Get back! Not one more step, pal! One more step and I will dose you with this shit, I swear to God!"

Baldy stopped short and eyed the little spray canister like it was a gun. Fuck, Esther wished she had a gun. Or even a taser.

The driver's door opened. Esther took another step back.

Goatee stepped out. His face was thunderous. He moved sideways, away from Baldy, putting space between them, and forcing Esther to swing her pepper spray from one to the other as she backed up.

"Guys, whatever you've done isn't going to be a patch on what you're about to do. A broken lamp is a thirty-five-pound ticket. You have a go at me, and I'll put you both on your asses and charge you with assault on police." Esther was proud at how calm and assertive she sounded, with her heart pounding so hard she was sure they must see it trying to leap out of her chest. She took another step back, struggling now to keep both men covered with her pepper spray; Baldy had taken his cue from Goatee and they were both inching closer to her while moving farther apart from each other.

And then suddenly there was another patrol car gunning up the road, its blue roof-lights flashing. Both goons spun to stare as it braked hard, right by Baldy, and the doors flew open. Two uniformed cops jumped out, barking commands—

"Get down!"

"Police! Get on the ground!"

Another police car appeared at the opposite end of the street. Esther watched Goatee tense up, clearly thinking of making a run for it, but as the second patrol car pulled up and more police emerged, batons out and shouting instructions, Esther could see him realise that the game was up. Almost in unison, both men put their hands out wide to show they were surrendering.

Esther only realised how tense she'd been when she felt the adrenalin drain out of her and her knees almost went. She lowered her spray as the others got Goatee and Baldy secured and handcuffed.

"Bravo Yankee Two-two from Despatch. Confirm those crews are with you and you're okay. Over."

Esther took a deep breath. Her hand was shaking as she lifted it to her radio mic and pushed the button. "Roger. Two in custody here."

"Roger that. You can go ahead and knock off your emergency transmit button."

"Yeah, okay, thank you." Esther knocked off the emergency transmit. She called out to the police restraining the two goons: "Go ahead and put them in separate cars. Defective lamp, obstruction under the road traffic orders and resisting police to start with, but I suspect they've got something in this van they didn't want me to see."

As Goatee and Baldy were placed into the patrol cars, Esther grabbed the keys from the van's ignition and unlocked the back doors. It was Jamie who joined her as she pulled them open. He shone his flashlight into the dark, cluttered space.

"What you think they're hauling, Sarge?" he asked, as Esther pushed aside two cardboard boxes full of old newspapers to reveal the black plastic packages beyond. She climbed into the back of the van to reach the nearest one, snapping on a pair of nitrile gloves and turning it on its side to examine it. It was heavy, and wrapped tight, with no obvious way of unravelling it. It felt solid too.

"Cannabis maybe?" she said. "You got a pen knife or something?"

He fished in his pocket and tossed her a Swiss army knife.

"Shine the torch on the package right here," she instructed, as she unfolded the blade.

Esther made a careful incision and peeled back the plastic.

"Whoa!" Jamie exclaimed when they both saw what was inside. "How many packs are in there?"

"Six," she replied. "All the same size."

"Fucking hell, Sarge," Jamie's voice had fallen to a whisper. "That's some haul."

Esther folded the knife up again and they both stared down at the cut-open pack. It wasn't cannabis. It was cocaine.

"Get me some evidence bags," she said.

"Yes, ma'am," he replied, and went to grab the bags.

Esther stared at the white powder, packed tight into the big plastic-wrapped block, and then took in the five other identical blocks lying next to it. Some haul, indeed. She took out her phone and rang Jared.

17

ESTHER STOOD IN the cramped monitor room, eyes fixed on the screen labelled INTERVIEW ROOM 4. It showed a wide-angle view from one corner of the ceiling, covering the whole room, where two of her detectives were interviewing Goatee. His name was actually Brian 'Buck' Furlong, but she still thought of him as Goatee. And they were not her detectives anymore, she reminded herself. Liz Fellowes and Kyle Harris were two of the best interrogators in CID, and Esther wasn't at all surprised by Jared's choice of personnel to haul from their beds at this ungodly hour.

"Where did you get the packages?" Kyle's voice was tinny in the monitor's speaker.

"No comment," replied Goatee. *Furlong.* He sat, arms crossed, coldly impassive. His lawyer—a young grease-ball in a rumpled suit—sat quietly, jotting notes in a legal pad and saying little. He didn't need to say anything, really, because it didn't matter how good the detectives asking the questions were when a client was as disciplined in his maintenance of a 'no comment' interview as Furlong was.

"Did you know what was in the packages?"

"No comment."

"Where were you bringing them?"

"No comment."

"Where did you get the van?"

"No comment."

Esther sighed. He'd even replied 'no comment' when Liz had asked him for his name and whether he'd been driving the van.

Esther turned as the door behind her opened and Jared stepped inside. He stood next to her and watched the interview for a minute.

"You had a passenger in your van. Isn't that correct?"

"No comment."

"Do you know him well? Can you tell us his name?"

"No comment."

"We've identified him as Gary Bradshaw. How do you know Gary?"

"No comment."

Jared grunted. "Same routine with Bradshaw," he muttered. "In fact, Mister Bradshaw didn't even give them the courtesy of a 'no comment'—fucker didn't say a goddamn word during the whole interview."

"What about the van?" Esther asked.

"Seized and on its way to the CSI garage. They'll give it a thorough going-over tomorrow. The plates are ringers, as I'm sure you guessed. We've already verified that the real van is locked up in the back yard of a supermarket in Aylesbury." He turned to her. "I take it you heard the prelim tests have confirmed the powder is cocaine?"

Esther nodded, eyes still fixed on the screen and Furlong.

Jared regarded her quietly for a moment. "That's twenty-four kilos of what looks like pretty pure stuff, Esther," he went on. "That's well over a million pounds worth, street value. Assuming they weren't planning on reducing the purity before distribution…"

She turned to look up at him, his face half-lit in the glow of the monitors.

"Smile, for fuck's sake," he chortled. "You've done well, Esther! This might get you back on the team!"

Esther frowned. "There's still Gorman, and the art gallery," she replied. "This is all linked to the murders of Rachel Gorman and Jack Barry, Jared. You know it is. Gorman is in this up to his neck. I don't think he killed his wife, but I'm pretty sure she was killed because of what he's involved in here. And I'm pretty sure he knows it."

Jared nodded. "Yeah, for what it's worth I think you're right. We've got a bit of a problem with how we go about pinning it on him though. We can't tell anyone you were tailing him on a day off, with no warrant, no authorisation. Or carrying out illegal surveillance on the art gallery either."

"I told you, I saw a light on—"

"I know, I know," he said, and sighed heavily. "But then you followed the van. For quite a distance. Covertly. It's too shaky. We need something more. A solid legal foundation to start this thing. This could be a really big bust if we do it right. But if we start with an illegal bit of police work, or breaching RIPA, it'll all unravel at Crown Court."

Esther grimaced. The Regulation of Investigatory Powers Act. Shoulda fucking called it the Hamstring-the-Police Act, Esther thought. It was frustrating how often the law got in the way of good police work. "Well, we can at least tell Intel about the links," she said. "They can run some checks on the art gallery and the owner and find out who he's connected to. I mean, think about it. It's perfect for money laundering. Anonymous buyers, confidential transactions, arbitrary sums of money for paint on a canvas. I bet the financial crime boys would have a field day with the books in that place. Fuck knows what they might find."

Jared shook his head. "We can't do anything with the art gallery yet. Not officially anyway. Not until we can make an above-board, legally watertight link to these guys, that van, and the art gallery." He brightened. "On the other hand, if we wash your info through as an Intel submission we can use CCTV and ANPR to put the Belfield truck and van together at that service station. With all the cash we seized at Charles Gorman's house—cash he still hasn't sufficiently accounted for—it should be enough to get a surveillance warrant on his office."

"The whole office?" she asked. "Or just Gorman?"

"Just Gorman. His office, his phone. His house and car. Can't justify the whole office. Too much collateral intrusion."

They both watched the screen showing Interview Room Four as Kyle reached over and knocked off the digital recorder. A little red light above the door went out, and the detectives and the solicitor began tidying up their papers. The interview was over, and they were no further along.

Esther yawned.

"Come on, Esther," Jared said as he pulled open the door to the monitor room and Esther squinted against the harsh white light of the custody corridor. They made their way out of the dungeon to the station yard.

Jared made a show of checking his watch as they stepped into a chilly predawn gloom. "It's, what, an hour to the end of your shift?" he asked.

Esther checked her own watch and nodded, stifling another yawn.

"Go get back to Yorkgate and get your handover done. Go home and get some sleep. With any luck, I'll have you off nightshifts and back with us next week."

"Porter will never go for it," Esther replied dryly.

"Who said anything about Porter?" Jared murmured. "I'm going straight to the superintendent."

Esther looked at him and raised her eyebrows.

Jared grinned and winked.

"There's still some fight in this old dog yet," he said.

18

As SOON AS she'd briefed the sergeant coming in for the early shift, Esther hurried to the locker room and got changed. Traffic would be building already, and she wanted to get to the hospital before there was a queue at the car park.

She made it in just under half an hour, and when she got to the eighth floor, she found her mother sitting up in bed having breakfast.

"You look tired," Hannah said, as Esther came in and sat down. She herself looked like death, but Esther didn't say so.

"Just finished a nightshift," she replied with a sigh.

"They'll be sending me home next week," Hannah told her. "They've done everything they can. I'll have home visits from a specialist nurse instead. Jean's getting her place ready. She'll be popping in later."

Esther frowned. "That's it. Just go home and wait?"

Hannah gave her a small smile. "We're all waiting,

hon," she replied. "It's just that some of us have a timetable in our hands." She gave a wink. Esther couldn't smile though. It was so weird. The voice brought back all the memories, and the eyes, but in some ways this woman was a complete stranger, an entirely different person to the mother Esther remembered growing up with. Here was the woman her mother *would* have been if she had kept her shit together, Esther thought sadly. She was starting to like this woman. *Now* she was starting to like her, for fuck's sake—*now,* when they had practically no time left.

She reached out and squeezed her mother's arm gently. Hannah patted her hand, and took another sip of her brightly-coloured smoothie.

"What is it?" Esther asked, nodding towards the smoothie.

"Banana, strawberry, and orange juice. Wanna try?"

Esther took a sip. "Mmm. That's good."

"I know, right? Since when was hospital food good? I'm going to have to try and work Jean's juicer when I get home, and make one of these bad boys myself." Hannah paused, and studied her daughter for a moment. "You should get some sleep, love. Too many of those nightshifts and you'll end up looking like me."

"It's just temporary. My boss, my old boss, is trying to get me back into CID."

"You're a detective?"

"Detective sergeant, actually," Esther replied with a mirthless smile, "not that it seems to mean much these days."

"What do you mean?"

Esther sighed. "I got kicked out of CID last week and put back on uniform duties. Hence the nightshifts. It's a punishment. I poked too hard at a murder case that the chief wants kept closed."

Hannah's eyes went round in a playfully dramatic way. "A conspiracy? Are you trying to uncover police corruption?"

Esther laughed. "Not exactly. Laziness and egotism, more like. I just... there was a murder a couple of weeks ago. Two, actually. But the chief closed one as a suicide and pinned the first murder on the guy who hanged himself. Or appeared to have hanged himself." She frowned. "I don't buy it, though. And last night... last night I stopped a van linked to it all, full of cocaine, and I think it gives my version a bit more credibility. It's a long story. Complicated. And I can't really go into it."

Hannah gave her a wide-eyed look. "I saw that in the news. The drugs recovery. That was you? It all sounds very exciting!"

Esther shrugged. "Like I said, I can't really go into it." Then she considered her mother's beaming smile, her eyes bright and curious in that gaunt face. She relented, and gave her the story in broad strokes, sticking to what was already in the public domain and adding a bit of first-hand flavour. She couldn't go into any detail, or use any names.

"What?" Esther asked suspiciously when she finished. "You don't believe me."

Hannah smiled. "I believe you. I just... I'm just amazed by you. What you've done with yourself, after the fucked-up childhood I gave you."

"Mum..."

"No. Really. Esther, you're an amazing young

woman. Don't ever forget that. Don't ever think you're any less than you are. This isn't sentiment talking. I know the shit you had to go through with me as a mother. The house you had to grow up in. And look at you now. You've beaten it. I almost can't believe you're my daughter. You're so much stronger than me. So much better." She took Esther's hand in both of hers. "In spite of me, you've become a good woman. A strong, smart woman. Hold on to that. I guess sometimes it won't feel like it means much. But it does. It means *so* much. Just keeping your life together. Don't ever be like me. If I gave you anything, let it have been a glimpse of what you're managing *not* to be."

Esther suddenly thought about the many times she'd woken up under strange ceilings with no clothes on. She thought about standing in the street, drunk, while hospital security guards eyeballed her. She thought about throwing up all over some strange man's penis... She felt her cheeks burn at the memory.

Her mother must have mistaken her blush for modesty. "Promise me?" Hannah persisted.

"Sure, Mum. Promise."

Hannah patted her hand again. She let out a long sigh. Then she perked up a bit. "So, what about men? You got a handsome young policeman you haven't told me about?"

Esther shook her head.

"Kinda between guys I guess," she offered lamely.

Hannah chortled. "Enjoy that too," she said huskily, and there was a reminder of the old Hannah in her tone. "Right guy will come along." She closed her eyes, clearly exhausted by the last half hour of storytelling and conversation. Her voice was sleepy when she went on. "You're smart and you're beautiful and thanks to me you've hopefully met enough scummy bastards to know one when you see one and avoid them."

Hannah went quiet then. Her eyes stayed closed. Esther waited a few minutes until she felt her mother's grip relax and was sure she was asleep. Then she got up, cleared away the breakfast, and slipped from the room. She needed sleep too, but there was something she had to do first.

*

Back at her apartment, Esther went straight for the fridge. Half the shelves were empty, and a lot of what was there wasn't food. She began clearing out the booze. Bottles of beer and chardonnay were poured unceremoniously down the sink. Two large bottles of vodka from her icebox followed. And then there were the empties scattered about her apartment. An empty vodka bottle under her bed, and a half-empty shoulder of the same brand in the bathroom. She wanted to be rid of it all, every bottle and every can. She stacked the empties into a basin and hauled them to her door. There were bottle-banks in the yard next to the apartment building.

She took the lift to the ground floor. She thanked the geeky guy in the bicycle helmet who held the front door for her and politely declined his offer of help. Then she hauled the basin full of empty liquor bottles around the side of the building and began shoving them one-by-one into the glass recycling container. Her ears were soon ringing with the sound of smashing glass, and she almost didn't hear her phone.

It was Jared.

"Hey," she answered, taking a break from her bottle-smashing.

"Hey. Wasn't sure if you'd still be asleep or not, but…"

"No, I'm awake. What's up?"

"I got a call from forensics half an hour ago."

"Yeah?" Esther asked. "And? They found something?"

"Jack Barry's DNA," Jared told her. "In the van. Quite a bit of it."

Esther felt goosebumps prickle her skin. *This* was the break they needed! "For real?"

"Yep. That and the fact that you found that bit of indicator up in the woods… well, that puts the van in the vicinity of Jack Barry's site of death, somewhere in and around the time he died, and it puts him *in* the van, sometime in the recent past."

"Enough for you to reopen the investigation?"

She heard him take a breath and hesitate.

"I hope so," he said at last. "I've got a meeting with Superintendent O'Halloran tomorrow morning to discuss it. Correction—*we* have a meeting with her."

Esther found herself nodding. "That's good, Jared. It's a chance, at least."

"It's all or nothing, is what it is. Porter will hear about it, if he hasn't already. So get some sleep and be at Central at ten a.m. sharp."

"Wilco."

"And stay focused?"

Esther glanced at the remaining bottles in her basin. "Stay sober, you mean?"

"That too."

"I'll see you in the a.m. Bright eyed and bushy tailed."

"Good work, Esther."

He hung up.

Esther allowed herself a little smile as she tucked the phone into her pocket and went back to dumping her empty liquor bottles.

*

Sitting in the black sedan at the far end of the street, they had a clear view of the front doors to the apartment building as well as the yard next to it. They watched the woman detective carry a basin full of glass bottles to the recycling enclosure and begin feeding them into the bottle bank. Watched her stop to pull a phone from her pocket and speak to someone for a few minutes.

The beefy woman in the passenger seat lifted a long-lensed camera from her lap and took some photos of her. This policewoman was a pretty one, she thought. Skinny. High cheek bones. Although it wasn't as if a woman like that would ever give someone like her a second glance. She touched the deep scar on her chin before she realised what she was doing and took her hand away. She found herself doing that sometimes when she thought about her appearance. Some people did a double take when she worked the door at the nightclub, not sure whether she was a man or a woman at first. She had started shaving the sides of her head and tying the rest of her sandy-brown hair back into a tight ponytail to add to the confusion. Made people hesitate. Even in a fight. Not that she needed the advantage. She could bench two hundred pounds easy and snap the neck of any fucker who thought she was an easier target because she was a woman.

She lowered the camera as the detective went back into her apartment building with the empty basin under one arm.

"How long we gotta sit here?" asked the beanpole of a man in the driver seat.

"Instructions are to watch her." She looked at him. He was a dangerous one, she thought, with his rat-like features and beady little eyes. But she could tell that he was intimidated by her all the same. Most men were. "So that's what we do until we hear different."

He might want to look tough, with his skinhead and neck tattoos, but he couldn't hold her flat stare for long. He sighed and made a show of settling back in his seat.

"Let's take it in shifts then," he said, closing his eyes. "Wake me in a half hour, or if she leaves again."

She stared at him for a long moment, but saw no reasonable argument against the proposal, so she said nothing. Turning back to the policewoman's apartment building, she watched and waited.

19

SUPERINTENDENT JANICE O'HALLORAN was a plain
woman, handsome rather than pretty. Her uniform
was spotless and well-pressed, her hair neatly tied in a
bun at the nape of her neck, exactly as per
regulations. She wore no makeup, or else wore so
little of it, so subtly applied, that she gave the
impression of not wearing any.

Her office was large enough to hold both her desk
and the small circular conference table at which they
all now sat. Framed certificates lined the walls. The
bookshelves, and the various police-themed
ornaments that adorned the tops of the filing
cabinets, were all in meticulous order; everything in
the room was a reflection of her own neat and tidy
appearance.

Esther sat next to Jared, with DCI Porter and
Superintendent O'Halloran opposite, although not
quite together, as if the four of them represented
three corners of a triangle. At a circular table.

Jared had warned Esther before the meeting that

O'Halloran had invited Porter. Anxious at first, Esther had quickly warmed to the idea of calling him out face-to-face. Still, her stomach was a little fluttery as they sat there and Jared explained the circumstances behind his request for the meeting. So much rode on this—not just for Esther, with the prospect of permanent banishment to Yorkgate and complete loss of her detective status, but for Jared too, putting his neck on the line for her like this. If the meeting went Porter's way, then Jared's life would become very miserable very quickly. The way the DCI glared at the two of them when O'Halloran wasn't looking told Esther of problems down the line either way.

"…and so, ma'am, I believe that Detective Sergeant Penman should be allowed to return to CID. I think she has demonstrated her ability and her dedication and, in spite of a few shortcomings recently, I believe she is still performing above and beyond what we expect of our officers. I think she would prefer to be back in CID, and I think she deserves that."

Superintendent O'Halloran was jotting notes. She turned to DCI Porter.

"Warren? What's your view? You're the one who sent her to Yorkgate."

"Ma'am, Sergeant Penman is a headstrong police officer," he replied, giving Esther a hard stare. She stared right back. "I think she would admit as much herself. She was sent to Yorkgate because she failed to follow instructions. She was interfering in cases that were not hers to investigate. Showing up late for work, on multiple occasions. I suspect she may be drinking heavily, and my threat to breath test her may account for further absences." Esther opened her mouth to speak, but he gave her no chance to interrupt. "And she ignored my summons to a meeting. All my supervisors are required to attend a quarterly review and she did not attend. She did not send me her reports. She may enjoy pro-active police work but when it comes to paperwork and the obligation to complete reports, she is woefully slack. I felt, since she enjoyed being out on the street more than getting her paperwork done, she should go back to uniform policing. I daresay that, given a chance, she might even find this is where she would rather stay."

Esther glowered at him. But it was Jared who cut in to respond.

"Ma'am, I feel there is a bit more to it than that," he began slowly, and all eyes turned to him. "When it comes to Chief Porter's reviews, DS Penman's reports may be hit and miss, but her files for the Crown Prosecution Service are always above standard. She has had some issues around punctuality, but I absolutely do *not* feel it warrants a forced position on night shift duties. I believe the issue here is a personal one for DCI Porter. And I feel it all stems from a decision about a case that he made, and then pressured us to accept, which may be critically flawed."

"Be careful where you go here, Jared," Porter growled.

"Be quiet, Warren," O'Halloran said sharply. "I called this meeting and I want to hear what all parties have to say. Go on, Inspector."

"The death of Mister Jack Barry last week," he said. "That's the case the chief is referring to when he accuses Esther of 'interfering' in cases that weren't hers. But that's not true. That case *was* hers, and he closed it down early in the investigation because he felt it was a clear-cut suicide. And, in fairness, the evidence tended to point that way. But in my humble opinion, Esther was well within her rights as one of the investigating officers to ask that she be allowed to follow up a few more leads. DCI Porter declined. In spite of this, Esther went ahead and looked into a few things anyway, and this is where the issue really began."

"Oh please," Porter interrupted. He was angry, but Esther saw signs of nervousness now too. "The issues with Sergeant Penman have been going on for months. Long before the Barry case. You know this, Jared. And I have been more than lenient with you for failing to address them."

Superintendent O'Halloran studied Jared's reaction to this. Jared nodded. "I accept that the punctuality thing has been an issue for some time. But again, I don't think it warrants the action the chief has taken here. And apart from all of this I think Esther has been vindicated in her continued investigation of the Barry death. Not only do we have a million pounds worth of cocaine off the streets, thanks to Esther, but we have tied Barry to the van it was being transported in. We found a considerable amount of his DNA in the back of that van."

Superintendent O'Halloran frowned. "The *back* of the van?"

"Yes, ma'am. Where the cargo is usually kept. That, together with the broken piece of indicator that Esther found at the scene of the hanging, which we've now confirmed came from this van... well, I think DCI Porter closed this case prematurely. I shouldn't have agreed to it. I'm not blameless here. I should have listened to Esther's concerns and backed her up. She was absolutely right to go against the DCI's instructions and to continue her enquiries. In fact, had she followed the DCI's orders, she would have been in dereliction of her duty to investigate."

Porter was seething, O'Halloran's brow creased in deep thought.

"Ma'am, if I may," Porter began, but O'Halloran waved a hand to silence him.

There was a long moment as the superintendent appeared to consider everything she'd heard. Then she turned to Esther.

"Do you think Jack Barry was murdered, Sergeant?" she asked.

Esther nodded. "Yes, ma'am. I do. I agree with most of the report that was filed—in that he is the main suspect in the Rachel Gorman murder, although he may not have been alone in that—but I don't buy into the suicide. I think he was killed when he either threatened to talk, or when he got in the way of… well, I think we can be pretty sure there's a drugs trafficking gang—some serious organised criminals— at the heart of this. I think Charles Gorman is heavily involved and that Jack Barry was too. I believe Barry was killed because of it, and his death was made to look like suicide."

"What else have you got to go on?" O'Halloran asked. "To prove he was killed?"

"We have a partial fingerprint on the suicide note which does not belong to Barry," Esther told her.

"We're running that print against the two men Sergeant Penman caught in the van the other night,"

Jared added. "They're still in custody. Superintendent Chambers has granted an extension until we get the results."

Esther looked at DCI Porter. He looked more nervous than angry now. They all knew he was going to cop a hit to his career for this. The way Superintendent O'Halloran was ignoring him, and nodding whenever Esther or Jared spoke, told Esther whose side she was on.

"I have to say, Esther, I admire your tenacity," she said. "You've shown insight and initiative, and you've persisted in chasing all possible leads. Which is exactly what a good detective does. I will speak to the commander and overturn your current transfer. You can go back to working with Inspector Wilcox. Reopen the case until you are satisfied that all lines of enquiry have been exhausted before taking a decision on it. But this reprieve comes with a condition. No more punctuality issues. If you have welfare issues you need to address, do what you need to do to address them now. DI Wilcox can provide you a referral to the Force Health and Wellbeing department if you need it. Understood?"

Esther nodded. "Yes, ma'am."

"Ma'am—" Porter began, but she cut him off again.

"Warren, you can stay. You and I are going to have a little chat about this Jack Barry case."

As Esther and Jared rose, Esther saw Porter shift uncomfortably in his seat. He shot Esther a look of pure hatred as O'Halloran went back to her desk and ordered him to pull up a chair.

Outside the office, she and Jared made their way briskly down the corridor and away from the offices of the top brass.

"You need to be careful now, Esther," Jared told her, as they got to the elevators and he pushed the button. "Porter will be gunning for you. You need to be in on time every day. And cut back on the booze."

Esther nodded. "It's fine. I can do that."

The elevator opened and they stepped in. They were alone.

Jared glanced sideways at her. He didn't try to hide his scepticism.

"Honestly," she replied. "I've turned over a new leaf."

"Oh yeah?"

"Yeah. I went to visit my mother in hospital. She… put some things in perspective for me."

"How is she doing?"

Esther shook her head, looked at the floor. "She's not how I remember her at all. She's like this other version of herself, how she would have been, if she'd done things differently. Lived a better life."

"Go easy on her," he said.

She nodded. "I know. I am. There are no recriminations or anything. We just talk. I think we just both want to be okay with each other again before… before the end."

Jared nodded. "That's good," he said. "That's something, at least."

The elevator stopped at the CID floor and the doors opened.

As they stepped out, Jared gave Esther a smile and a wink. "And the prodigy returneth," he murmured. "Now let's go get your desk back."

20

THE ROOM WAS dark. The blinds were drawn. Only the light from the laptop screen illuminated their faces. They were watching footage from the night that Gary and Buck were lifted, and a million quid's worth of *his* coke was seized.

The first thing he did when he heard about it was check his own CCTV. No. That wasn't entirely true. He had raged and shouted curses and smashed a few things in his apartment first. Then, when a few minutes had passed and he'd got a handle on his temper, he'd logged into his computer and downloaded the footage remotely. Just in case it wasn't a random stop. That was how he'd discovered the video of the policewoman snooping about the yard behind the gallery. His blood had run cold at the sight of her.

After that, he had packed his things and spent the rest of the night at a hotel. Some phone calls from there and he soon had a couple of his associates' best operatives tracking the policewoman down.

He'd left his things at the hotel and approached his gallery cautiously that morning. He'd gone to a coffee shop across the road, and sent two of his men in to open the store and check the locks. He had spent no less than two hours sitting at the café window, watching every car, every window in the street, and every other person in the café.

Nothing happened. There were no raids and no police cars. There was no sign of any watchers.

Cautiously, warily, he had crossed the street and gone into the store as if he was just another customer. He stood by a piece near the window—a banal landscape by some local wannabe that he had placed a ridiculously high price on—and studied all the windows across the street for any signs of surveillance. He saw nothing.

At least the van couldn't be linked to him or to the gallery. Not on paper, anyway. But she had seen it parked there, and there was every chance she had seen *him* too. The doors in the back yard were not signposted, they were just anonymous blank portals. If she hadn't seen him, or hadn't linked the door to the art gallery, they might still be working out a strategy to carry out surveillance on the whole block of premises. That would take them longer, and give him some time to figure things out. The possibility that the police had not yet singled out the gallery might explain why there had been no raids.

Eventually, he had retreated behind the counter and then back to his office.

He'd been jumpy all day. Every time the phone rang, or the little bell above the door chimed, his heart beat just a little faster. But by the time he had closed up shop for the day, there still hadn't been a sign of a single copper. That wasn't to say they weren't monitoring the place already. He thought it best to behave as if they were, and so he had arranged this meeting here, away from the gallery, at a separate apartment that he kept specifically for meetings like this; usually it was because he didn't want the people he was meeting to know where he lived or where he worked—now it was because he didn't want the police to see who he was meeting…

The woman was as big as a house, with a nasty looking scar on her chin. She was ugly. There was no way around it. It didn't help that the sides of her head were shaved close—it made her look more like an ugly man than an ugly woman. The skinny man with the tattoos said very little. She was the one who gave the report.

"She pretty much goes from her apartment to the police station," the woman concluded. "There's one other thing, though. Her mother's in hospital. Cancer ward at Belfield Regional. Ward Eight North. She visited her later that morning."

Peter Darren glanced at the photos the woman had given him along with the scribbled addresses and hospital room number. He paused the CCTV. Most of the yard was dark, the footage black and white, but the image of the policewoman's face was clear. She hadn't seen this camera. Everyone saw the big CCTV camera at the gate and assumed that was it—very few spotted the hidden ones dotted around the walls, at head-height and angled to capture faces. He studied the still on the screen and the photos on the desk. *Esther Penman.* Miss Penman was about to discover her uniform wouldn't protect her. She had fucked with the wrong organisation this time. Whether to have her removed from the picture, or bring some pressure to bear? It might be useful to have a local cop under his thumb. He felt his left eye twitch and pressed a finger to it until it stopped.

"Keep following her. I need something I can use against her. If we can't get something to turn her, or things get too hot... I'll let you know. Keep your phones on, and stay close to her. I'll be in touch."

They nodded and left. When the door closed behind them, he picked up the photo of Penman. She was standing next to a bottle bank with her phone to her ear. Turning her would be more useful in the long run, but he might not have the luxury of time. He wondered what she knew, and whether she knew who he was. Perhaps it was pure coincidence. He had considered phoning in an attempted burglary, to throw any suspicions off the gallery, but it was too messy, too risky, and too difficult to stitch a good story together at such short notice, especially when he had no idea what they already knew.

Not for the first time, he thought it might not be *cops* at all, but only her. That would explain why he'd had no visitors yet. Perhaps, for one reason or another, she hadn't told anyone, or hadn't linked the gallery to the drugs yet.

And if *that* was the case, it might be far more expedient if she just disappeared altogether...

*

The community hall smelled faintly of antiseptic and cheap air freshener. They were all sitting in a circle, since there weren't very many people here tonight. They numbered twelve in all, including Esther, and a more eclectic mix of people she could not imagine. Barbara, a plump housewife and mother of four, dressed in her pearls and her Sunday best, sat next to a homeless man called Felix—pale, gaunt and unshaven in his grubby, ill-fitting army surplus gear. Next to him was James, sporting an expensive pinstripe suit, his tie loose and the top button of his silk shirt undone.

Esther felt awkward and out-of-place. She had come here determined to get through this meeting. She had promised herself she was going to give this a proper go. But right now, listening to Felix recount a story about a time he had been so desperate for dope that he'd burgled a house with two small children in it, frightening the little things out of their wits and talking about how bad he had felt afterwards, Esther was not at all sure she could do this. At the very least, she was going to have to keep her job a secret. She was relieved to hear him say the police had picked him up since, after he'd left fingerprints at the scene, and that he had been charged with it and had pled guilty and had written an apology to the family— allowing her to dodge an ethical dilemma on her first visit here.

Felix didn't end his story so much as trail off into an embarrassed silence, but Reverend Thomas—a chubby man who wore a cheap brown corduroy suit jacket over his wool sweater—immediately began praising the man for his honesty, and thanked him profusely for sharing the story with them. He began clapping, and everyone else joined in. Felix gave them all a grateful smile.

Then the Reverend turned to Esther. He had told her to sit next to him for the first meeting, for support, but even still she had been dreading this moment.

"We have a new member joining us. I want to introduce you all to Esther. Esther, would you like to say something? Even just to introduce yourself. You don't have to share any stories with us just yet if you don't want to, although we'll all be very grateful when you feel ready to." He placed his hand gently on her knee. She twitched her leg away, then gave him a tight smile and a short nod, before clearing her throat and taking a deep breath. She was doing this. She was going to give it a proper go. She had promised herself.

One step at a time. Just introduce herself. That was all she had to do.

"Hi," she said. "My name is Esther. And I'm an alcoholic."

The chorus of voices replied "Hello, Esther" and there was an encouragement in that response that made her think maybe, just maybe, she could actually do this.

21

CHARLES GORMAN WAS trembling as he made his way down the corridor to his supervisor's office. Rajesh Patel was normally a very soft-spoken man. A man who had gone out of his way to support Charles throughout the ordeal of recent events. There were other managers—some quite senior ones—who had made little effort to hide their hostility, or their desire to find some way to terminate his employment completely.

But something had changed. Mr Patel had not been soft-spoken when he summoned him just now.

The corridor felt hot and stuffy as Charles stopped at the door to his supervisor's office. Through the glass pane he could see Mr Patel on the phone. He was talking animatedly. The usual smile was gone, replaced by a deep frown. Charles's breath quickened and his palms grew sweaty. This summons was not going to be about his health or mental wellbeing, he realised; those meetings began when Patel tapped gently on Gorman's door and slipped in with his trademark look of concern. No. A summons to Mr Patel's office in clipped tones meant something else.

Charles took a deep breath and knocked on the door.

Still on the phone, Patel looked up and waved him in. He gestured for him to take a seat. Charles closed the door gently and slipped into one of the two chairs facing the desk.

"Yes, sir," Patel was saying into the phone. "Yes, I understand that. I'm looking into it." The voice on the other end of the phone was loud enough for Charles to hear the anger, but not so loud that he could make out the words. "Don't worry. I will get it straightened out. I have Charles here with me now." Charles's heart began to thump. He felt fat drops of sweat pop out on his forehead. "Yes, sir," Patel finished. "I'll get back to you this afternoon with a plan."

He hung up, still frowning, and gave Charles a long, searching look. Charles had to force himself not to look away. He licked his lips. Patel's jaw was clenched, and when he finally broke the silence, he spoke through gritted teeth.

"Charles, I've noticed some irregularities in the routes you're managing," he said, clearly choosing his words carefully. "I'm hoping you can straighten a few things out for me..."

Forty minutes later, Charles emerged from Rajesh Patel's office shaking and sporting dark sweat stains beneath his armpits. Patel's careful, generous approach had not lasted long, as Charles had stammered to make excuses as to why he hadn't discontinued superfluous routes, or made obvious merges, or utilized their air cargo partners to cut costs. He had been berated about the damage such wastage was causing to the business and the economic pressures they were under. About how foolish oversights and sloppy management like this could cost dozens of people their jobs. Charles was unaccustomed to such harsh chastisement. Patel was cutting him some slack because of his recent trauma—he said so—and although it wasn't spelled out, Charles knew that the only reason he wasn't packing up his desk right at that moment and heading to the job centre was because of Rachel's death.

He made his way unsteadily down the corridor towards his own office. The air felt close and heavy; it was like wading through soup. He avoided eye contact. He got into his office and closed the door. The room was spinning. He leaned back against the wall and sank to the floor. His heart was somewhere down around his stomach.

He might have kept his job—and only just—but he had lost his ability to manage the routes he had run for years. He was being shuffled sideways into sales. How was he going to tell Mister Darren?

As though the very thought had been a summons, the cheap, old-style Nokia—the 'burner'—began to buzz in his pocket. It buzzed and buzzed.

Reluctantly, Charles dragged himself to his feet, fished it out, and pressed the answer button.

"Gorman," Darren said on the other end, his voice icy and crisp, "we've had a setback. We're going to need a second truck and more papers. And I need to talk to you. Meet me in half an hour."

Charles opened his mouth to speak. Nothing came out. His mouth was arid, his throat sticky.

"Gorman. Answer me. Do you understand?"

"Y-yes, h-half an hour. The art gallery?"

There was an irritated hiss on the other end. "Not the gallery. The quarry. As usual."

"O-okay, but… M-mister Darren, I… I have bad news." He was sweating again. The silence stretched. "Mister Darren?"

Charles took the phone from his ear and saw that the call was already terminated. He stared at the mobile in his hand for a long time. It suddenly looked strange to his eyes, this device that could deliver such terror so easily. His hand began to shake.

Abruptly he dropped the phone, rushed across the room to his wastepaper basket, and threw up.

*

Esther had been back at her old desk, going over the crime scene report from the Rachel Gorman murder again when she'd got the call. Now she and Jared were in a cramped, windowless room in the bowels of the station, listening back to the recording of Charles Gorman. Farooq Kabir, a rake-thin cybercrime officer in his late twenties who smelled strongly of Old Spice and stale cigarette smoke, was at the desk operating the playback for them.

Esther studied Kabir's computer monitor as they listened to the recording from Gorman's office for a second time. The display had a list of devices in use. This recording had been picked up by one of the bugs on his desk. They had heard the buzz of a phone on vibrate, except—according to Kabir's onscreen display—Gorman's mobile phone was not active at the time.

"What phone is he using?" she asked Kabir. "I don't see his mobile lighting up on that screen of yours."

Kabir shook his head. "He's using another phone. One we don't have. That, or he's talking to himself."

Jared shook his head. "No, we heard it buzzing. It must be a burner, an unregistered pay-as-you-go."

"So, we can't ID the caller? Or get a tap on the line?" Esther asked.

Kabir shook his head.

"You heard him mention the art gallery," she said to Jared, who nodded.

"We've got him," he replied. "Sounds like a meet in half an hour at the gallery."

Esther turned to Kabir. "Do we have a unit on him today?"

Kabir nodded. "Plainclothes, unmarked car." He clicked at his computer. The list of audio devices and equalizer controls vanished, and a map popped up on the screen. It showed Belfield's industrial zone to the west of the city, centred on the Southwest Estate and Belfield Logistics. "They're parked up two hundred yards from Gorman's office in one of the neighbouring lots." As they watched, a small icon lit up at Gorman's office.

"What's that?" Esther asked.

Kabir frowned. "That's the subject in his car and moving." He picked up a radio handset that sat next to his computer monitor. Hit the transmit button. "Bravo Victor One, Bravo Victor One from Bravo Charlie."

"Send."

"That's our subject on the move."

"Roger. We have eyes on."

Esther turned to Jared. "Let's go." To Kabir: "What radio channel are you using?"

"District channel five."

"Okay, we'll use callsign Bravo Victor Two," she told him. "Keep us updated with his movements."

"Yes, ma'am," Kabir replied.

She was already out the door as Jared got to his feet.

*

The room felt like a sauna. His collar was too tight. Charles pulled at his necktie and fumbled with the button at his throat. His fingers felt like sausages. Abruptly he tugged hard, popping the shirt button off altogether. It landed on his desk and bounced across the room.

He sucked in the air. His face was coated in sweat and he could feel his shirt sticking to his back. As he stared at the cheap Nokia on his desk, a cold realisation crept over him. He knew what he had to do.

Tears formed and fell unchecked down his sweaty cheeks as he snatched up a page from his jotter and began scribbling a note to Charlotte. He told her how sorry he was, that he loved her, but that he'd made some terrible mistakes, and the mistakes had led to her mother's death. He wrote without thinking too much about what he was writing, wiping away the tears that blurred his vision as he spewed his thoughts onto the page in a messy scrawl. When he was finished, he tore the page from the jotter, folded it neatly and sealed it in an envelope. He wrote Charlotte's name on the front and placed it at the centre of his desk. He was focused now. Resolved. He snatched up his jacket and briefcase, more out of habit than anything else, and headed for the door.

Mr Patel was standing next to Penelope at reception. They both looked at Charles as he crossed the room. Patel looked concerned, but Penelope Newman looked as if she was watching an adder dart towards her through long grass.

"Charles, are you okay?" his boss called out, as Charles made a beeline for the front doors. "You look—"

"Yes, fine, thank you."

"Where are you going?"

Charles didn't slow or turn, just called back over his shoulder, "Meeting. Clients."

Patel must have known that was bullshit, but Charles didn't give him any chance to counter. He was out the doors and hurrying across the car park. He tossed his briefcase and jacket into the back of the car, collapsed into the driver's seat, and started the engine. He backed out of the space too quickly, narrowly missing a truck rolling into the yard. The driver blasted his horn, but Charles didn't wait—he accelerated out through the gates and away.

*

Jared was fumbling with the police radio, trying to tune it to channel five as Esther slipped through the gates of the police station and into the traffic. The industrial estates were to the west of them, Marigate to the southeast, so they could get ahead of Gorman and make it to the gallery before him.

Abruptly Jared found the channel and Kabir's

voice came through the speakers. *"He's out of the industrial estate and heading northeast on the A-Niner-Five-Niner."*

Esther frowned. "He's not heading into the city."

Jared pointed out a junction. "The A-Nine-Five-Nine is north of here. We can take Parliament Street and maybe still be able to get to him."

Esther hit her blue lights and sirens to help her cut through the traffic, as she spun the wheel and followed his directions. Jared picked up the radio mic.

"Bravo Charlie from Bravo Victor Two, what exit is he at?"

"Crossing the West Canal Bridge now. Staying on the A-Niner-Five-Niner."

Another voice on the radio, one of the officers who had been sitting at the industrial estate: *"Bravo Charlie from Bravo Victor One, we've got him. We'll take over the commentary. Note for the log: no lights activated at this time, no sirens. Subject vehicle travelling eastbound on the A-Niner-Five-Niner, east of the West Canal Bridge. Five-zero miles per hour. Traffic is light, conditions dry, risk low. No pursuit at this point. No sign that the subject is aware of our presence."*

Esther kept her blue lights and sirens on as she weaved through the heavy city-centre traffic. They were several miles away from where the covert pursuit was happening. She forced her way into the centre of the road, steady but bullish about urging cars to either side as she pushed her way onward from one street to the next.

Another transmission from the officer in Bravo Victor One: *"That's left, left, left onto Old Woodland Road. Four-five miles per hour. Traffic medium, risk low."*

"Bravo Victor One from Bravo Victor Two, that's all overheard," Jared transmitted. "We're making our way north on Parliament Street. Keep us apprised."

They reached the intersection at the end of Parliament Street, a narrow junction that was jammed with traffic. A delivery truck with its hazards on and doors open was the cause. Esther cursed and edged out slowly into the oncoming traffic, forcing cars coming against her to mount the kerbs and let her through the junction. As they reached the crossroads, Jared waved towards the road on the left.

"Take Fethwick Avenue," he instructed her. "It'll take us straight to Old Woodland Road."

Esther swerved to the left. The traffic was lighter on Fethwick, and she began to cover the distance faster.

"Approaching Woodland South Roundabout, four possible exits, stand by for directions."

"That's a mile south of where we'll come out if he stays on Old Woodland Road," Jared told her. He'd spent five years as a sergeant in the traffic unit in Belfield and knew the roads better than Esther. She knocked off the lights and sirens as she reached the junction with Old Woodland Road.

"Not one, not one. The second, the second. Still northbound on Old Woodland Road. Speed five zero now. Traffic medium. Risk low."

"Cut across and pull in over the road," Jared directed. "He'll come right past us."

Esther did just that, but wondered aloud as she pulled in, "Old Woodland goes up into the mountains, doesn't it? Isn't it the road that leads over the Valley Bridge? To those winding tourist routes with the viewing points over the nature reserve?"

"The meet must be somewhere else," Jared mused, "not the art gallery. We only heard half the conversation. We must have missed something. If you were a drug baron, would you meet in your front-company's office, or at one of those viewing points?"

Suddenly, a slightly more urgent tone from Bravo Victor One: *"Callsigns, subject at seven-zero miles an hour now... Speeding up... Maybe he spotted us, but he's really taking off. Loss of visual, wait."*

A moment later the silver Mercedes appeared in Esther's mirrors. It was travelling much faster than the other traffic, overtaking erratically, clearly breaching the speed limit. Esther hit the accelerator and shot forward, hitting fifty-five and rising as Gorman raced past her. She pushed the police car hard, into the outside lane and up to seventy, the silver Merc directly ahead of her.

Jared lifted the radio mic again. "Bravo Victor One from Bravo Victor Two, we're behind the subject now. He's seven zero miles per hour, traffic medium, risk medium. We're unmarked. Not sure whether he knows we're police. Bravo Charlie, can you get Traffic Unit on the line? See if we can't get him stopped for his driving, and we'll stay covert."

Kabir replied: *"On it!"*

That's when Gorman started to drift into the wrong lane, into the path of a large articulated truck coming straight towards them...

*

The blare of a truck's horn alerted Charles to the fact that he was drifting across the central line towards oncoming traffic. He snatched at the wheel and the whole car wobbled as he overcorrected before getting the Mercedes back under control. He glanced at the speedometer and forced himself to ease his foot from the accelerator.

Could he actually hear himself wheezing? He tugged at his collar, but it was already open. He pulled at it again anyway, stretching it wide, desperate for air. His chest felt too tight. He was struggling to fill his lungs. Maybe God would be merciful and give him a heart attack. That's how much of a spineless coward he was; he wanted the job done for him. He realised he was crying, sobbing uncontrollably. It sounded like someone else. He felt like someone else. In truth, he hadn't felt like himself for a long, long time…

The houses of north Belfield fell away. He was speeding up again without realising it, fast approaching the Valley Bridge. To the unfamiliar eye, the enormous suspension bridge would appear suddenly around the curve of the road, looking every inch the majestic feat of engineering that it was. It was a sight to behold, spanning a beautiful, tree-coated valley that plunged half a mile or more towards the blue waters of the River Bale below. But for Charles there was no beauty to be seen in the world. Not anymore.

He needed to do this now, he realised. He was such a failure, such a coward, that if he left it any longer, he would lose his nerve. Now—*right now*—he knew what he needed to do. And he needed to do it *right now*.

Halfway across the bridge, Charles veered onto the narrow strip of hard shoulder and hit the brakes, skidding to a sudden stop. He threw open his door and staggered from the car.

*

The abruptness with which Gorman pulled over and skidded to a stop took Esther by surprise. When he tumbled from his car and made a run for the bridge barrier, she realised exactly what was happening.

"Shit, Jared, he's going to jump!" she yelled, as she pulled up sharply in front of his abandoned Mercedes. She leapt out without switching off the engine. The other unit, Bravo Victor One, pulled in behind Gorman's car and hit their blue lights, bracketing the vehicle off from the rest of the traffic.

Gorman was already climbing onto the wall, a four-foot-high platform of steel that was not designed to prevent people from getting over it. The bridge served road traffic only—there was no pedestrian access. Apart from drivers who got out of their vehicles...

"Charles!" she called out. He stopped and turned. He looked a total mess, collar and tie tugged wide as if he'd been wrestling with them, hair dishevelled, forehead slick with sweat, cheeks wet with tears. His eyes were red, and snot and spit fell from his nose and chin unheeded. Esther was quick to recognise the signs of a man who was truly at the end of his wits... *Shit, what was his daughter's name again?* "Charles, take a moment for me," she called. "Take a breath. You don't want to do this. Think of your daughter..." *Charlotte!* "Think of Charlotte."

The officers from Bravo Victor One—two men in casual clothes with radios in their hands—were out of their car now. They had the good sense not to approach, giving Esther the space she needed to try to communicate with the hysterical man on the bridge. She heard them mutter into their radios, but they were just on the edge of hearing, doing their best to relay information without upsetting their suddenly suicidal subject.

"Come on, Charles," Esther said, more softly. She inched closer to him. "Come on down for me. We can help you. I know you didn't kill your wife, Charles. I've always believed you about that. I know you didn't do it. You're innocent."

Gorman gave a bark of mad laughter which quickly turned to sobbing. He shook his head.

"Not innocent. Not innocent. I didn't kill her, but I've made a mess of things all the same. No, I'm not innocent."

"Okay, well, nobody's completely innocent, are we, Charles? We all do things we shouldn't from time to time. Make mistakes. Hurt people. Doesn't make us bad people. See, if you've made some mistakes, I'll bet you've made them for the right reasons? Yeah? For Charlotte, probably? Am I right?"

Gorman shook his head, face crumpling, crying more quietly now. "I've fucked up. I don't know how it got this far, I really don't."

"We can help you, Charles. Come down and we'll talk it through, and we'll help you get it all straightened out. That's what we're here for." She was still several yards from him. She crept forward steadily, trying to close the distance without spooking him.

Gorman just kept shaking his head. "You can't fix it. They'll get me, and they'll go after Charlotte. This is the only way. This is the only way I can protect her from them." Suddenly he wiped his eyes and stared hard at her. "You need to be careful too, detective. They're more powerful than you think. They'll come after you too."

Esther shook her head. "We're the police, Charles. We *can* protect you. *And* Charlotte."

Gorman smiled at her sadly. "Just be careful. And look in on my daughter. Have someone keep an eye on her, please. Keep her safe. And tell her I'm sorry. Tell her I love her."

"You can do that yourself, Charles," Esther replied calmly, edging forward. She was close now. Only four or five feet away from him… "We can help you both, just—*NO!*"

Gorman had taken a deep breath while she was speaking, and then calmly stepped backwards and out of sight.

Esther ran forward. She leapt onto the top of the steel barrier, knowing already, deep down, that there was nothing on the other side. She was right. Just a sheer drop to the rocky riverbank far below. She watched Charles Gorman's body hit the rocks and spread out in an abrupt bloom of red. A flock of birds in a tree nearby, startled by his landing, took to the sky on a cloud of white wings.

22

THE WOMAN FROM the Independent Office for Police Conduct stood about fifty yards away, clipboard in hand, watching the photographers and mappers and her own IOPC investigators going about their work. The Valley Bridge was closed and cordoned off. Police cars stood with blue lights flashing at both ends of the suspended roadway, all the lanes clear of vehicles apart from Gorman's car and the two unmarked police cars that had been involved in the chase. The sun was setting, washing the whole grim scene in a ruddy glow.

The IOPC agent was a particularly sour old harridan, Jared thought, as he watched her. Was it because she didn't like Mondays? Or because she didn't like police officers? Some IOPC agents were like that. In this case, Jared couldn't be sure. She'd appeared very distrustful of his account when he'd given her his debrief, probing every little detail.

He had not been allowed to listen in on Esther's version of events, obviously, but judging from the expression on her face, Esther was just as angry as he was. He'd placed himself nearby, not close enough to overhear, but close enough to intervene in case his headstrong DS suddenly punched the old bitch out.

Eventually the woman had dismissed Esther with a wave of her hand while she finished jotting her notes. Esther had grimaced at Jared and stomped off towards their new police car; another unmarked sedan had been brought up by a crew, since the car they had used during their pursuit of Gorman would have to remain in situ as part of the scene for a while yet.

A voice in his ear suddenly reminded Jared that he was on the phone with a duty inspector from Cambridgeshire Constabulary, a man whose name he'd already forgotten. He turned away from the scene on the roadway and looked down over the side of the bridge into the valley below, where a more gruesome task was underway.

"Okay, Jared, I've spoken to my sergeants. They're going to get a crew back, give them a quick brief and send them out to the house to deliver the message. But we won't be able to babysit her forever. Is there any plan once we're with her?"

"Not yet. I'll have our superintendent review the threat and we'll get a decision. This gang were after her father, not her. As far as we know, with him gone, she's no use to them." Jared watched the body recovery unit pick their way up the forested slopes from the river towards the remains of Charles Gorman. They would have some job, he thought grimly, as he considered the mess the poor man had made of himself on the rocks below. He sighed and scrubbed a hand through his hair. It was growing cold, autumn turning slowly to winter, and there was a slight fog on the air from his breath. "Let's get the death message to her first and take it from there. Make sure the crew know the background. We can have one of our callsigns come and meet you halfway if she wants to travel home."

"Okay, Jared, I'll let you know how it goes."

"Thanks. I appreciate the help."

Jared hung up, still unable to remember the man's name. He trudged over to the car and sat in.

"That's Cambridgeshire Constabulary on their way out to speak to Charlotte and deliver the death message," he said. "They'll keep a crew with her tonight. Or we'll get a couple of Belfield officers to go and pick her up if she wants to come home. Both parents in less than three weeks. Poor girl's going to be beside herself."

Esther was slouched low in the driver's seat, staring at the activity, arms wrapped around herself and coat collar zipped up to her nose.

Jared turned and looked at her. "You okay?"

She nodded. "Fine," she replied, voice muffled behind the zipper of her coat.

He frowned. "If you need that referral to Occupational Health, or some time off or anything—"

"I'm fine, Jared," Esther replied tersely, emerging suddenly, turtle-like, from her coat collar.

Jared hesitated, then nodded and sighed. "Gorman was our link to the art dealer," he pointed out. "Possibly the only link, unless the guy's stupid enough to use a registered phone."

Esther didn't reply for a long moment, then abruptly she reached forward and turned on the engine.

"Not necessarily," she said.

She pulled out suddenly, doing a big U-turn that made all the uniform officers at the cordon tape straighten up and stare at them. Esther appeared not to notice. She just spun the car around and sped away down the hill back towards town.

"Where are you going?" Jared asked, unable to hide his alarm at Esther's unexpected burst into action.

"To get a new link," she replied simply.

*

Esther pulled up just short of the Marigate Art Gallery. It was early evening now but the gallery's lights were still on, the shutter still up. The street bustled with bohemian activity as the daylight faded—tattoo parlours, sex shops and seedy bars drawing more custom as the quaint little cafés and the charity stores locked their doors for the night.

"What are you planning to do, Esther?" Jared asked, and she could hear a touch of apprehension in his voice.

"Just wait here," she replied, pulling on a pair of thin leather gloves that she kept in the pockets of her coat.

"Like hell" she heard him growl as she got out of the car. He caught up with her as she reached the door to the gallery. She pushed open the door, a brass bell tinkling brightly as she stepped inside.

Peter Darren was stacking leaflets on a wall-mounted stand next to the door. He looked up at her as she entered, and she saw the recognition light his eyes before he schooled his features and fixed a polite smile on his face. He didn't seem quite as short up close, and although he was rail-thin there was something about the way he held himself that made him seem dangerous. The glasses and cashmere turtleneck did nothing to conceal it. There was a deadness to his eyes, a dangerous intelligence. She did her best to hide her uneasiness as she heard Jared step into the shop behind her. Fixing Peter Darren with a hard stare, she met his cold eyes without flinching.

"You know me," she said flatly. "You know who we are."

Darren put on a dramatic frown. "I'm sorry, madam, I'm not sure… Have we met before? I don't recall."

"Don't play games, Mister Darren," she replied. "Charles Gorman is dead."

Darren froze. His left eye began to twitch. He licked his lips. "I beg your pardon? Charles who?"

"Threw himself off a bridge a couple of hours ago," Esther went on, as though he hadn't spoken. "You and your business associates drove him to it."

Darren stiffened, his jaw clenched. His left eye was twitching furiously now. He half-raised a hand to it, but stopped himself. Taking a deep breath, he forced another smile—a smile that never touched his eyes—and shook his head. "I don't know what you're talking about, madam. Are you interested in purchasing a piece of art? If not, then I must ask you to leave."

Esther smirked. The news about Gorman had shocked him. His left eye still twitched sporadically, despite the calm in his voice. And from the clench in his jaw, belying the smile… yes, she had definitely rattled him with her little stunt.

She turned and picked up a couple of the leaflets he had been stacking on the display.

"Supporting local artists, I see," she said, making a show of studying them. "Very noble of you, Mister Darren. Is that to make up for all the damage you do to the community with your drug dealing?"

She heard Jared inhale sharply behind her.

Darren's smile vanished. "You're crazy," he snapped.

He turned and marched back to the counter, and the phone next to the till. He lifted the receiver.

"If you are not here as a customer, I must ask you to leave," he repeated. "If you do not, I shall call the police." He said that last part softly, as close to an acknowledgement that he knew exactly who Esther was as she was likely to get.

Esther made a show of scanning the paintings on the wall, just to irritate the man a little more, daring him to start dialling. Then, looking back at him, she smiled.

"We'll be back, Mister Darren," she said. "Count on it."

With that, she turned on her heel and left the shop, ignoring the look of consternation on Jared's face as she passed him. He looked relieved to be getting out of there, but he didn't speak until they were back in the car.

"What the fuck was that about, Esther?" he barked. "Have you lost your mind?"

She said nothing for a moment, just studied the art gallery, where Darren had skulked to the window to watch them getting into their car. She stared back at him until he moved out of sight again.

"Esther," Jared growled, "tell me what purpose

that served, please?"

Without taking her eyes from the art gallery, she lifted her gloved hands to show him the two leaflets she'd taken from the display that Darren had been stacking.

"A new link," she told him.

When he didn't reply, she turned to him.

"Fingerprints, my dear Wilcox," she explained. "Fingerprints."

Jared's hard expression began to soften as he stared at the leaflets.

"Did you see how he was stacking them?" Esther asked. "I took this leaflet from the top and this one from the bottom. And if you didn't notice, then neither did he. This one will have his thumb prints, and this one will have the rest of his fingers." She grabbed an evidence bag from the glove box and carefully slipped the leaflets into it.

Jared grunted, a grudging concession to some good police work. But he still wasn't happy.

"You could have done that without blurting out the whole bloody thing the way you did," he grumbled.

"Did you see how rattled he was when I told him about Charles Gorman?" she asked. "I think that might be just the thing to push him into doing something stupid."

"Or going to ground."

Esther shook her head. "I don't think so. Something tells me Mister Art Dealer is not the kind of man who can just walk away with his tail between his legs. We'll get him, Jared. I think our little encounter will set things moving. And then we'll have him."

"I hope you're right, Esther," Jared muttered. "For your sake."

*

He watched them go to their car, the bitch detective and her grizzled old counterpart. But he couldn't hold her stare when she caught him watching. His left eye was twitching madly, and it was all he could do to keep himself from lifting a hand to it until he'd moved back into the store and out of view. He was glad there were no customers. He was shaking with rage as he locked the door, twisting the sign from 'open' to 'closed' and heading back behind the counter to his office. Swearing aloud, he pressed the heel of his left palm hard against the jumping nerve in his eyelid. *Fucking eye! Fucking bitch!*

He tugged open the bottom drawer of his desk and pulled out one of half a dozen pay-as-you-go sim cards lying inside. At least now he knew the place wasn't bugged. No way she'd have spouted off like that if her words were being recorded. He ripped open the packaging, slipped the sim into his cheap burner phone, and dialled. He knew most numbers by heart. Better that way. Better to write as little down as possible.

"Hello?" came the man's voice on the other end.

"What's happened with Gorman?" he asked.

"He hasn't turned up yet. Still waiting, boss."

Peter Darren let out a long, slow breath. He hadn't really doubted what the policewoman had said, but now he knew it for sure.

Picking up the remote control on his desk, he turned to the television that hung on one wall and flicked until he found a local news channel. There on the screen was the Valley Bridge, crawling with police and blocked off with police cars, their blue lights flashing. The caption read: *Local man falls to death from Valley Bridge. Roads closed.* Darren could see Charles Gorman's silver Mercedes sitting in the background, its driver door lying open, investigators in white CSI suits photographing it and picking over the interior.

"Get out of there," he told his man on the end of the phone. "Go lie low for the evening." He hung up and immediately thumbed in another number.

A woman's voice this time. "Yes?"

"I thought you were watching her."

"We're at the station. We can only cover one entrance. She could be in and out in any number of patrol cars using the other gate."

"She's just been here," he said, doing his best to keep the anger, the boiling rage, from his voice. "It's time to deal with her. Tonight. You know what to do. Meet me at the warehouse."

"Yes, sir."

Darren hung up, pulled the sim from the phone, and snapped it in two. Then he tossed the phone onto his desk. He stared at the TV screen, where a local reporter was trying to fill his airtime minutes with what tiny morsel of information he had about the local man who'd jumped to his death. But Darren wasn't really listening to any of the inane drivel. He was thinking about that cunt of a detective, Penman, and how she'd smirked at him before she'd left.

The whore wouldn't be smirking this time tomorrow. She'd be on her knees, begging for the pain to stop.

23

HALF THE CID floor was in darkness. The old sodium lamps in the street outside cut through the venetian blinds, casting lines of orange light across the ceiling tiles. The desks in the main workroom were all empty. Esther was alone, the lamp on her reclaimed desk in the sergeants' office creating an island of light in the gloom.

She had just finished filling out an order for an overnight fingerprint exam of the pamphlets she'd lifted from the art gallery. She'd had to bend a few truths on the form to get authorization, but with any luck one of Peter Darren's prints would come back to Jack Barry's suicide note. Esther was banking heavily on it.

She heard Jared's laboured breathing and tired shuffle even before he popped his head in the door.

"You done?" he asked. "Fancy a drink down at the Crown and Lion?"

Esther shook her head, momentarily terrified at how quickly she had been about to say yes, and at how much she *wanted* a drink right then.

"Off the drink for a bit," she told him without looking up. It took every fibre of resilience to say those words. Even now, she felt herself wavering, only half a second from changing her mind and grabbing her coat. She pushed away thoughts of the sweet sharp sting of vodka in her throat, and the fuzzy warmth that would follow…

"You okay?" Jared asked, leaning against the door frame.

"Fine."

There was a moment of silence.

"You couldn't have stopped him," Jared said at last. "No one could have. Don't blame yourself."

She just nodded. If she started turning over all the things she *could* have said to Charles Gorman in his last seconds, instead of the words she actually *did* say, it would never end, and she would drive herself crazy. She knew that already. It was done—she'd tried, she'd failed, he'd jumped. It was done.

"If you need anything, you let me know," Jared added softly.

She looked up at him and forced a smile. The look of concern on his face was touching.

"I know," she said. "I'm fine, Jared. Really. Just need to get things back in order here. Back where I left off."

He nodded reluctantly, then straightened up with a grunt. "Well, I need a pint," he said.

"Okay, see you later," she replied, staring fixedly at her computer screen again, clicking open random emails without reading them, just to seem busy.

Jared hovered for a moment, then disappeared.

Esther let out the breath she hadn't realised she'd

been holding.

She picked up her mobile and tried her mother's number. Straight to voicemail. After a moment's hesitation and a quick look at her watch, she picked up the phone on her desk and pressed star to dial out. Pulling a search engine up on the screen in front of her, she sourced the number she needed.

A clipped female voice with a strong Welsh accent answered.

"Belfield Regional Hospital, Ward Eight North."

"Hello, I'm looking to speak with Hannah Penman."

"It's late. Who's calling?"

"Her daughter."

"One moment till I see if she's still up." There was a click and a moment of silence, and then the Welsh woman came on again. "Okay, putting you through to her room. Keep it short. She needs her rest. It's late."

Another click.

"Mum?"

"Esther?"

"Sorry I haven't called in the last couple of days. Been busy."

"Everything okay? You sound as tired as I feel."

"Rough day. Guy jumped off Valley Bridge earlier. Me and Jared—my boss—we were there. Tried to stop him, but... wasn't close enough, or quick enough."

"Oh God, Esther, I'm sorry. I'm... I'm sure you did all you could."

Esther sighed. "Yeah. He had his mind made up, I think. How are you doing? Has Jean been around?"

"She was here earlier, but not for long. Double shift at Delilah's. They work her to the bone, poor woman. I've told her she needs to start looking about. Bound to be better jobs."

"I'll call in tomorrow," Esther said. "Promise."

"Okay, but only if you can. You're a busy police detective."

"I'll make the time."

"See you tomorrow then."

"Tomorrow."

Esther hung up.

*

Hannah set the phone down and picked up the remote control. She turned on the television and found a local news channel. There was a sports bulletin on, but she read the caption rolling across the bottom of the screen. The local man who fell from Valley Bridge was being named as Charles Gorman. *Gorman's wife was recently killed in a home intrusion.* Hannah waited for the main bulletin, but it didn't add much to the scrolling headlines. She flicked through the channels for a bit and felt herself begin to drift.

A tap at the door woke her. She wasn't sure how long she'd been dozing—sleep caught her off-guard these days—but when she opened her eyes she saw that someone had been in and closed the blinds and turned off the television.

She turned towards the door as it opened. In walked a hospital porter pulling an empty wheelchair with her. Hannah didn't recognise the big, hard-faced woman with the scar on her chin. But then, Hannah didn't know the nightshift people as well as she knew the day shift ones.

"Missus Penman?" the woman queried, as she brought the wheelchair to the bed.

"Yes?"

"I need to take you for a scan."

Hannah frowned. "At this time? That's strange. I thought I was a lost cause," she quipped dryly, although her attempt at humour seemed lost on the woman.

"Yes, ma'am. Apologies. Someone must have ordered it last minute. I just do as I'm told. I gotta take you down for the last scan this evening because they're full up tomorrow."

Hannah muttered again about the time, but allowed the woman to help her out of the bed and into her dressing gown.

"Will it take long, do you think?" she asked.

The porter shook her head. "I think it's just you. Should be back up in twenty minutes."

Hannah sat into the wheelchair and let herself be pushed out the door. Instead of going towards the nurses' station at the entrance to the ward, the woman wheeled her towards the back elevators. This was also strange, but Hannah didn't think much of it. Nightshift people. Evidently, they did things a little differently.

It was only when they rode the lift down all eight floors and emerged into an empty service corridor on the ground floor that Hannah realised something was wrong.

She was being wheeled towards a back exit.

"You've gone too far," Hannah protested. "Radiography is on third. Excuse me? Miss?"

Abruptly she realised there was a man walking next

to them. He was wearing a paramedic uniform. He was skinny, with a shaved head and tattoos on his neck. There was something rodent-like about him, and Hannah was immediately sure he was no paramedic.

"Hey, what the—"

And suddenly the big woman in the porter uniform had her hand over Hannah's mouth and they were racing towards the back exit. The rat-man in the paramedic uniform ran ahead and pushed open the doors. There was a dark car waiting outside. The engine was running but there was no one inside it. The service road was empty. An ambulance dock fifty yards away was well-lit, but there was nobody about. Hannah could see the back of an ambulance truck sitting there. If she could have screamed perhaps someone might have heard, but the woman's hand was like a vice over her mouth.

Rat-man threw open the back door of the car as the giant porter-woman lifted Hannah out of the chair—none too gently—and dragged her into the back seat, one hand still pressed firmly over her mouth. Rat-man shoved the door closed and hopped into the driver's seat. And as quickly as that they were moving towards the main road.

The porter-woman finally took her hand from Hannah's mouth and Hannah gasped for air.

"What are you doing?" she cried, in shock and in pain. Her whole body felt pummelled.

"Sit quiet, and don't move," the woman said sternly.

Hannah tried the handle. Child-lock.

The woman moved as quick as a snake and punched her swiftly on the forearm, causing Hannah to howl. It had not been a full-strength punch, but Hannah's bones were brittle and weak, and the big woman might well have broken one with that punch.

"I told you," the woman repeated. "Sit quiet and don't move."

They slipped out into the traffic of the main road and Hannah turned to watch the hospital disappear behind them.

24

HE HAD BEEN waiting patiently for over an hour. That was a big part of the job: waiting patiently. That, and a talent for blending in. Standing there in his beige anorak, grey woollen hat and dark slacks, staring at his phone through fake glasses, he was perfectly inconspicuous. Not worth noticing. And now, finally, his patience was rewarded. He could hear footsteps on the tiles behind the main doors to the apartment building. He slipped his phone into his back pocket and pulled out a key. It wasn't a key for this door, but the person coming out would never suspect this. He was holding it to the keyhole as if he was just about to use it when the door was snatched open from the inside. He looked up as though startled, and stepped back with a muttered apology and an embarrassed smile.

"Sorry, no, after you," said the Asian gentleman in his fifties who had opened the door. Despite the late hour, he was dressed in an evening suit and highly-polished black shoes, and he held the door open to allow the man inside first.

The man muttered a thank you, ducked his head in gratitude, and slipped in past him. He did not need to turn around to watch the Asian man leave—he could hear the click of his brightly-polished brogues fading away across the pavement outside.

There was only one CCTV camera in the building, or so he'd been briefed, and it covered this small, tiled vestibule just inside the main door as far as the elevator. He was careful to keep his face turned down and away from it as he made his way to the stairs.

The police detective's apartment was on the third floor. His plain, unbranded sneakers allowed him to move silently down the tiled corridor. The tiles would hold his footwear impressions, but he would burn the shoes afterwards. He paused at her apartment door for a long time, head cocked, listening. There was a television on inside. A political satire show he sometimes liked to watch himself. Good. This told him two things: where she was inside the apartment, and that she was distracted. The TV would also help to mask any inadvertent sounds he made on the way in.

He pulled the hat lower over his ears, making sure that none of his hair was sticking out. Retrieving a pair of latex gloves from his pocket, he pulled them on and tried the doorknob. There was the faintest click as he twisted it. Unlocked. Perfect. Lock-picking could prove tricky and time-consuming, so an unlocked door made his job all the easier. He pushed it open slowly. He was tensed for a squeaky hinge, but the door opened soundlessly to reveal a short hallway beyond, with two doors to one side and light spilling from an open door at the end. The sound of the television came from that doorway. The kitchen-living room. He stepped inside and closed the door, turning the knob as he pressed it gently against the jam. No sound. All good so far. He turned and waited, listening once more, before he began making his way carefully down the corridor. The floor was carpet over concrete, so he had no concerns about creaky floorboards.

He stopped when he thought he heard something behind him. A glance over his shoulder showed him that the front door was still closed, and the light in the communal hall beyond betrayed no movement outside. Perhaps noise from another flat. He turned and continued.

Carefully, he peered around the door frame and into the living room. The open door blocked some of the kitchen behind it, but gave him a full and unimpeded view of the living area, where he spotted her straight away. She was not watching the TV, but her back was to him nonetheless; in PJ bottoms and a T-shirt, she was whipping out a blanket and draping it over the couch.

He crept towards her. He was reaching for the syringe in his pocket when she turned, as if suddenly aware of his presence. She opened her mouth, eyes wide with alarm. He moved quickly, closing the last couple of yards between them in a flash. He punched with his left fist, because his right hand was still in his pocket groping for the syringe. It was a clumsy strike, but it caught her on the cheek and was enough to turn her scream into a gasp and send her stumbling backwards. He gave her no chance. He pounced on her, taking her to the floor.

*

Hannah's left arm ached badly, but the tremendous pain that had racked her whole body as she'd been bundled into the car was subsiding. And a quick check confirmed she was able to move all her fingers. She worked on breathing steadily now, calming herself. She needed to think.

This craziness was all about Esther. It must be. Whatever was happening, it had something to do with her daughter's work, and these people were going to try to use Hannah against her as leverage. What other use would she be? She resolved then and there, as she calmed herself by counting out each slow breath, that she would not let them use her. She had failed her daughter, her only child, in so many ways over so many years; here and now she had an opportunity to make amends. For some of it, at least.

She risked another sideways glance at her hefty captor. The woman was staring straight ahead, making a point of ignoring her now. Hannah was no match for her strength, it was clear. She was probably about three times Hannah's weight and clearly saw no threat in her prisoner. But she didn't realise that Hannah had something far more dangerous than size or muscle: Hannah had the knowledge that she was going to die very soon no matter what happened, and that she had nothing left to lose.

The skinny, tattooed driver was taking them up the winding, forested roads of the Norwick Mountains. He was taking the bends at speed, reckless and confident, as though he'd driven this route many times before. The road itself was narrow, with tree-covered slopes to either side—uphill to the right, and down into a steep gorge on the left. The borough council had erected crash barriers at some of the sharper bends, but for most of the route there was nothing but grassy verge to either side, shadowy and pale in the sweep of the headlamps. There was almost no other traffic this high up the mountains at this time of night.

Hannah leaned forward and put on a prim voice. "Where are we going? Can't you slow down, young man? You're driving awfully fast."

"Sit back," the big woman said, as she pushed Hannah roughly back into her seat, away from the driver, who ignored her.

Hannah risked a quick glance down at the cigarette lighter on the console between the front seats. The woman hadn't seen her reach for it before shoving her back into her seat. Hannah had only got her fingertips to it, but it had been enough to press it down. She could see that the button was still depressed now. Heating slowly.

"He's driving much too fast," Hannah went on. "It's dangerous." She reached for her seat belt. The woman did nothing to stop her, just watched with a contemptuous smirk as Hannah fastened herself in. Neither she nor the driver were wearing seat belts.

Hannah reached up and gently adjusted her belt at the shoulder, giving herself plenty of slack, as she kept one eye on the cigarette lighter.

Click.

The button popped out. The big woman heard the click, but she didn't know what it was. She frowned stupidly, and was slow to react as Hannah leaned forward and snatched it from the console. Her frown turned to a look of annoyance. She reached out to push Hannah back into her seat again—but not before Hannah had tossed the glowing cigarette lighter down the back of the driver's shirt.

His howl of pain coincided with a total loss of control. There was a smell of burning fabric, burning flesh, and the car swerved madly as he twitched and shrugged desperately, trying to reach back to fish the lighter out of his shirt.

There was a terrible jolt as the car hit the verge on the left side of the road. There was no crash barrier here.

Time seemed to slow down. Hannah's seat belt pulled and locked, holding her in place as the car went over the edge and the other two went flying. The world spun. Up became down, and then sideways, as the car tipped, landed on its roof, and began to roll down into the gorge. Both of Hannah's captors looked like rag dolls being tossed about. Hannah felt oddly calm as she watched them, until a sudden crash jerked the big woman's body towards her, and her meaty shoulder connected with Hannah's face. Then everything went black.

*

Pain exploded in Esther's jaw, stunning her as she fell to the floor. Her attacker was on top of her in seconds. She tried to gather her breath to cry out, but he clamped a hand firmly over her mouth. Somehow, he had both her arms pinned too. She tried to bite the hand muffling her, but his thumb dug under her chin, forcing her jaw shut. She tasted latex. He was wearing gloves. She tried to bring up her knees, but he was straddling her waist and she couldn't get any power into her strikes. She lurched and writhed, but it was useless. He was too heavy.

"Stop struggling," he hissed. "We can do this the easy way, or I can beat you to a pulp. Decide."

Esther's roar of outrage was muffled by his hand. She tried to knee him in the back, but to little effect.

He struck her again. This time it was a sharp blow to the ribs that made her eyes bulge. She grunted and sucked in air through her nose.

"Decide," he hissed again.

Through the pain and the panic, Esther forced herself to assess the situation. His left hand was over her mouth. He was sitting on her hips, pinning her right arm tightly to her body with his left knee, his position on her hips taking the strength out of her legs. He had taken hold of her left arm with his right hand and was holding it flat against the floor. He wore a wool hat and glasses and latex gloves. But no mask. That worried her.

Suddenly, she caught sight of movement over his right shoulder. She tried to keep her eyes on him, but she must have given something away—some shift in the tension of her muscles or the briefest flick of her glance—because he abruptly seemed to register the blanket and pillow on the couch for the first time. His eyes went wide, and he spun.

Jared's meaty fist met the man's face in mid-turn, sending him sprawling. Jared lifted his arm again, ready for a second blow, but the smaller man lay still. Jared's punch had knocked him out cold.

Esther pushed herself up, gasping for breath. Her right ear was ringing from the earlier blow. She worked her mouth to try and ease the pain in her jaw.

"I'm so glad you took me up on that offer now," she rasped.

Jared still smelled of booze, having arrived back from the pub less than an hour ago. He just nodded, the effects of the drink beginning to wear off quickly now.

"Yeah, me too," he replied. "We need to call the station."

"Let's get him handcuffed first," Esther replied. "Watch him."

Jared frowned as she went to her bedroom.

"You take your handcuffs home?" he called out.

When she reappeared with a set of fluffy pink handcuffs, she glared at him and dared him to speak.

"Shut up," she said.

Jared made an indignant face. "I didn't say anything."

"You're thinking too loudly."

His mouth twitched, but all he said was, "Will they hold him?"

"They're proper handcuffs," she replied tersely, "under the... under the pink..."

Jared chuckled.

"Shut up," Esther repeated. "Just ring the station."

She grabbed the burglar's hands, tugged them around to the small of his back and slapped the cuffs on, making sure they were secure.

She patted him down, checking his pockets. No wallet, just one cheap, old-style mobile phone. And a syringe full of clear liquid. Esther was staring at this, her skin pebbling with goose bumps, when the phone suddenly lit up, blinking silently with an incoming call. No name, just another mobile number.

She looked at Jared, who gave the slightest shake of his head, and then back at the blinking phone...

*

Hannah woke up, confused and nauseous. Everything felt wrong. When she threw up, the vomit fell over her eyes and face. She was upside down, held in place by the seat belt. She groaned in pain, wiped the vomit from her eyes and blinked.

Both her captors were out cold. Possibly dead. In fact, when her vision cleared, she saw that the driver definitely *was* dead; he lay with his neck bent at an unnatural angle, and half his head was lodged in the broken and bloody windscreen.

The other one, the woman, was lying above her, or below her rather, on the ceiling of the car. Hannah, sobbing and shaking, felt for her seatbelt buckle. When she eventually managed to unclip it, she fell onto the woman with a thump and a cry of pain. Gasping, her heart hammering so hard she thought it might break through her weakened ribcage, she clambered over the motionless woman and made for the window and the muddy ground outside.

She was almost free when she felt the hand grab her ankle. She screamed and spun. The big woman had come round. Hannah shrieked and kicked, kicked with all her might, dealing the woman blow after vicious blow to the face with her soft-slippered feet. The woman, her face covered in blood already, seemed dazed and unable to react. Eventually, after maybe the fifth or sixth kick to the face, she slumped, eyes closed once again, and her grip on Hannah's ankle loosened. Hannah scrambled free, cutting herself on a shard of glass as she pulled herself clear of the car window.

She struggled to her feet, whimpering as a sharp pain shot down her neck and shoulder. But it wasn't just her neck and shoulder—*everything* hurt.

She looked around. The car lay on its roof, wedged between two giant spruce trees. The slope was still steep here, the car's headlamps doing little to penetrate the gloom of the valley below. Its taillights illuminated the trail of wreckage that lay uphill. Broken branches and crushed undergrowth led upward into the darkness.

That's when she spotted it, lying in the dirt next to the car. A mobile phone. It must have fallen from one of her captors' pockets and been flung from a window with the force of the final impact. It was a cheap, old-fashioned sort of phone, with plastic buttons instead of a touchscreen.

She grabbed it and dialled 999.

A woman's voice on the other end answered after the first ring.

"Nine-nine-nine, what's your emergency?"

"I've been kidnapped," Hannah gasped. "They've crashed and I've managed to get free. We're somewhere on the mountain road north of Belfield."

There was a moment's pause, as if the operator was trying to decide whether this was a hoax call or not.

"Hello?" Hannah sobbed. "Hello, can you hear me?"

And then the voice returned, business-like and matter-of-fact. "Okay, ma'am, I need you to stay on the line for me, can you do that? We can get a location on your phone if you stay on the line. We'll find you. What's your name?"

"Hannah Penman."

"And your address?"

Hannah rattled off her personal details, told her that she was a patient at Belfield Regional Hospital, and that that was where her two captors had grabbed her, pretending to take her for an X-Ray. "My daughter," she said, "My daughter is in the police. She's a detective. They did this because of her. You need to send someone to check on her. Please! Quickly!"

"What's her name, Hannah?"

."Esther. Esther Penman."

"Okay, I'll get a car out to her. But we need to get you safe, so let's concentrate on that. You've crashed on the side of the mountain road? Do you know how far you are from Belfield?"

"A couple of miles, I think. I'm not sure."

"And can you move?"

"Yes. Yes, I can move."

"Can you see the road, Hannah?"

Hannah squinted uphill again. "I'm not sure. We're in the trees. I can't hear any cars. Wait…" She saw it then, glinting in the moonlight up above— a break in the trees, and a broken road sign hanging askew where the car must have struck it. "Yes, I see where the car came through the trees. There's a road sign."

"What does the sign say?"

"It's just a… one of those… an exclamation mark!" she remembered suddenly.

"Hannah, if you can move and you're not too badly hurt to try it, can I ask you to make your way to the road for me? Can you do that?"

Hannah began staggering up the slope, slipping and pulling herself up again. "Yes, yes I think so."

"Good, but stay on the line for me, please. We have a unit en route to you now. I want you to stay on the line until they're with you, okay?"

"Okay," she replied breathlessly. She kept the phone to her ear as she pulled herself up through the trees, towards the red-bordered sign with its fat black exclamation mark warning of danger ahead. She kept checking over her shoulder as she worked her way up the hill, but there was neither sound nor movement from the car-wreck below.

25

THE CRUNCHING OF grit under his boots echoed in the large empty space, rebounding off the aluminium roof far above. Keeping his footsteps even, Peter Darren affected an air of calm that he did not feel. He was pacing in the darkness, beyond the island of light, where a single battery-powered spotlight illuminated a carefully arrayed collection of items. A large sheet of plastic covered the floor there, in the centre of the abandoned quarry warehouse. On it were two chairs, a fold-out table, several lengths of thin rope, and a bucket. Set out neatly on the fold-out table, just at the edge of the light but close enough to make the objects glint, were a set of pliers, a pair of scissors, some nails and a hammer... Elaborate preparations for a show he had been dearly looking forward to watching, even more so after the policewoman's last visit to his art gallery.

Nicco, a slight man of Romanian extraction, was one of the Board's interrogators. Darren had seen him at his work on two previous occasions. He was a man with a gift for applying pain, and gaining quick compliance thereby. He stood next to one of the broken windows on the south side of the building, keeping a lookout for any sign of tonight's guests. Guests who were now running worrisomely late.

Darren couldn't help himself: he checked his watch again. Out of the corner of his eye he saw Nicco do the same, and then glance over at him. Something was wrong. They both knew it. The mother should have been here by now. And he hadn't received any message at all from the man he had set on the policewoman herself, which was even more concerning.

When Darren began pacing again, Nicco turned back to the window and continued his patient vigil.

Darren took out his mobile. He phoned the woman first. The phone was engaged. Odd. He tried the next number, the man he had sent to capture the detective bitch. The phone was on and began to ring. A cold sweat formed on Darren's back as he listened to the phone ring and ring, and a creeping dread stole over him. The nerve in his left eyelid twitched once, twice, and he pressed his hand against it.

The call rang out. He hung up and put his phone away. Took a deep breath.

"Something's wrong," he announced, his voice thin and reedy in the big empty warehouse.

Nicco nodded. "Yes. I think so. They should have been here by now. The hospital is not so far, I think."

"Gather the things. Go."

Nicco did as he was told, without question, without hesitation. He strode from his post by the window, grabbed an oversized duffel bag from the shadows nearby, and set to work. The tools went in first, then the ropes. The chairs were tossed into the darkness, where they landed with a clatter. The table folded neatly, and the stand for the spot-lamp collapsed to a third its full size, so that both became compact packages that fit into the bag. The plastic sheet, clear of any blood or bodily fluid on this occasion, was folded over and over until it too fit snugly atop the rest. All that remained was the fat spotlight, shining up into the rafters.

"You be okay, boss?" Nicco asked, as he zipped up the duffel and hoisted it carefully over one shoulder.

Darren nodded. "I'll lock up. You go."

Nicco went to the spotlight and flicked the switch. They were both plunged into blinding darkness.

Darren's eyes adjusted slowly, until he could finally make out Nicco's shape by the grey moonlight filtering through the broken windows. The Romanian had hefted the spotlight with his free hand and was making his way across the empty warehouse at a brisk trot, his broad shoulders bearing the heavy duffel bag as if it weighed nothing. A moment later, he slipped through the door and out into the night. Darren waited a few seconds before he crossed to the windows, the ones Nicco had been standing sentry at, and peered out cautiously.

Nicco marched briskly across the yard, to where he had parked his red panel van in the open space beyond the litter of junk and rusted machinery. Darren scanned the treeline beyond the dilapidated chain-link fence. The forest was dark and motionless. No blue lights, no spotlights. No police loudspeakers breaking the silence. He watched Nicco place the duffel bag and spotlight carefully into the back of the van and close it up, then walk around to the driver's door and clamber in. The engine rumbled to life and the van's headlamps came on. And still there was no movement from the trees. Darren glanced up at the cloudless sky, where constellations twinkled, and a half-moon sat low over the forest roof. No police helicopters either.

As Nicco executed a quick three-point turn and drove out through the gates unmolested, Darren decided it was safe. His car was out the back. He would need to move quickly now, and to proceed as if the worst had happened…

26

HER ASSAILANT WAS not on the police system. His fingerprints didn't match any file on their database. Esther wasn't sure which she found more alarming: that, or the fact that the syringe he had been carrying had been full of a potent sedative. They were dealing with serious, organised criminals here. It seemed that Peter Darren had powerful associates, and that Esther was going to have to find a new place to live…

She had been unable to take part in the interviews herself, but the detectives who were running the investigation had kept her in the loop. The man was not saying anything. He wasn't talking, period. They had assured her that they had escalated the case, in light of the circumstances, and notified the National Crime Agency.

Esther had been at the station, getting a fresh ice-pack for her face from the kitchenette on the CID floor, when they told her about Hannah. She took a police car and used the blue lights and sirens to get to the hospital as quickly as she could—policy could go fuck itself. Only when the nurses on the ward had reassured Esther that her mother was okay was she placated.

She peered tentatively around the door of her mother's room now, unsure whether to disturb her or not. If Hannah had looked bad before the attack, now she looked like she'd been hit by a train. She was in a neck brace, her face a mass of bruises, and her left arm was in a sling. Her bandana had been replaced by a thick wrapping of bandages, pink along the edges where the blood had seeped through.

Her eyes fluttered open, and she looked sideways at Esther, standing in the doorway.

"Sign my cast?" she asked.

Esther laughed in spite of herself.

"Come in," her mother said. "I can't turn my head much and you're standing right in the annoying bit of my peripheral vision."

Esther walked to the bed.

"You look terrible," she said.

Her mother gave her a wry grin and replied, "No change there then."

"How do you feel?"

"Terrible," her mother replied, and they both laughed. Then she noticed Esther's swollen cheek. "What happened to your face?"

"Bad guys came after me too," Esther told her. "But Jared slugged him good. A flashback to his old boxing days, he says. We had him in handcuffs in no time."

"Sounds like you dealt with your bad guy better than I dealt with mine," Hannah said.

Esther scrunched up her face. "Not sure about that, Mum," she said. "I'd say you were a bit more thorough with yours." Both her mother's attackers had been confirmed dead now—one at the scene with half his head missing, and the woman shortly after arrival at hospital, from internal injuries.

Hannah smiled. "I can afford to be," she said. "That's the thing about being told every few months that you've only got a couple of months to live. Gives you the courage to go out on your own terms, in a situation like that."

There was the sound of a throat being cleared. They both turned to see Jared standing in the doorway.

"This is my boss, Detective Inspector Jared Wilcox," Esther announced. "Jared, this is my mum, Hannah."

Jared nodded politely. "Ma'am, nice to meet you. Your daughter is a credit to you. Best police officer I've worked with in all my years, without a doubt."

Esther rolled her eyes, about to retort, but her mother forestalled her with a gentle touch on her hand.

"She *is* a credit," Hannah agreed, giving Esther a broad smile. "I'm very proud."

Esther blushed.

Jared went on. "And from the sounds of it, she's inherited her backside-kicking genes from your side of the family," he said. "I'm sorry to see you hurt, but your stunt on that mountain was quite heroic, I'd say."

"Why, thank you, Detective Inspector Wilcox," Hannah replied coyly, eyes suddenly bright as she studied Jared. Esther couldn't believe it: her mother was flirting with her boss.

She interrupted quickly, nodding towards the

paper in Jared's hand. "What's that?" she asked.

"This, Detective Sergeant Penman," he replied, flourishing the page dramatically, "is your vindication. And the evidence that's going to send DCI Porter away to a back-office job for a while, I reckon. Funny how things move a lot quicker when the NCA get involved."

"The fingerprint report," Esther said, and it wasn't even a question.

Jared nodded. "Partial on Barry's suicide note is a match for Peter Darren," he told her. "And there's a second partial on the whiskey bottle. Neither are complete prints. Looks like he's wiped the bottle down, and used gloves with the note, but he's not been careful enough."

"That'll be enough to get him in," Esther said suddenly.

"Sure will."

Esther turned to her mother, but Hannah already knew what she was going to say. "Go get him," she told her daughter before Esther could say a word. "Go!"

Esther nodded, and she and Jared headed quickly for the door. "I'll stop by later," she called back.

"Be careful!" Hannah shouted after them.

27

His hands were trembling as he opened the drawer in his bedside table and took out the notepaper with the ciphered number on it. Every week at the same time on a Monday morning he received a message to his work phone. A string of seemingly random letters. Every week he scribbled this coded telephone number onto his notepaper and deleted the text message, then brought the notepaper home. The old pages were burned when the new number arrived.

He rarely needed to use it. He rarely needed to contact them. They contacted him. That was how it worked.

He did his best to ignore the twitching in his eye. He allowed the tremor in his fingers to subside, and then he dialled the number.

It rang once. There were no words spoken when the phone was answered. It just stopped ringing, and there was breathing at the other end.

"It's the Art Merchant," Darren said quickly.

"Speak," said the older male voice on the other

end.

"Inform the Board. I need to take a vacation. The competitors may have my business plan. Statutory agencies are involved. I'm sending my staff on their secondments."

He waited a moment, holding his breath.

"Received."

And then the connection was cut.

Darren let out a long, shaky breath. There would be no way to know *how* the Board would take that news until he received a message from them. Or a bullet. He may have just signed his own death warrant. It was fifty-fifty, though; had he *not* told them, and things went badly wrong, then a bullet—or a makeshift blade in his prison cell—would have been a one hundred percent certainty.

He pulled the phone apart, and did the same with his other phones. He snapped all the sim cards into two pieces and threw the devices and the broken sim cards into a plastic carrier bag. He would toss them all separately, in public bins far away from this neighbourhood.

He began packing. Just the essentials. Basic toiletries and basic clothing; he left the expensive stuff in his wardrobe. Peter Darren would be no more. His whole history—his clean criminal record and everything that had made him such a valuable asset—was gone. Either the Board supplied him with a new identity, or they finished off the Art Merchant for good. He'd just have to wait and see.

Stopping suddenly, he pressed the heel of his palm against his twitching left eye. *Goddamn eye!* He pressed it so hard that it hurt. Abruptly he cried out and punched the nearest wall. He drew his hand back, shaking, and stared at the blood that trickled from cuts on two of his knuckles. It wasn't the wall he wanted to hit. He had toyed briefly with the idea of finishing off the bitch detective who had ruined everything for him. But going after her meant he risked getting caught, and she wasn't worth that risk. He didn't want to spend his life—or even half a dozen years of his life—in prison. Prison meant he was worse than a lost asset. Prison, especially if he was sentenced to a long stint, meant he was a liability. And the Board did not like liabilities. Even if he avoided prison, what worth would he be to them now, he wondered. And if he was of no worth... was he likely to end up in a ditch anyway? Another unsolved missing person case to join the thousands, a case that would become neglected and grow cold, even as he grew cold in some unmarked grave.

He realised he had stopped moving. He was standing, frozen, in the middle of his bedroom, staring into space. What the fuck was he doing? He needed to move faster. He needed to go *now*.

The safe in his wardrobe held a measly twenty thousand. He was going to need much more. In order to stay out of prison and make himself a valuable asset once again, he was going to have to show some initiative and buy himself some time. He was going to have to run. He was going to have to run far, and he was going to have to run fast. And he needed all his money to do that. He had another hide at the art gallery. It held around five hundred thousand in various currencies. There was a fake passport there too, hidden under the false bottom of a drawer in his desk. He would need a different one when he got over the Channel and onto the continent, but the passport at the gallery would be enough to put him beyond the reach of the police to start with. Yes—with enough cold hard cash a man could disappear and buy a new life. With enough cold hard cash, anything was possible.

He would go to the gallery first. He would do it now, straight away. In and out. Ditch his car afterwards and get new wheels. No. A bus to Dover and the train to France. Public Transport only for a while. No cars. The money would keep him on his feet long enough to find a job somewhere. Somewhere far away. Somewhere sunny.

He chucked the envelope full of cash into his suitcase along with the bag of broken sim cards and mobile phones. Then he snatched up his keys and wallet and hurried from the apartment.

Twenty minutes later, after a quick stop by some litter bins to dispose of the phones and sims, he pulled up on Marigate Street. He saw nothing out of the ordinary around the gallery, if you could call the life around Marigate Street at this hour ordinary. Clubbers in patched denims and spiked leathers, or in wigs and in drag, stood in clusters at the doors to the various dives, most of them pierced and tattooed to within an inch of their lives. Any cop would stand out a mile in these parts.

There were only a handful of cars parked in the street at this late hour and the garish lights from the nightclubs showed Darren that all of them were empty. But he waited a full five minutes nonetheless, watching the comings and goings, and studying all the windows above street level for signs of surveillance. Finally, when he saw nothing to cause him concern, he rolled down the street, turned into the alleyway and pulled up in the back yard of the art gallery.

As he stepped gingerly from his car, engine still running, he watched for any movement in the alley. Nothing. The only sounds were the pulsing beats from the clubs and the laughter and talk of their patrons in the street out front.

Confident now that there was nobody in the yard or alley waiting to pounce on him, he took the key from the ignition and went to the back door. He looked it over. It was secure. There was no sign of forced entry. With another quick glance over his shoulder, he unlocked the door and slipped inside.

He flicked the light switch and the fluorescent bulb flickered on, lighting up the corridor's raw concrete walls. There were no windows in any of the back rooms.

By the time he got to his little office he was beginning to relax a little. In ten minutes he would be motoring towards London. Or maybe Edinburgh or Glasgow first, before doubling-back on the train to throw off any pursuers. All thoughts of vengeance and bloody retribution had disappeared. It was all about self-preservation now, and he was suddenly focused completely on getting away from Belfield, away from England, with the security of a bag-load of cash to see him to safety. There would be time to think about vengeance later, once he was far away from here.

He unlocked his desk, lifted the false bottom on the middle drawer and took out the fake passport. Not a UK passport, but an Australian one. He would be Peter Blake until he managed to get a new set of documents on the black market wherever he wound up. It would be tricky—making contacts discreetly in any new city always was—but the Board had people everywhere, and with a bit of prudence he could manage it. And Peter Darren could do prudence. His little insurance policies were a testament to that. And his not-so-little insurance policy...

He turned towards the boiler closet at the back of his dingy office and began to move quickly. Grabbing one of the empty rucksacks from the shelf above his desk, he snatched open the closet door. The hinges squealed. Years had passed since he had stashed this cash away and since then the cabinet had only been opened for the boiler's annual servicing. He reached behind the boiler itself and removed a section of the drywall. The plasterboard was awkward to unscrew and difficult to manoeuvre out of the way, which was exactly why he had chosen this hide in the first place. Behind the wall was insulation of the most magnificent sort: solid blocks of cash, packed and sealed in cellophane. Sterling, dollars, and euros for the most part. Some other currencies. Roughly half a million, maybe a little more. Enough to get set-up all over again, and to do it in comfort.

He froze when he heard something outside. Creeping carefully to the door of his office, he peeked out into the corridor. It was empty. The door to the gallery floor was ajar, but only the garish neon lights from outside shone through the crack, and there was nothing moving there. He waited, holding his breath. A full minute passed and all he heard were the whoops of the revellers and beats from the clubs. Just noises from the street.

He hurried back to the boiler closet and began pulling the cellophane-wrapped blocks of cash from the wall and dropping them into the rucksack. Queen

Elizabeth and Benjamin Franklin tumbled together with euros and Turkish lira. When he had cleared it all out, he set the panel of drywall back in place and locked the closet door again.

He slipped out of his office and back down the corridor. At the back entrance, he reached out and flipped the switch. The corridor went dark. He stepped out into the yard.

28

"POLICE! STAND BACK from the door!"

Esther watched as the entry team used the heavy enforcer bar—their miniature metal battering ram—to smash the door from its hinges. There'd been no reply to her knocking, even though she'd called out Darren's name loudly enough to wake his neighbours. Bewildered residents, woken from their sleep by the racket, had emerged from their apartments along the corridor to watch the show. The spectators in this high-end apartment building were all older folk, and their nightwear was high-end too, with plenty of silk dressing gowns and monogrammed pyjamas on display.

High-end or not, it took only a handful of thumps from the steel bar to knock the door—frame and all—out of the wall. It collapsed inward with a crash. The entry team stepped back, and uniformed officers swarmed the apartment, shouting that they were police and for anyone inside to stay where they were.

A minute later, the sergeant in charge came out,

shaking his head.

"Not here, Guv," he said to Jared, who cursed.

"The art gallery," Esther announced. "Did you send a patrol?"

The uniform sergeant nodded. "Drove by there about ten minutes ago," he replied. "Said it was all in darkness, locked and shuttered."

"Did they check the rear yard?"

The man hesitated, realising he'd fucked up. Esther didn't waste any time.

"Send them back," she ordered. "Tell them to check the back yard, and get another car to watch the front." She turned to Jared. "Let's go."

They kept their sirens off on the way across town, but with their blue grill lights flashing they overtook what few cars there were on the road and made it to Marigate Street in about five minutes. As reported, the art gallery was dark and the shutter was pulled across the front.

"Let's go around back," Esther decided.

They pulled up at the entrance to the rear alleyway just as a marked patrol car pulled in across the street. The two uniform officers that stepped out looked a little embarrassed.

"Sorry, ma'am, we didn't realise—"

"It doesn't matter," Esther said, waving away the young woman's apology, "Just come with us."

Esther began to make her way gingerly up the alleyway with the young officer by her side. Gingerly, because she couldn't see what lay on the grimy concrete ground but didn't want to use a flashlight and risk alerting Darren to their arrival. She skirted the dumpsters, which were no more than vague shapes in the darkness.

There it was. His black Audi. Even as it came into view, the back door to the gallery opened and Peter Darren stepped out into the yard. He had a bulging rucksack clutched close to his chest. Drugs or money, or both. As soon as he stepped outside, he squinted into the darkness, as if looking for them, and even cloaked in darkness he could make them out, only yards from the gate.

His eyes went wide.

"Peter Darren!" Esther called out. "Stand where you are! Don't move!"

The officer at her side pressed her radio. "Suspect is in the rear yard."

Darren darted for his car. He tossed the rucksack in and jumped into the driver seat as Esther and the young officer ran towards him. The uniform cop had her baton out, ready to smash some glass. But they didn't get close enough. The engine roared to life and the Audi's reverse lights came on. Within seconds, the car was speeding backwards towards them.

"Watch out!" Esther shouted.

The other officer was directly in the path of the Audi. Esther made a move to grab her, but she was too far away. The girl's leap was a moment too late. The car clipped her, and she was thrown to the ground at Esther's feet.

The Audi's headlamps lit up the yard briefly as it raced backwards down the alley. The girl was out cold, baton lying on the gravel nearby. Lying there in that moment, before shadows covered her face again, she looked like a teenager. A rookie. Esther knelt and felt at her neck. Her pulse was strong, and she was still breathing. Esther checked the back of her head and was relieved not to find any blood when she took her fingers away. She reached down and used the radio mic on the girl's shoulder.

"Officer down. Rear yard of Marigate Art Gallery. She's been struck by the suspect's car. Unconscious but still breathing. Send an ambulance."

With the earpiece still stuck in the young woman's ear, Esther couldn't hear if any reply came. The girl's colleague appeared and knelt down next to her, an older woman in her late forties or fifties.

"Did that transmission go through?" Esther asked.

The woman nodded. Then both of them spun toward the sound of a loud crash from the street.

"Stay with her until the ambulance gets here," Esther ordered. Scrambling to her feet, she started running towards the street. "Jared?" she called. "Jared!"

She spotted Jared as soon as she emerged from the alleyway. He was yanking open the door to their unmarked sedan. Darren's Audi had hit the liveried patrol car on its way out of the alley and was at the far end of the street now, careening madly towards the intersection.

"Come on!" Jared shouted. "He's getting away!"

Esther darted over and hopped into the passenger seat. Jared revved the engine and pulled out, blue lights flashing.

Esther snatched the radio mic from its hook on the dash.

"Suspect is headed southbound on Fortuna Street, driving a black Audi A4, registration juliet-victor-two-two-foxtrot-foxtrot-romeo. Approaching junction with Herisham Road. Wait for direction... That's right-right-right onto Herisham Road."

Darren had taken the corner too wide. He'd lost

control. As they came around the corner, they saw the Audi spin out of control and smash against a parked car halfway down the block. The driver's side of the car was pinned against the wreckage. Jared gunned their sedan towards it, but not before Darren had managed to scramble out the passenger side and disappear down a nearby alley. He was still clutching that rucksack.

Esther got on the radio again. "Suspect on foot now, heading northbound from Herisham Road. IC-one male. Approximately five foot seven, thin build, dark hair, dark clothing, glasses. Believed to be a Peter Darren, twenty-nine years. He's in the alleyways. Get a helicopter up."

She tossed the radio mic down as Jared skidded to a stop at the entrance to the alley. Snatching open her door, she took to her heels. She heard Jared coming after her.

"Careful, Esther!" he called out, already sounding out of breath.

She caught sight of movement up ahead, a figure flitting into the light of the next street and around the corner. Here, away from the nightclubs, the streets were empty. It had to have been Darren. She ran faster, leaving the sound of Jared's puffing and wheezing behind her as she emerged onto the next street. The deserted strip of shoulder-to-shoulder boutique shops left nowhere to hide. She spotted him immediately. He was almost at the far junction. Still running hard, he had that rucksack slung across his back now. If he got to a street with enough small entries, he could lose her before the helicopter was up and the backup arrived. She pressed on.

She had cut the distance between her and Darren

in half by the time she turned the next corner. He glanced over his shoulder and saw her. He tried to run faster, but he was flagging. She would be on him within two blocks. He seemed to realise this too. He darted sideways into another alleyway.

Darren was clambering onto a brick wall as she rounded the corner. He'd tossed the rucksack up ahead of him and had climbed onto a dumpster to reach the top. Esther bolted forward, but she was too late. He disappeared over the other side, tugging the rucksack with him. Esther scrambled onto the dumpster and jumped, catching hold of the top of the wall, and scuffing the toes of her boots all to hell as she hoisted herself up. As she pulled herself onto the top of the wall, she saw that the other side was an enclosed yard. Darren was already on top of the far wall. There were no bins or dumpsters in the yard, just an old wooden ladder. Esther watched as Darren pulled the ladder up after him, tossed it ahead of him. It landed on the far side of his wall with a clatter. He glanced at her as he turned around to lower himself down after it, and she fancied he smirked at her before he disappeared from view.

What Darren didn't know was that Esther had patrolled this area as a beat cop, years ago; she remembered most of these alleyways, and the alleyway he'd just lowered himself into split in two. One route would double back and let him out around the corner, and the other end was blocked by a fifteen-foot-tall city council gate which was always locked at night.

She heard the sound of a helicopter approaching as she turned and hopped back down onto the dumpster. Dropping to the ground, she hurried back out onto the street. Jared appeared from around the corner, limping and looking miserable, but Esther didn't wait for him to catch up. She turned and raced around the next block to where she was sure Darren was going to reappear.

A moment later she heard his footsteps approaching at a dead run. She poised herself. The entry was narrow. She just needed to listen... and to time it right...

She darted forward, crashing into her quarry as he burst from the entry. Taken by surprise, Darren tumbled to the ground. She tried to grab him, but he spun quickly and Esther lost her footing. As she landed next to him, he managed to trap her left arm. He brought his elbow down hard. There was an audible snap, and pain shot up Esther's forearm. She cried out.

Darren scrambled to his feet. Despite the pain, Esther had the presence of mind to reach out and catch hold of his shoe as he tried to make off. The tap-tackle brought him crashing to the pavement a second time. But as Esther was getting to her feet again, he was already up, his fists swinging. She backed away a couple of steps, trying to ignore the pulsing agony in her left arm. Pivoting, she brought her foot up hard, catching him in the ribs. She used the advantage to shoulder-charge him with her right side, head low, right arm over her face. It was enough to wind him, but he was already turning to run again. She needed to buy time. Where the fuck *was* everyone?

She kicked out again, low and hard this time, and caught Darren squarely on the calf. He stumbled once more, the weight of the bulging rucksack unbalancing him.

And still, he wouldn't give up. He was getting to his feet for a third time when the helicopter emerged above a nearby rooftop, the thunder of its rotors deafening her as it dropped low overhead. Its spotlight found them, and they were both caught in a sudden blaze of white light. A moment later, the patrol cars appeared, blue lights flashing. Jared finally caught up to her as uniform cops spilled out of their vehicles and ran towards them.

Darren turned. He was surrounded. He knew the game was up. There was fury in his eyes. The glare he gave Esther was full of unmasked hatred; when they locked eyes, he stared at her as if there was no one else in the street. Esther stared back. She didn't blink. They were both breathing hard, but Esther found her voice, and said what she needed to say. "Peter Darren, you're under arrest for murder and conspiracy to murder, for your role in the deaths of Jack Barry and Rachel Gorman. You do not have to say anything but if you do not mention, when questioned, something which you later rely on in court, it may harm your defence. Anything you do say may be given in evidence. Turn around please. Put your hands behind your back."

He didn't move. Just stared.

"Turn around, Mister Darren," she insisted, "and put your hands behind your back. If you do not, I will take it to mean you are resisting and you will be taken to the ground and handcuffed that way."

Darren's left eye twitched once. He continued to stare at her for a moment, but then slowly did as he was told.

Esther stepped forward, tugging the rucksack from his shoulder with her right hand. It came open as she did so, and they all stared at the plastic-wrapped bundles of cash inside.

Jared whistled. "That's a hell of a lot of dough, Mister Darren," he said, as he moved in to handcuff him and pat him down. From the man's pockets he took a set of keys, some loose change, and a passport. He handed the coins and the keys to another officer. Flipping open the passport, he frowned. "Or is that Mister Blake?" he asked. "I didn't know you were Australian. Must've lost your accent, eh?" Darren made no reply. He was just staring at the ground now, refusing to look at anyone or speak. Jared grunted. "You're further under arrest for possession of a false identity document, Mister Darren, as well as dangerous driving, failing to remain at the scene of an accident—two accidents—assault on police and resisting arrest, and I'll remind you that you're still under caution." He turned to the uniformed officers who'd moved in to take him away. "Get him out of here."

Two PCs took Darren by either arm and escorted him to a waiting patrol car. Jared indicated to the bag in Esther's hands. "We'll need to get that sealed up here and count it down at the nick under the custody cameras. Must easily be a couple hundred grand in there."

"Easily," Esther agreed.

Jared took the rucksack from her and went to speak to the sergeant who'd arrived on the scene. He needed to make arrangements to have the rucksack conveyed to the police station, have the crashed Audi recovered, and get a full search of the art gallery organised.

Esther watched as the police car with Peter Darren

in the back drove away, before finally lowering herself to the kerb. She winced at another jab of pain from her left arm.

Jared returned.

"What about the PC back at the gallery?" Esther asked him, as he hunkered down in front of her with a grunt of discomfort. "Is she okay?"

Jared nodded. "She'll be okay. Possible broken leg, but the duty sergeant said she was conscious and talking when the ambulance arrived. Speaking of which," he said, nodding to the arm she was cradling against her stomach, "we'll need to get you up to the hospital too. You're holding that arm like it's broken."

Esther grimaced. "Yeah, Darren caught me good."

"We'll have to further arrest him for that," Jared surmised with a frown. "As for the murders, it's going to be tough to get convictions on the prints alone, unless one of his henchmen rats him out."

Esther shook her head. "Not much chance of that. If my unwanted guest earlier is any indication, then our art dealer is part of a very big, very sophisticated drugs gang. In which case, no one's going to talk. But it doesn't matter."

Jared raised his eyebrows. "No?"

"No. We have enough to stick charges on him and get him remanded," Esther reasoned. "It'll buy us time to find the evidence we need." She nodded towards the Australian passport he was still holding in one hand. "And with that, and all the money in the rucksack, we'll have no trouble convincing a judge he's a flight risk. He's going to prison straight away, is Mister Darren. And it might take a couple of months, but I'm pretty sure our finance guys can dig up all sorts of money laundering offences when they go through the books for that art gallery."

Jared nodded. "Bound to find something."

Esther smiled. "We got him."

"We should celebrate," Jared said, grunting again as he pushed himself upright. "Come on, I'll buy you a smoothie."

Esther laughed. "Not yet. I want to be the one to book him in before I have to go to the hospital."

"Now *that's* dedication," Jared chortled, as he took her right hand and hauled her to her feet. "Let me sling that arm up for you in the meantime."

As they made their way slowly back up the street, the last few uniformed PCs got into their patrol cars, moving away to help secure the crime scenes at the art gallery and the crash site. The helicopter had lifted. By the time Esther and Jared had trudged to the end of the block and turned the corner, the street was empty and silent once more.

EPILOGUE

ESTHER SMILED AND thanked the male nurse who was finishing off her cast. He told her he'd be back in fifteen minutes to check it was set and put it in a sling for her.

The X-rays had revealed a simple fracture of her left ulna four inches above the wrist, right where Darren had struck her. It was going to take at least six weeks to heal.

Jared had taken her to the hospital straight from the police station, but booking Peter Darren into custody had taken a little longer than expected, and it was already midmorning. He'd got a call from the superintendent's office shortly after they'd arrived at the Emergency Department and gone in search of a place with better reception to take the call.

As the nurse bustled out, Hannah appeared, still in her neck brace and cast, being pushed along the corridor in a wheelchair by one of the hospital porters. She pointed at Esther and the big man duly steered Hannah towards her.

"Thank you, Angelo," she said, as he parked her in front of Esther's cubicle. "Just give us a few minutes and then you can take me back up to Eight. Promise."

Angelo shuffled off, muttering good-naturedly about being a taxi service.

"You look terrible," Hannah said to Esther when they were alone.

"Thanks," Esther replied.

"How do you feel?"

"Terrible."

They grinned at each other, both of them sporting their new casts and fresh bruises.

Hannah picked up the iPad sitting on her lap. "Here," she said, as she passed it to Esther. "You're almost famous."

Esther looked at the screen. It was a Belfield website that purported to dish out local-interest stories and breaking news faster than the mainstream national and regional broadcasters. The headline read BELFIELD COPS SMASH MAJOR DOPE RING, and there was a picture of the Marigate Art Gallery, with cordon tape and uniform police all around it in the early morning light. A second picture showed Peter Darren's wrecked Audi being hoisted onto a recovery truck during the night. Esther scanned the article quickly, but the reporter was vague on detail; he cited the recent cocaine haul, and mentioned that a significant amount of cash had been seized overnight. Most of the article was about the car chase that had taken place in the streets of downtown Belfield in the small hours, a car chase which had ended with the arrest of a local businessman. Scrolling down the page, Esther saw more pictures of damaged cars, as well as a shot of the smashed-up patrol car. The only name mentioned in the whole article was that of Superintendent O'Halloran, who had confirmed that a man had been arrested and was 'assisting police with their enquiries'.

"Almost famous," Hannah repeated, "as in, you're not mentioned, but I know it was all your doing."

"Thanks, Mum," Esther said, "but it wasn't just me. It takes a lot of police to pull off a job like this."

"I already bumped into Jared in the corridor on my way here," Hannah replied. "It was your bust. He said so."

Esther arched an eyebrow. "'Jared' now, is it?"

Hannah gave her a look of wide-eyed innocence. "It's the man's name, is it not?"

Esther grunted, but couldn't help smiling as she handed back the tablet. "No one uses the word 'bust' anymore. Anyway, how are *you?*"

"I'm being discharged as planned. Jean's picking me up later. Another short reprieve. You'd think all the battering and bruising my body's taken would've been enough to finish me off. But no. Still hanging in there." Hannah smiled as Angelo reappeared. "Well, here's my handsome taxi man," she announced and gave the porter a wink.

"You're a terrible woman, Missus Penman," he said with a smile.

"I'll see you on the outside, my dear," she said to Esther, as Angelo kicked off the brakes and backed her out of the room. "We'll make a date."

"I look forward to it," Esther replied, as her mother was wheeled away.

Jared appeared a minute later carrying two bright pink drinks with colourful straws sticking from them.

"What's this?" Esther asked as he handed her one.

"A smoothie," he replied. "As promised. To celebrate."

Esther chuckled. "Ta," she said, and took a tentative sip. "Mmm. Strawberry?"

"Strawberry and banana. I think."

"Nice. Sweet."

"And I've got something even sweeter," he announced. "I've just spoken with Superintendent O'Halloran. It's official. Porter's getting moved."

"Shut the fuck up!"

Jared smiled and nodded. "He's being moved to the Statistics and Quality Assurance Department."

"That's like…"

"It's like being sent to live in a cupboard somewhere for a few years, counting crimes and clearances."

"He'll be pissed."

"He already is," Jared said with a wry twist to his lips. "Apparently he's off on sick leave in protest."

Esther smiled. "Ding-dong the prick is gone," she said with a happy chortle, and they touched their smoothies together in a toast to his departure.

"And that's not all," he went on. "You, DS Penman, are getting a commendation. Ma'am is already in agreement with me. It was excellent police work, getting Peter Darren collared. Especially in the face of resistance from the head of department. She thinks it's worthy of a full commendation."

Esther gave Jared a grateful smile. "Thanks, Jared."

"You deserve it, kid," he replied, as he sat on the bed next to her.

"Kid?"

"I'm an old man. Everybody's a kid now."

"You're not that old."

He grunted. "Too old for foot chases, that's for sure."

"You just take the car next time. Cut him off."

"Next time?" He shook his head. "I left all that shit behind when I left uniform. Twenty years ago. I'll just stick to the detecting, thanks very much."

"Uniform or CID, suspects are generally the same, Jared. They tend to run."

He sighed and nodded. "I suppose they do." He gave her a nudge. "Luckily, I have you to catch them."

She raised her smoothie again. "To catching them," she declared.

"To catching them," he echoed, and they sat quietly next to one another, sipping their strawberry and banana smoothies until the nurse reappeared.

When the nurse did reappear it wasn't the one who'd put the cast on and left it to set. Esther stared at the elfin brunette in scrubs who stood in the doorway watching her with a small, pixie-like smile on her face. Even with all her clothes on, Esther recognised her straight away. Jared took their empty smoothie cups away in search of a trash can as the nurse stepped into the room.

"Hi, Esther," she said.

Esther opened her mouth, "Um, hi…" *Trish? Tanya?* It was something beginning with T, she remembered that much.

"Triona," the nurse replied with a little laugh. "It's okay, I'm not offended. Bit disappointed not to have seen you around, maybe." She didn't give Esther a chance to reply as she set about her work. "Let's have a look at this cast." She had an Irish accent. Esther hadn't noticed that before. And she really was very attractive, with those azure, almond-shaped eyes and those dimples. Even if Esther wasn't gay, she could at least see that the woman was beautiful.

Triona leaned in to test the plaster, and then began assembling the sling. She studied Esther coyly. "Work-related?"

Esther cleared her throat. "Yeah. Work. Did I...?"

Triona smiled. "Yes, I know you're a cop. A detective, you said."

"I'm sorry, I don't remember much from that night."

"No?" Triona replied, eyebrows rising dramatically. "Gosh, lucky for me I'm so thick-skinned. You're just full of compliments."

Esther blushed. "Sorry."

Triona laughed. "I'm joking," she said, as she put the sling together with the speed of a practised professional. "I guess you were working pretty hard on that bottle of vodka towards the end." She hung the sling's wider loop over Esther's head and then gently, tenderly, worked her broken arm into the lower loop. "There. Try to keep it elevated. Use the sling to take the weight off it for a day or two, then you can probably go without. The receptionist will give you a date to come back and have the break checked and get your cast off."

"Thanks," Esther said. "Triona."

The nurse grinned, then hesitated. Seeming to suddenly decide something, she plucked a pen from the neckline of her scrubs, took a gentle hold of Esther's cast, and wrote something on it.

"Call me," she said, giving Esther another one of her bright pixie smiles as she turned on her heel and left.

Esther stared down at the phone number jotted on her cast. She was still staring at it when Jared reappeared in the doorway a few moments later.

"All good?" he asked.

Esther looked up and nodded, and realised that she was smiling too.

"All good," she said.

J.K. FLYNN

DON'T MISS the NEXT EXCITING CHAPTER in the Detective Esther Penman series…

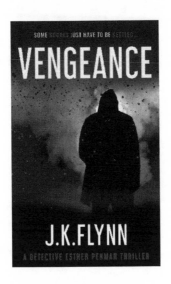

AVAILABLE ON AMAZON FROM SEPTEMBER 1ˢᵗ, 2023

Follow the author on **Amazon** *and* **Bookbub***, or subscribe to the newsletter at* **www.jkflynn-author.com** *for updates on all new releases & promotional offers!*

ABOUT THE AUTHOR

I spent over ten years as a frontline police officer in the UK. It's a job unlike any other, a job that exposes you to aspects of life and society that most people don't get to see.

My time in law enforcement made me want to write a crime fiction character with an authentic voice, raw and unvarnished. D.S. Esther Penman is that voice.

I hope you like her stories...

— J.K. Flynn

Made in the USA
Middletown, DE
26 September 2023